Oh, why were things so difficult?

If he *had* confided in her, she asked herself, could she really have gone back to New York with the information? Things weren't so clear-cut as they had been when she'd taken this assignment. When she wanted to say so much more, all she could allow herself was a soft, "I understand. Some things are private."

Chris looked out over the desert night again. "I wish I understood," he muttered.

He looked so unhappy that she couldn't think of her job; this was the man she was falling in love with. Tentatively, she put her hand on his arm. "I wish there was something I could do," she said quietly.

"You already have done something," he answered, pulling her into his arms. "You're here. Just stay with me...."

ABOUT THE AUTHOR

Superromance veteran Risa Kirk never ceases to delight readers with her wit and lighthearted touch. This successful writer of mainstream fiction as well as category romance makes her home in California with her husband and an assortment of horses, dogs and rabbits!

Books by Risa Kirk

HARLEQUIN SUPERROMANCE

200–BEYOND COMPARE
238–TEMPTING FATE
273–DREAMS TO MEND
300–WITHOUT A DOUBT
361–PLAYING WITH FIRE

Don't miss any of our special offers. Write to us at the following address for information on our newest releases.

Harlequin Reader Service
901 Fuhrmann Blvd., P.O. Box 1397, Buffalo, NY 14240
Canadian address: P.O. Box 603,
Fort Erie, Ont. L2A 5X3

Undercover Affair

RISA KIRK

Harlequin Books

TORONTO • NEW YORK • LONDON
AMSTERDAM • PARIS • SYDNEY • HAMBURG
STOCKHOLM • ATHENS • TOKYO • MILAN

Published June 1990

ISBN 0-373-70408-9

CHAPTER ONE

GAIL SULLIVAN WAS SITTING at her desk listlessly going over some surveillance reports when her boss, Roger Brenner, poked his head in the door. "Got a minute?"

Did she! As an investigator at the corporate intelligence-gathering firm Brenner and Company, based in New York, she'd been at the boring task all morning, and she was beginning to wonder if she'd ever be promoted to a more exciting position. She was thirty years old, and she'd been with the company nearly two years now. She wanted to do much more than analyze data on competing computer businesses, or confiscate counterfeit products for rock stars. Although, she thought, the latter assignment had been interesting. It had been a little out of Brenner's line, but Roger had allowed the firm to be hired by legal counsel for one of the newest rock group imports, Juba-2, before their sellout tour played New York earlier in the year. The purpose was to clear the streets of contraband, like T-shirts and posters displaying the band's copyrighted photograph, and it had turned into a full-scale operation. She wouldn't have believe it if she hadn't been involved herself, but before the rock stars left the city, Brenner agents had confiscated a warehouse of paraphernalia with a street value of more than a million dollars. Hoping Roger had another assignment for her, Gail shoved the files aside and invited him in.

"What's on your mind?" she asked with a smile. She liked Roger, with his paunch and his receding hairline, about which he was so sensitive; he was a good boss, even if—in her opinion—he vastly underutilized her talents. She reminded him of that at every opportunity, pointing out that with her hazel eyes and dark hair—such average coloring—she could blend easily into any background. He always thought that was hilarious.

"You, blend in?" he'd exclaimed one time. "Maybe, if the competition was a Roman candle. But even then, I don't know."

"You mean because of my height?" she'd said, disappointed. She was five foot six, a little taller than average, and because she was slender, she felt she looked even taller.

"Your height has nothing to do with it," Roger retorted, enjoying himself. "Go take a gander in the mirror. It could be a certain look in your eyes."

Well, she was determined; she couldn't deny that. But in this business, that was an asset. Wondering if Roger had finally reached that conclusion himself, she gestured to the only other chair in her tiny cubicle of an office.

Roger sat down with a sigh. Rubbing his head for a moment, as he was apt to do when deep in thought, he surprised her by saying, "You used to be in the hotel business, didn't you?"

She laughed. "I wouldn't say 'in the business,' Roger, I was a reservations clerk, and that's about it."

"No, it was more than that. You took classes in hotel administration, as I recall."

He recalled correctly, but since all that information was in her personnel file and he hadn't commented on it before, she was suddenly cautious. "Yes," she said. "But I didn't like it. That's why I quit."

"But you learned a lot about it, didn't you?" he persisted.

Now she knew she didn't like the drift of this conversation. Hoping he wasn't going to suggest that she take a hotel job to investigate pilfering, she hesitated. It wasn't that she had *disliked* hotel work; after all, she had put nearly five years of her life into a hotel management career. It had taken her that long to admit it just wasn't for her. By the time she resigned, she had worked her way up from the housekeeping department to front office manager, and she could have gone much higher with those classes. But halfway into the course, she had realized she wasn't interested. She'd been restless and bored, but she hadn't known what to do about it until she saw an article about corporate intelligence work. She'd known instantly that was for her. Corporate intelligence had everything she'd unconsciously been searching for: action, excitement...adventure! She couldn't wait to get started.

Her fiancé, Stanley Meller, had been horrified when she told him she wanted to change careers. A data processing manager for an insurance company, he couldn't understand her sudden desire to leap out from behind her sedate hotel desk and fly off to...heaven knew what. He convinced himself she was going through some crisis, that it would pass. It hadn't. She loved this work—even the boring routine of it—and now she could no longer pretend that things would work out between her and Stanley.

He was a nice man; she knew he loved her. In her own way, she still loved him. Who wouldn't love Stanley? He was like a big, overgrown puppy, so anxious to please.

But marrying him was impossible, unfair to them both. Even though they had tried to compromise, to hold on, to work things out, they'd grown too far apart since she started at Brenner and Company, and she knew they would never get back on track again because now they wanted different things. Stanley longed for a wife who aspired to nothing more than keeping his house, raising his children and maybe—for thrills—attending the local PTA meeting now and then. In short, he wanted a homebody, while she...she wanted to be where the action was. That meant that he viewed her work as a threat, which of course it was. She couldn't be home and on a stakeout; she couldn't be away on assignment and still do the grocery shopping. For his sake, she'd tried to do everything but it wasn't working, even at the junior level she was at now. She could imagine how much more strained their situation would be when she was given more difficult assignments, so she knew she had to do something about Stanley soon. But first she had to listen to what Roger had to say.

"Why are you asking about my experience?" she asked warily. "Did we just get a hotel client?"

"Maybe," Roger said. "Have you ever heard of the Kalliste resorts?"

"Those wonderful theme resorts? Who hasn't?" She sat back searching her memory. "Aren't they owned by someone named...Damion?"

"Yes, Harlan Damion. He wants to sell them all."

"Who's buying?"

"A man named Christian Van Der Kellen."

She raised an eyebrow. "The owner of VDK Enterprises. He's been in the financial columns a lot lately."

Roger wasn't surprised that Gail was well informed; he expected his people to keep abreast of the news. "Yes, mainly because his company has been involved in several deals that fell through. One was Fallbrook Lumber, and another—oh, that hardware chain, what was it—?''

"Barrington Brothers. 'If we don't sell it, you don't want it.'" she said, quoting the jingle that had insinuated itself into practically every American home. She leaned forward again. "As I recall, VDK Enterprises hasn't been interested in hotels before. Why now?"

"That's what Damion wants to know," Roger said. "Van Der Kellen has approached him with a preliminary offer, but because VDK has been in the news so much lately, Damion wants to make sure the deal will go through."

"Is anyone else interested?"

"Not according to Damion. Van Der Kellen is the only one who's made an offer so far, but then, Damion hasn't really publicized the fact that he's planning to sell."

She thought again. "As I recall, there are about four or five Kalliste resorts, aren't there?"

"Yes, and all doing very well. Each one is identified with a sports theme—Kalliste Bahama, for instance, is water sports, while Kalliste Scottsdale is tennis and golfing. I believe there's a dude ranch resort in Southern California, and another in Colorado that's devoted to skiing. They're all under the Kalliste International umbrella."

"And worth a substantial sum, I imagine."

Roger gave her a significant look. "As is the fee."

Now she understood why he was interested in her hotel background. It seemed obvious that he needed more information before taking Damion on as a client, and since she had experience, he wanted her input. But he hadn't said anything about assigning her to the account, and she struggled to hide her disappointment when she said, "If you want to bone up on hotel administration before you talk to Damion, I've still got some books at home, I think. I'll be glad to help any way I can."

"I'm happy to hear you say that," he said, giving her a broad smile. "Because I've been thinking of sending someone in undercover on the assignment, and the job seems to be right up your alley."

She tried to hide her sudden excitement. Investigating the pilfering of hotel towels was one thing; going undercover on an important assignment was quite another. "You want to assign me?"

"Don't sound so surprised. You know you've been angling for fieldwork for months now. I thought it was time you proved what you could do."

Now she didn't care if he wanted her to be a hotel maid for the rest of the year. She was so thrilled at the thought of actually going out on a case that she leaned forward, eyes aglow. "When do I leave?"

"Hold on a minute. Don't you want the details first?"

"I don't care what it is, I'll do it!"

"I think we'd better meet with Mr. Damion," Roger said hastily. "He's got to approve."

Approve? Of what? If he wanted her to cut her hair, she would; if he wanted her to dye it dishwater brown, she'd do that, too. If her eyes weren't the right color, she'd get contacts. Oh, there were lots of things she could do to alter her appearance, if that was what was required. She was prepared to do anything—well, almost anything. Her nose was a little too long and straight for her taste, but as her mother said, she'd inherited the Sullivan looks, and she had a right to be proud. He wouldn't want her to change her nose, would he?

Embarrassed, she reined in her galloping thoughts. Roger hadn't said anything about her appearance. She was just so elated at the thought of finally getting a chance to do something important that she was going off half-cocked. Taking a deep breath, she said, "When do I get to meet him?"

Roger stood. "Right now. He's in my office, waiting. We'll discuss what we want you to do there."

Harlan Damion was waiting as promised, sitting in a chair by the window; he turned when they came in. Gail saw an old man with mottled skin and heard a voice that quavered when they were introduced. Even so, his eyes still pierced, and he seemed to know exactly what he wanted to say. He immediately took charge of the meeting without wasting words.

"I want to sell my resorts, Miss Sullivan," he said when they sat down by Roger's desk. "But I only want to go through the process once. I'm an old man, and these things tire me now." His slight smile was more of a grimace, really. "There was a day when I thought it was all so exciting, but I leave the chase to younger men—and women—now. That's why I came to Brenner and Company. As I told Mr. Brenner, I don't want to be involved—I just want to make sure my resorts are sold."

Gail already knew this man's reputation as a recluse; she was surprised that he had actually come to the office. According to sources, he rarely did business in person, preferring to use the phone. But she had herself in hand now, and she said, "I understand completely, Mr. Damion."

He gave her a sharp, penetrating look. Then, as though she'd passed his personal inspection, he nodded. "Yes," he said slowly. "I believe you do. The problem, of course, is that Chris Van Der Kellen has expressed an interest in buying my resorts, but with the difficulties his company has been having lately, I have to wonder if he's prepared to see that the deal does go through. That's why I need you people." He coughed suddenly and gestured to Roger. "Mr. Brenner, if you don't mind..."

Roger took over, explaining to Gail. "Mr. Damion has already told Mr. Van Der Kellen that he's assigned a special representative to handle this matter. He's made sure Mr. Van Der Kellen understands that his representative will have complete authority to answer questions, provide information and relay discussions or offers back to him personally." He glanced quickly at his client, who nodded in confirmation, then he went on. "We've decided that because of your background in hotel administration, Gail, that special representatives will be you."

Even though she'd known this was coming, once the words confirmed it, she barely prevented an exuberant hurrah. "Thank you," she said calmly, though her heart was racing. "I'll certainly do everything I can."

Damion entered the conversation again. "I want to make sure you understand exactly what I need, Miss Sullivan. The sale of my resorts involves quite a...substantial sum. Are you prepared to spy for me to make sure Chris Van Der Kellen holds up his end?"

She didn't look at Roger. Any agency involved in corporate intelligence shunned the word *spy* like the plague. They all preferred *information gathering* or *competitive intelligence*. But what did a word matter? He was asking her if she was prepared to do anything necessary to accomplish the task, and the answer, of course, was a resounding yes! She didn't have to think about it; she'd do everything in her power to see this through!

"That's my job, Mr. Damion," she said, trying not to grin like an idiot from sheer elation. But she couldn't help thinking what an opportunity this was—an undercover job, an important one, with prospects of promotion. She couldn't have done better if she'd designed it herself! "When do you want me to start?"

They agreed she'd begin right away, as soon as things could be arranged with Mr. Van Der Kellen. Damion was anxious to get the details settled as soon as possible, and as he and Gail shook hands and she left the office, she felt as though she was walking on air.

She didn't remember until she left work that night that she still had to explain all this to Stanley. Her euphoria vanished, and she hit ground again with a thump. Glumly, she took the subway home.

CHRISTIAN VAN DER KELLEN stood thoughtfully at a huge plate-glass window that made up one wall of his Tampa, Florida, office. It was almost noon on a warm October day, and the pink flamingos that often visited the man-made pond on the grounds of VDK Enterprises languished in the midday sun. Lifting his eyes to the glittering ocean not far away, Chris imagined that he could glimpse Kellen Key, the island on which the family estate was located. Thinking of its calm waters, its shaded paths and the blissful quiet of the huge house, he frowned. He would much rather have been there than at work, trying to deal with sabotage and treachery and deceit.

With that thought, he took a deep breath and turned around. Two men were sitting at the conference table at the opposite end of the room, and a third was bending over the other two, distributing copies of the report they were to discuss before lunch. They were all suspects, Chris thought grimly. His expression unreadable, he watched them for a moment before his mouth tightened. After months of quiet investigation on his part, he had determined that one of them was a traitor. Which one, he had yet to find out.

"Gentlemen," he said. He had a deep voice and spoke quietly, but they all looked up instantly. His eyes, so dark they appeared almost as black as his hair, touched each man in turn. His father had been fair-haired, blue-eyed, Dutch, but despite the difference in coloring, his own an inheritance from his European mother, they looked very much alike. It was said—or had been, until recently— that Chris was indeed his father's son. That had been both a blessing and a curse, for Kerstan Van Der Kellen had been a brilliant and innovative man who had turned VDK Enterprises from a back-room operation into an international conglomerate. He'd been merciless in business, demanding no less where his only son was concerned, and it had been understood from the time Chris was very small that he would one day head the company. He'd taken the helm ten years ago when he was twenty-five, right after his father died. The transfer had taken place without fanfare or fuss. Why not? He'd been groomed for the job for years.

Since that time, he'd developed his own reputation. He was thought to be as brilliant and sharp as his father, but decidedly more human, even if he did expect the best from his people. He didn't have to guess how his father would have handled this current situation; Kerstan would have cut a swath through the entire company until he discovered the informant, who would then have been heartlessly dispatched without a qualm.

But despite all the endless conjectures and comparisons, he wasn't his father, and he had to deal with this in his own way. "Is everyone ready to begin?" he asked.

His executive assistant, Nicolas Sierra, turned to him with a smile. He and Nick had known each other for years. They had grown up on Kellen Key together, the Sierras in service to the Van Der Kellens as far back as—

farther than—Chris could remember. As boys, they'd gone to school together, had swum and sailed and fished together, had in fact been nearly inseparable until college. Then Chris had gone off to Harvard for his business degree, and Nick had stayed home. When Chris returned to Tampa to take an executive position under his father, he'd invited Nick to be his assistant. When he became president of the company, Nick had stayed with him. He had been the perfect choice; now Chris didn't know what he'd do without his old friend, who knew him so well that he seemed to read his mind at times. Glancing covertly at Nick now, he wondered, with a pang, if Nick was the one.

"Ready, Mr. Van Der Kellen," Nick said now, as formal as he always was in the presence of others. He took a position at the end of the table, discreetly buzzing for the secretary to come in. A woman appeared, silently taking her place to the side, pencil and pad poised.

As he came to his place, Chris glanced at the other two men, his executive vice president, Patrick Delaney, and Daniel Harris, VDK's comptroller. Both men had been with the company for years; until recently, he'd trusted them implicitly. Now he didn't know whom to trust. Someone was giving out advance information about VDK's plans; they'd lost a lot of ground—not to mention money—because of it, and lately, in a perverse blow to his pride, he'd been hearing speculation that he wasn't the man his father was. He didn't know why that should bother him, but it did. For as long as he could remember, he'd done his best to prove that he *wasn't* his father. But that didn't mean he wasn't as good—or that he didn't know how to handle himself.

He looked around the table again. "I had an outline concerning the purchase of the Kalliste International resorts sent to each of you," he said, watching them all closely. "All the details—or those we're aware of at the moment—are contained in the report, which is the reason we're meeting today. I know you've had time to study it, and I want your opinions."

As always, Patrick Delaney was the first to speak. He'd worked with Chris's father, Kerstan, and felt familiar enough in his place to be frank. Tall, broad, sandy-haired and blue-eyed with freckles, he had a sharp mind and business grasp Chris trusted. Or had until recently.

"Well, Chris," he began, "I've read through the thing, and I'll be damned if I can understand why you want to get involved with a chain of theme resorts like these. The figures aren't all that spectacular, the overhead is high, and it doesn't seem like such a good deal to me. If you're interested in hotels, an economy chain might be a better way to go."

Daniel Harris spoke up. The stereotypical picture of a dedicated accountant, he even had a closetful of bow ties, and wore a different one each day. He'd been the head of the accounting department for as long as Chris could remember; he was a wizard with figures and, disdaining calculators, was able to add columns in his head down to the penny. He knew where every cent went that the company spent, and although Chris had had to rein him in on some of the austerity programs he proposed with monotonous regularity, he knew Harris would have already formed a financial picture down to the last dime.

"I'm with Pat on this one," Harris said. "If you must get into the hotel business, economy is the way to go."

"And we should do it right," Pat continued. "Send out a surveillance team to check out various locations. Have them travel around the country logging strengths and weaknesses. We'll analyze the data and decide then if the idea is feasible.''

Chris nodded, acknowledging each view. But his expression was unreadable as he turned to his assistant. "What do you think, Nick?''

Nick glanced quickly at the other two men, who were suddenly occupied with the folders in front of them. Chris often asked Nick's opinion about mergers or acquisitions or other business matters that affected VDK, but usually when they were alone. Obviously uncomfortable, Nick said, "I'm sorry, Mr. Van Der Kellen, I don't think it's my place to—''

Chris made an impatient gesture. "Don't give me that, Nick. You prepared the report—you know what it says. I want your opinion.''

Nick looked around uneasily again. It was clear that he didn't want to say, and he muttered hesitantly, "I . . . I'm afraid I don't know that much about it.''

To his relief, Chris let it go. With a glance at the expressionless secretary, whose pencil was poised again over her pad, Chris said, "Well, I do. These theme resorts appeal to me, and I want to buy them, maybe expand the chain in the future. I've studied this, and statistics on the millions of Americans who will travel this year, in this country alone, seem to prove this opportunity is tailor-made. The chain is small now, but the figures aren't that disappointing. And we would be going into it with our eyes open, no surprises.''

"So you've already made up your mind," Delaney said.

Chris shook his head. "No, not yet. Damion and I can't get together on a preliminary bid.''

Harris looked horrified. "You've already put in a bid—without telling accounting?''

Chris was brisk. "I know that's heresy, Dan, but accounting will survive. I haven't spent the money yet, after all. I'm waiting to meet with Damion's representative."

"And who might that be?" Delaney asked.

"A woman named Gail Sullivan. She's Damion's executive vice president at Kalliste International and supposed to have all the answers. Naturally, I would have preferred to meet with Damion himself, but as you're aware, he's been reclusive for years. So we'll have to make do with Ms Sullivan."

"When is she coming?" Delaney asked.

"Soon. I plan to meet with her at Kellen Key, unless any of you have objections."

Delaney threw up his hands. "Hell, Chris, it's your company. If you want to become an innkeeper, that's your business."

Harris still looked scandalized. "I really think we should...er..."

"Don't worry," Chris assured them. "You'll all meet her. I wanted to present my case in a more...relaxed setting before I overwhelmed her with VDK reps intent on information gathering."

"You seem anxious about this, Chris," Delaney said. "Is that because someone else is bidding?"

The question seemed casual enough, but Chris wondered if Delaney was as nonchalant as he appeared. "I don't know," he replied. "I don't intend to take that chance." He picked up the untouched folder in front of him, tapped it decisively against the shining tabletop. "That's all, gentlemen. Unless you have other questions..."

"I'll wait until I get to Kellen Key," Delaney said, rising.

Harris got to his feet, too. Giving Chris a significant look, he said, "And I'll go over the figures again. But it would help if I could get a complete financial statement on Kalliste International, Chris. If not on Harlan Damion himself."

Was Dan fishing, or not? Keeping his expression neutral, Chris answered, "You'll have it, Dan—on Kalliste, at least. I'll make sure Ms Sullivan brings all the pertinent information with her. But I can't promise more than public access on Damion, you know that."

"But..."

Watching the man closely, Chris said, "You wouldn't willingly give out such information on VDK, would you?"

Harris straightened indignantly. "Absolutely not!"

"Then we'll have to settle for what we can get."

Looking unhappy, Harris nodded. "All right."

With Nick holding the door, the other two men started out, but Chris stopped Nick for a moment. "I think we should give Damion's representative the red carpet service, Nick. Find out when she's coming, and make first-class reservations, please—and have my plane and car ready for the leg to Kellen Key."

"Yes, sir," Nick said, following the others out. The secretary had already unobtrusively left, and as soon as he was alone, Chris went to his desk and sat down.

It had gone about as he'd expected, he thought, tiredly rubbing his eyes. The hard part now was going to be waiting to see what would happen. He'd baited the hook, making sure they all knew how much he wanted this acquisition to go through. Only three people besides himself—and the secretary, whom he had deliberately selected at random from the pool—knew about his desire to purchase Kalliste International. And, despite Pat's and Dan's objections, the deal was a good one; he knew it, and they knew it, too. Granted, VDK had never been involved in the hostelry business, but that didn't mean it couldn't be. And he could always say it was a whim. His mouth tightened. The Van Der Kellens were known for their whims.

Well, he'd done what he could to dangle the bait. One of those three men was a traitor, selling private information to the highest bidder. Which would it be? Wearily, he put his head back against the soft leather of the chair. He couldn't think about the problem anymore; he'd just have to wait and see.

LATER THAT NIGHT, safely away from the VDK offices, where there was always at least a chance that someone would overhear or that a line might even be tapped, one of the men who had been at the meeting with Chris stopped at a pay telephone and dialed a number he'd called several times. The phone rang at the other end just twice before it was picked up, and a voice hoarse from cigarettes said curtly, "Sutton."

The caller had no need to identify himself; he and Wade Sutton had spoken before. "I thought you'd be interested to know about a meeting I attended at VDK," he said.

Sutton didn't hesitate. "Go on," he said.

"Have you ever heard of Kalliste International?"

"Don't be cute. Just tell me what's going on."

The caller paused. He hated to be spoken to in that tone, and it was a moment before he controlled his anger enough to respond. "Van Der Kellen wants to buy the chain."

Sutton was silent for a few seconds. "Why?"

"I don't know why. Does it matter? He just does—enough to meet with a Kalliste representative to discuss details."

"Do you know who this representative is?"

"Some woman. Chris is pulling out all the stops—first-class, private plane, limo, a visit to Kellen Key—the whole bit."

Sutton laughed. It wasn't a pleasant sound. "In that case, it might be interesting to put a spoke in the wheel right off—until we figure out what's going on. How about a little mix-up in travel arrangements? Do you think you could manage that?"

The caller smiled, and his smile was no more pleasant than Sutton's laugh. "Consider it done."

CHAPTER TWO

WHEN GAIL RECEIVED the first-class ticket to Tampa, with a copy of her itinerary from there to Kellen Key, she wanted to hug herself with glee. The ticket made her new undercover assignment real, not something she wondered at times if she had dreamed up because she wanted so much to prove herself at Brenner and Company. But now she knew she wasn't dreaming, and after a week of preparation, she was ready to leave. She shook her head wonderingly. Who would have thought that her background in hotel management would lead to something so exciting?

Now all she had to do was tell Stanley, she thought, and grimaced. She had put off saying anything until she was sure she was going, but she couldn't avoid it any longer. Tonight, she thought; no matter what, she'd tell him tonight when she got home from work. She had to—she was leaving in the morning. After a frantic week of memorizing all the facts and information Damion had given her about the resorts—not to mention a hasty review of her hotel management courses—she was ready to go. Or would be, once she finished a few details here at the office. She was still working when Roger stopped by.

"All set?"

She looked up with a grin. "I will be by tomorrow morning."

He lounged in the doorway. "I hear Van Der Kellen is pulling out all the stops. First-class all the way."

She nodded, thinking of the ticket in her purse. She wanted to frame it, especially when she remembered her original plans: a commercial flight to Florida, then a transfer to a small air service, or a ferry ride to Kellen Key, the Van Der Kellen family's private island. But it hadn't turned out that way. VDK Enterprises had taken care of everything: now she was going first-class from Newark to Tampa, where she'd be met by Chris Van Der Kellen's private plane, of all things, which would take her to the private airstrip on Kellen Key, whence she'd be whisked by limousine to the estate. It was another dream come true. Not only was she taking on a special assignment—undercover yet!—with a lot of responsibility and a chance finally to prove herself, but she was being treated like royalty in the process.

Realizing that Roger was smiling at her, she smiled back and said, "I guess he believes in doing things right."

Her boss's smile faded. "Yeah, well, watch yourself. I hear the guy's a smooth operator."

She was confident she could handle anything. It was the opportunity she'd been waiting for, and she wouldn't let anything stand in her way. "I'll manage."

"I know. But just remember why you're down there. Did you read that last report Damion sent over about Kalliste International?"

She tapped her forehead. "I've got it all right here."

"And you've boned up on your hotel management theory, so that no matter what Van Der Kellen asks, you'll have an answer for him."

"I've been studying every night."

"Because as Damion's special representative, you're supposed to know all about the resorts."

Rolling her eyes, she said, "Don't *worry* about it, Roger. I know what I'm doing!"

"I know, I know," he said, rubbing his head. "I wouldn't be sending you if I didn't. It's just that Van Der Kellen has such a reputation—"

"I can take care of myself," she boasted, and waved on the way out.

Her apartment was dark when she got home, and as she fumbled with the key and the groceries she'd stopped to buy, she was glad Stanley hadn't arrived yet. Even though they hadn't exactly been living together—he had his own place, she had hers—he would often be here when she got home from work, and she needed a little time by herself tonight to plan. She'd bought the things for his favorite lasagna dinner in the hope that a good meal would make things easier, but as she started preparations in the kitchen, she had the sinking feeling that tonight wasn't going to go well at all.

Thirty minutes later, she was proved right. Anxious to get the ordeal over with, she had just blurted out the story when Stanley came in. Now he was sitting at the kitchen table in his three-piece suit, his briefcase by his feet, a mutinous expression in his blue eyes.

"Undercover? What does that mean, undercover?" he asked for what she was sure was the tenth time. He was looking at her as though she'd told him she wanted to fly off to Africa to study gorillas.

She tried to be patient. "I told you, Stanley. We landed a case involving a lot of money, and I'm to investigate the intentions of...of someone who wants to buy... something."

Her explanation sounded weak to her own ears, but she couldn't make it better. She couldn't tell him all the details; she was sworn to secrecy. Employees of Brenner and Company never discussed cases outside the office. Corporate intelligence work demanded discretion, and while it sometimes made things awkward, they all had to accept that. She had. Stanley, unfortunately, hadn't.

"But where are you going to go?" he asked petulantly. "And how long will you be gone?"

She couldn't answer those questions, either—the first because it was privileged information; the second because she didn't know. "I can't tell you where I'll be," she said, trying to make it sound unimportant that she planned to depart for an undisclosed location for an indeterminate amount of time. "I don't know how long it will take. But there's no danger, and I promise I'll be safe."

He flushed with sudden anger. "Well, that's just great!" he exploded. "My fiancé—my wife-to-be—is going off *somewhere*, but she can't tell me where, and she's going to be gone a *while*, but she doesn't know how long! What am I supposed to do in the meantime? What will I tell our friends?"

She tried to hold on to her temper. She'd known he was going to be difficult, but she'd hoped he'd at least try to understand. "You don't have to tell them anything," she said. "It's none of their business."

"Oh, wonderful! You just…disappear for God knows how long, and I'm supposed to tell everyone we know that you're having a little vacation? No, no, this isn't going to work, Gail. You'll just have to tell your boss that you can't do it!"

She was dumbfounded. "Can't do it! Do you know what you're saying?"

"I know exactly what I'm saying! Oh, I knew this would happen if you took that job—"

"It isn't a job, Stanley, it's my career!"

"And what about me? What do I do when you're gone?"

"What you always do—go to work, come home, watch TV. It won't be forever."

"How do I know you'll come back?"

Despite her best intentions, she was losing patience. "You're being ridiculous, Stanley. Of course I'll come back. I'm not going on a wilderness expedition, you know."

"How do I know? You haven't told me anything!" Abruptly, he stood. His mouth tight, he went to the kitchen telephone.

She looked at him in alarm. "What are you doing?"

He lifted the receiver. "I'm going to call your boss and tell him you've changed your mind."

"What? You can't do that!"

"Watch me."

This was absurd! Reaching over the counter, she took the phone from his hand and put it back in the cradle. It was an effort not to slam it down. She made herself take a breath and say, somewhat reasonably, "Stanley, you're overreacting here."

"No, I'm not! I'm not going to have the woman I love traipsing all over the country—" He stopped suddenly and looked at her. "It *is* this country, isn't it?"

"Of course, it's this country!" she exclaimed. "Don't be ridiculous!"

"I'm not, I'm not. What would you say if the situation were reversed?"

"I'd be excited for you."

"Ha! You wouldn't, and you know it!"

She tried again. She wanted him to understand; if they were going to quarrel, maybe she should tell him now that she wanted to break their engagement. She shook her head. One thing at a time, she told herself, and said, "I'd at least try, Stanley. You know how much an assignment means to me. You know how anxious I've been to get ahead at Brenner. It's my chance to prove myself. Why can't you support me? I'd support you."

"I did support you!" he cried. "But I thought you'd get tired of this...this intelligence business. I thought you'd come to your senses. You'll have to, you know, when we get married!"

She felt a silence descend on her. The moment had arrived. She'd known it was going to happen; it was futile trying to postpone it any longer. Quietly, she said, "And what if I don't want to quit after we get married? What if I want to keep working?"

He looked more agitated than ever, beginning to pace back and forth between the little kitchen and the equally cramped breakfast area. Fortunately, he was a small man, barely taller than she was; otherwise he wouldn't have been able to turn around. She couldn't get out of his way; she had to lean back against the counter every time he passed.

"I've no objection to you continuing working for a while, Gail—at least until we're married," he said, walking furiously, his face red. "I know how much your independence means to you. I know how much responsibility you feel to contribute. But when I agreed to your working, I meant in the hotel. You were happy there; you used to like it a lot—until you got involved in this...other business."

"I wasn't happy in the hotel business and you know it, Stanley," she said. "And I've told you before, I've found my niche. I love my work now. I don't want to quit."

He looked at her for a long moment. "Then we've got a problem, Gail. If you won't quit Brenner and Company, I'm afraid it just isn't going to work."

She almost felt relieved. "You don't want time to think about it?"

"Will you quit?"

She shook her head.

"Then there's nothing to think about," he said. "It's obvious that we don't have the same goals. I thought we did, but..."

He held out his hand. She looked at it. "What's that for?"

"I'd...I'd like my ring back," he said.

She looked at him in disbelief. "You...what?"

He looked unhappy, but still determined. "I want my ring back. It's obvious our relationship is over, and—"

She could feel herself getting angry all over again. "And you want to find some other woman to give my ring—*my* ring—to?"

"Well...yes."

She was so indignant that she jerked the little diamond off her finger. She had a right to keep it, but she didn't want it anymore. Grabbing his hand, she put it in his palm and then curled his fingers around it so tightly that he winced. "You wanted the ring? Well, here it is, Stanley. I hope you're both going to be very happy!"

Too late, he tried to apologize. "I'm sorry, Gail. If you change your mind—"

That was too much! "I think you'd better leave, Stanley," she said, her voice shaking.

He took one look at her face and left. It wasn't until he'd gone that she smelled something burning. Whirling around, she jerked open the oven door. The lasagna that she'd lavished so much precious time on had become charred into oblivion. Muttering to herself, she pulled it out and threw it, pan and all, into the trash. Then, still angry, she want into the bedroom to pack. She got as far as pulling the suitcase down from the closet shelf before she burst into tears. Throwing the suitcase on the floor, she sank onto the bed and had a good cry.

She had loved Stanley once; she still did, in a way, even after what had happened tonight. She'd hurt him; that was why he'd asked for the ring back. She knew that once he thought about it, he'd be sorry, but by then it would be too late. It already was, she thought, reaching for a tissue to wipe her nose. They had grown so far apart since she started working for Roger that she knew they could never go back, even if they wanted to. The simple truth was that she had changed, but Stanley hadn't. It wasn't the fault of either of them; it had just happened. People didn't stay the same all their lives. She shuddered. At least, she hoped not. But when one person grew, the other had to grow—or adapt—or the relationship became unbalanced. She knew that was what had happened between her and Stanley. Her job had opened up exciting possibilities, new horizons. She was thrilled by that, delighted, looking forward to fresh challenges. Stanley just felt threatened. That wasn't his fault, either; he just wasn't ready to change.

So it was better this way, she thought, wiping her eyes. Stanley would find someone who wanted the things he did; it was just a matter of time. And in the meantime, she'd have her work. At least now she could leave for Florida without feeling guilty about leaving him behind. And who knew what thrilling things she was about to encounter?

Buoyed by the thought, she tackled her packing again. It wasn't until then that she realized she didn't have the wardrobe for a visit to an island estate. She'd been so busy cramming facts and figures into her head that she hadn't thought about what she'd wear. She glanced in panic at the clock. It was too late to go shopping, but she was leaving tomorrow. What was she going to do? The itinerary had mentioned a "get-together" with some of VDK's executives once she arrived at Kellen Key, but what did that mean to a man like Chris Van Der Kellen? A business meeting or a party? Formal or semiformal? Maybe, since it was an island, it meant casual. Oh, why hadn't she asked before now?

She was still staring in dismay at the paltry contents of her closet when the doorbell rang. Hoping it wasn't Stanley coming back already to apologize, she went to answer and let out a sigh of relief when she saw a friend, Suzanne, who lived down the hall, making faces in the door peephole. Jerking the door open, she grabbed Suzanne by the arm and practically hauled her in.

"Do you have anything to wear to an informal, semiformal business-type meeting or party on an island estate?" she asked breathlessly.

"Hi, to you, too," Suzanne said. "Is that a trick question, or do I get points for answering all three parts?"

She wasn't in the mood to joke. Time was running out, and she didn't have a thing to wear! "I'm serious!"

"About what?" Suzanne said, giggling. She was a color and makeup consultant for several exclusive Manhattan boutiques, and looked it. Unlike Gail, she was blond and blue-eyed, with a figure that in other decades might have been enviously termed voluptuous. She was proud of it, and enhanced her assets with tight-waisted, peplum-style dresses, and high, high heels, relaxing at home in designer velour lounge outfits with matching satin slippers. Gail loved her friend, but she still joked that it was a good thing Suzanne lived alone; her wardrobe filled half her apartment. Which Gail was glad about now. They didn't have the same taste at all, but maybe Suzanne could suggest something.

"Suzanne, I really need your help," she said. "I'm leaving tomorrow, and I've got nothing to wear!"

Suzanne laughed. "When other women say it I know it can't possibly be true. But in your case..." She paused, looking the slender Gail up and down. "You don't really think anything in my wardrobe is going to fit, do you?"

"You must have something!"

Suzanne shook her head in mock exasperation. "It's just like you to leave something so important to the last minute. Well, come on, maybe we can find something. I can always wrap one of my belts around you four or five times."

It was after midnight by the time Gail got back to her own apartment. She and Suzanne had finally found the perfect outfit—an apricot-colored silk dress with a matching beaded jacket—stuffed at the back of one of Suzanne's bulging closets. Her friend pulled it out with a whoop of triumph.

"I'd forgotten all about this!" she exclaimed, and held it out to Gail. "It's perfect. I bought it about twenty pounds ago. It'll be a little big on you, but with your eyes, who'll notice?"

Dashing over to the full-length mirror in the corner of the cluttered bedroom, Gail held the dress up. It really did look good with her coloring, and she turned to Suzanne with relief. "You won't believe it, but by some miracle, I've got shoes to go with it," she said. "You sure you don't mind if I borrow it?"

"Borrow it? Keep the darn thing. Then I won't feel guilty about those twenty pounds."

"Thanks, Suzie. You're a true friend."

Suzanne waggled her fingers. "Wear it in good health. You—" She stopped suddenly, staring at Gail's hand. "Why aren't you wearing your ring?"

Flustered, Gail looked at her bare hand. "I . . . I gave it back to Stanley tonight."

Suzanne looked shocked. "What! You broke your engagement?"

She really didn't want to talk about it. "It's a long story."

Suzanne grabbed her and dragged her down onto the edge of the bed. "Tell me."

"Oh, Suzie—"

"*Tell* me!"

Gail was still holding the beautiful dress. Smoothing the rich material with one hand, she avoided looking at her friend when she said, "We got into a fight about my work."

Suzanne sat back. "I'm not surprised. Stanley never did like all this cloak-and-dagger stuff."

"It's not cloak-and-dagger!"

"Okay, okay—corporate intelligence," Suzanne said agreeably, then she gave Gail a mischievous look. "But it's the same thing."

"It is not!"

"Hey, you don't have to be so defensive with me. *I* think your work is exciting."

"So do I, but Stanley doesn't."

"I know. He's certainly complained about it enough times," Suzanne said, and hesitated. But, being Suzanne, she had to say it. "Well, at the risk of sounding heartless and all that, maybe this is for the best. Stanley was never right for you. We both know it.''

Despite the fact that she knew, deep down, that Suzanne was right, Gail couldn't prevent an indignant ''How can you say that?''

''Because Stanley, bless his little chauvinistic heart, is basically a homebody who wants a meek little wife to stay home and keep house for him.'' She gave Gail another wicked look. ''And you, my friend, are about as willing to do that as you are to become an archive custodian. You need excitement, adventure in your life. You've said so yourself.''

Gail looked away from Suzanne's knowing glance. ''You make me sound so...shallow,'' she muttered.

''Why, because you want to do something different? Pooh. I think it's wonderful. So should Stanley.'' She pursed her lips. ''I take it this latest dustup was because of your new assignment?''

Gail sighed. ''Yes, but it's been coming for a long time. I just didn't have the courage to tell him before now.''

Suzanne patted her hand. ''Well, if it's any comfort, I think you did the right thing. Stanley will find someone else—someone who wants the same things he does.'' She paused. ''And so will you.''

''Oh, no, not me,'' Gail said. ''Now that I've finally made the decision, I plan to concentrate on my career.'' She stood dramatically. ''Now I only have to be responsible to me!''

''We'll see,'' Suzanne said knowingly.

''What does that mean?''

Suzanne walked to the door with her. ''I said you didn't want to spend your life in the archives, Gail. I didn't say you wanted to be a nun.''

''Suzanne!''

"Don't sound so scandalized. There's nothing in the rules that says you can't have a career and a man, too, you know. You just haven't found the right one. Man, I mean."

"Well, I don't intend to look," Gail said firmly. She held up the apricot-colored dress. The beads on the jacket caught the light and glinted, as though sharing a private joke. Hastily, she folded the dress under her arm and raised her chin. "I've got a job to do, remember?"

"Absolutely," Suzanne said. But her eyes sparkled and it was obvious that she was trying not to smile. "By the way, where is the island?"

"I'll tell you all about it when I get back—maybe."

"Aha! I was right! You *are* on a cloak-and-dagger case!"

Gail gave up. "My first—but not my last," she said, grinning at her irrepressible friend. Waving goodbye, she went back to her own apartment to finish packing. When she looked at the clock again, it was almost one.

WITH AN EXCLAMATION of impatience, Chris put down the book he was reading and got up. It was two o'clock in the morning, but he couldn't sleep, and he walked to the sliding glass doors at one end of the master bedroom, wondering why he felt so restless. He had a lot of work awaiting him in the study that he should have attended to after dinner; tomorrow was going to be a busy day. Damion's representative was scheduled to arrive, and he wanted to be ready. Knowing he should try to get some sleep, he stood at the doors for a moment instead, then opened one and went out to the deck.

The air was warm, even at this time of night, and a crescent moon hung low in the black sky, casting a wavering silver ribbon of light on the sea. The house was built on a small rise so that it looked out over the bay that nestled in the curve of the island. He'd taken this bedroom not because it was the biggest, but because it had such a wonderful view of the beach.

The sight was especially restful tonight, for along with the lightest of breezes on his face, it was so quiet that he could hear the gentle lapping of the waves against the shore. The beach spread out on either side of him, beckoning, the sand gleaming palely under the moonlight. For a second he was tempted to go for a swim, but it seemed too much of an effort, so he leaned against the deck rail, enjoying the play of moonlight on water, thinking how much he loved this place. He'd grown up here, and even though he had several other houses scattered over the world, he'd always regarded this one as home, the place to come to when he needed solace, or peace, or rest. He'd been so grateful to have it, especially during the worst of times, when his father died ... or when Celeste asked for a divorce.

His mouth tightened at that last thought, and he turned and looked the other way. But his eyes didn't see the beach now; he was thinking of his wife, the beautiful Celeste, and now, even after two years, their failure to make their marriage work still galled him. He'd never failed at anything in his life, and to think that his marriage had been such a disaster was painful and humiliating even yet. Worse, because he knew it was mainly his fault.

I love you, Chris, but it's just not working. You're married more to VDK than you are to me!

He could hear her voice ringing in his head again, as he had so many times since the night she'd told him that; he closed his eyes, willing away the words, and the accusation behind them. But as always, once he let her in, he couldn't easily rid himself of her presence, and he put his head down on his arms, which were folded on top of the deck rail, and cursed.

He *had* been at fault; he could admit that now. He never should have married Celeste when he did. It had been too soon after his father died. He'd tried to do too much—he knew that now. Marriage and taking over a company the size of VDK had been incompatible. He'd been so determined to succeed in his father's place that he couldn't see anything else. He'd been trained to take over VDK; he'd prepared for it, and anticipated it. But what he hadn't foreseen was the effect his father's death would have on him. Without realizing it, he'd started to feel overwhelmed. Kerstan had been such a powerful influence in his life; everything he'd ever done seemed to have been with his father in mind, and suddenly that overpowering presence was ... gone.

There hadn't been time for grief, if that was what he had truly felt; there had been too much to do. Hundreds of details had had to be taken care of—business had had to go on whether he was ready or not. He'd had so much to learn, so much to prove. He knew everyone at VDK was waiting to see how he would handle things, and he was just as eager to demonstrate to them all that he was as much a man as his father had been.

Remembering how fierce his desire to prove himself had been, and what it had cost him, he shook his head. That was ten years ago. He'd do things differently now. His mouth twisted. For one thing, he wouldn't get married. Celeste had left him because of all the time he spent at VDK; he couldn't blame her. He rarely did it any longer, but he could still remember the nights he'd slept on the couch in his office, too exhausted to come home, too driven by that need to prove to everyone—especially himself—that he could take his father's place.

Maybe that was why he'd been so vulnerable, why he'd convinced himself that marrying Celeste would help balance things. But agreeing to marriage had been a colossal mistake—one he wasn't going to make again. For all her faults, Celeste had been right about one thing: he had been more married to the company than he ever would be to any woman. Things hadn't changed, he thought with a sigh. For better or worse, VDK was still his wife.

CHAPTER THREE

THE FLIGHT WAS ALL Gail had imagined, and more. She'd never been treated so well; her smallest wish seemed to be anticipated, and the service was sublime. She lost count of the courses offered on the double-width, pull-down trays; everything was served on linen, with real china and silver, and with individual tiny vases of miniature fresh flowers. The flight attendants handed her slippers to put on when she boarded, and every wide seat came with earphones for the first-run movie. She had a choice of music if she wanted, or she could settle back with a pillow and soft blanket and just sleep the flight down.

She was far too excited to sleep. This was the only way to travel, she thought, as the attendant offered her more coffee—fresh-brewed regular or decaf, her choice—and promised that the dessert cart would be around directly. Settling back with her cup, she closed her eyes and just reveled in the luxury. The plane was so quiet she could hardly hear the engines, and there was no turbulence.

By the time the big plane touched down at the Tampa airport, Gail was so enchanted with flying first-class that she wanted just to take off again and go back the way they had come. The assignment had started off so beautifully that she was sure it was an omen. If things went this well the whole time she was in Florida, she'd have no problems at all.

Things fell apart the instant she stepped off the plane.

She wasn't too concerned when she went to the gate and found out that plans had been changed, and that she was to take a small commuter plane to someplace outside Sarasota. She was disappointed to miss traveling in a private jet, but she'd been treated so well until then that she couldn't complain. And she wasn't even too worried when she finally found the gate at the extreme end of the concourse and saw the plane. It looked very old and very lonely sitting out there by itself on the tarmac, but still she told herself it would be an adventure. After all, she was almost there; how bad could it be?

She found out soon enough, when the flight was called and she had to fight a rising wind to get out to the plane. Things weren't quite so fancy here; she had to carry her own luggage, and climb up a shuddering set of steps to get inside. A single frowning flight attendant abruptly gestured her to her seat, and she nearly hit her head when she tried to sit down. There were two small seats on each side of the narrow aisle, and when she glanced down and saw metal glinting from under the threadbare carpet, she hastily averted her eyes. Was this a regulation plane? she wondered.

Her sinking feeling intensified when only two other people got on; as they strapped themselves in and the attendant stood at the front and shouted emergency instructions at them over the increased whining of the propellers, she wondered if she'd made some dreadful mistake. Was this the right flight? She managed to snag the attendant when he came down the cramped aisle as they taxied out for takeoff.

"Is this Flight 414 for—" she started to say. But just then the engines increased their high-pitched whining and the plane began to shake and bump from side to side as it headed ponderously down the runway. They were obviously on their way—or trying to be, and it was too late to change her mind now. She'd have to ride it out.

The ride was rough, and they weren't even airborne yet. Gripping the worn arms of her seat as the plane bumped and jolted, she looked out the window, expecting to see the scenery starting to slide by as they picked up speed. It looked like a slow-motion show instead, and when nothing seemed to be happening, she began to wonder if they were even going to get off the ground. She found herself leaning forward, practically willing the plane into the air; it seemed to take forever, but finally she felt a tiny jolt, a bigger thump as the landing gear retracted, and they were tentatively on their way.

"Thank God," she muttered, and glanced out the window just as the pilot banked sharply and steeply into the wind. Quickly she closed her eyes again. They seemed to be about ten feet off the ground and already out over water. If the window had opened—did it? she shuddered at the thought, but nothing would surprise her at this point—she could have reached out and gotten her fingers wet.

"Would you like a mint, miss?" someone said an endless time later.

She forced her eyes open. The saturnine attendant was by her seat, looking impatient. She wanted to ask what else he had to offer, but didn't dare; instead she said faintly, "How...how long until we land?"

"What?"

The clamor of the engines made anything less than a scream impossible to hear. She shouted her question at him again, and he nodded and glanced at his watch.

"Oh...soon," he said vaguely, and went off.

It was the longest few minutes she'd ever spent in her life. Once she looked up and saw steam—smoke?—drifting out of the vent over the door to the cockpit, and quickly looked away again, telling herself that since no one else seemed disturbed, it might be better to ignore it. She concentrated instead on just enduring the awful flight until they landed again.

Finally—finally!—they began a bumpy descent. When the attendant opened the doors and she was able to get off, she was so grateful to have survived that she nearly dropped to her knees and kissed the ground. She didn't get the chance: a blast of wind hit her as the plane turned to taxi off again, and before she could get her bearings, she heard someone shout. The man who had pushed the stairs from an equipment shed to the plane and back again was now standing at the edge of the airfield gesturing to her. The plane's engines were blasting away behind her, blowing her hair; she brushed it out of her eyes and started toward him. When she reached him, he pointed to a battered old car with an equally battered Taxi sign only half-attached to the roof.

"Miss, miss, you going to Kellen Key?"

"Yes, but how did you—"

"Then take this taxi, or you'll miss the ferry!"

There wasn't time for debate. Before she could reply, he took the bags from her hands, threw them in the back seat of the car, directed her inside, and away they went, careering down the single lane at a speed that pressed her against the seat. Hoping she hadn't made a terrible mistake, she gripped the window handle and held on as best she could. Moments later they rocked to a halt in a spray of gravel.

"Is this—" she started to say, stopping short when she got a better look at their surroundings. She couldn't see any landmarks, only a concrete landing ahead and water beyond that. They seemed, quite literally, to have come to the end of the road.

The driver jumped out of the car, opened the door and held out his hand. "That ten dollar, miss."

"Ten dollars!" They hadn't gone a mile!

"Better hurry, miss. Ferry waiting," he said with a toothy grin as she stared at him in disbelief. He still had his hand out, but he gestured with the other toward a dilapidated old boat banging against the concrete dock they'd parked near. A man who had to be in his seventies if he was a day was obviously the pilot; he was casually balanced, one foot on the sagging roof of the boat, the other on the pier. He was holding a rope that was tied to the bow to keep the boat from drifting out, but considering the condition of the vessel, she wondered why he bothered. It looked as though all it deserved was a decent burial at sea—as quickly as possible.

"You, miss! You want ride to Kellen Key?" the ferryman shouted.

Even though he was going where she wanted, she wasn't sure she could force herself to board that shabby little boat. This was the ferry? The paint had long since peeled away, and while the benches looked as though they had been designed to transport at least ten passengers, the craft didn't look seaworthy enough to hold her and the pilot. Swallowing, she looked around. The taxi driver was still waiting to be paid; the ferryman was obviously anxious for her to board.

Abruptly, she made her decision. She'd come this far, and the plane was long gone. She might as well risk it, she thought, and dug in her purse for some money. The driver grinned his thanks when she handed him a twenty—all she had—and kept the change; he then magnanimously decided to help her with her bags. Glaring at him, she turned toward the ferry. The aged pilot held out his hand, and before she could think about it, she closed her eyes and jumped aboard. She was just turning around to help with the bags when the taxi driver casually tossed them onto the roof.

"Wait!" she cried, sure they would fall off.

"Don't worry," the pilot said, and revved up the diesel. She wasn't prepared for castoff and fell sprawling onto one of the benches as the taxi driver shoved the little ferry away from the dock with his foot. With a hoot from the horn and a big black puff of smoke from the engine, they were off.

"Oh, Lord!" Gail groaned moments later. She was hanging on for dear life. The wind seemed to have come up, for the run-down little boat wallowed in the troughs made by the waves, throwing her back each time she tried to make her way forward. She wanted to ask the pilot how far it was to Kellen Key—if indeed that was where they were going—but even if she could have stood and clutched at his sleeve, the roar of the diesel engine would have made conversation impossible. Her hair damp from the spray tossed up from the bow, she peered through the cracked windows and wondered if this was the way everyone down here traveled. If so, she wanted to go home!

It wasn't far to Kellen Key; it only seemed forever. They arrived at a pier after a journey of about ten minutes.

"You have to go forward and climb out, miss," the boatman said. She looked at him in disbelief.

"Forward, and climb out?" she said, horrified. The front of the boat was pitching in the water; waves were slapping against the hull. A ladder of sorts was attached to the pier, but she'd have to make a grab for it between waves. She knew she'd never be able to do it.

"It's the only way," the pilot said. "I'll help."

She couldn't allow that; the man was more than seventy years old! "No, I'll do it," she said hastily, and started out. By some miracle she made it, snagging the ladder with one hand while the boat dipped under her. But at last she was on the dock with the luggage he tossed her, and just as he reached for the helm again, she bent over and shouted, "What do I do now?"

He made a vague gesture. "They say they leave a car...."

"A car? But someone was supposed to meet—"

He didn't hear her. Waving cheerily, he tooted the horn and pulled away. Left alone on the dock, Gail fearfully looked over her shoulder. Yes, there it was—a vehicle of sorts. It was parked under the trees, a sort of battered brown conveyance that should have been abandoned years ago. Surely, the ferryman didn't mean . . .

Fighting that sinking feeling again, she approached the wreck. A piece of paper was tucked under the steering wheel, and even before she reached for it, she was resigned. Drawn on the paper was a map to the Van Der Kellen estate; it seemed the limousine had disappeared with everything else. Obviously, the map meant she had to drive herself.

Wearily, she hefted her luggage again and glanced up at the sky. By this time it was late afternoon and she knew she had to hurry. But when she reached for the door handle, it came off in her hand. As she looked at it in dismay, her already taut nerves snapped. She'd come this far, endured this much, only to be greeted at the final leg of her journey with a . . . with a broken car?

"This is unbelievable!" she muttered furiously, and threw down the handle on the ground. Reaching through the window, she jerked at the inside handle, just *daring* that to come off, too. But with a loud shriek of metal, the door opened, and she tossed her luggage inside with a curse. She'd had it. When she got to Kellen Key—if she ever did, she thought, enraged—she'd give Chris Van Der Kellen a piece of her mind. More than a piece! Throwing herself onto the seat, she angrily pumped the accelerator to bring the coughing, choking engine reluctantly to life, thinking direly that Van Der Kellen didn't know how lucky he was. If she had really been Damion's representative, she would have turned back right now and told her boss never, under any circumstances, to sell *anything* to a man who treated his guests like this!

Finally, the ancient engine caught. With a wheeze and a cloud of dust, she was off.

AT THE OTHER END of the island, Chris paced back and forth, glancing every few seconds from his watch to the sky and back again. He swore. If he didn't hear his plane soon, he was going to charter another one and fly to Tampa himself!

"I can't imagine what happened, Chris," Nick said. He was leaning against the gleaming Cadillac, his legs crossed, squinting at the sky like Chris. "I told Darby to meet the flight in Tampa. Maybe she wasn't on it."

"She was on it," Chris growled. "I called the airline to make sure."

"What did Darby say then?"

Darby was Chris's pilot, the one he was going to fire as soon as he landed. If, indeed, he ever did. "He said he couldn't find her," he said tightly. He looked at the sky again. "Where in the hell is he? Better yet, where is *she*? Damn it, Nick, how could this have happened?"

"I don't know, Chris. I gave instructions, just as you said. First-class all the way. I'll find out what went wrong in the morning."

Chris was so furious he could hardly speak. "And in the meantime? What do you suggest we do about finding her? Hire a detective? She's Damion's executive vice president, for God's sake! What is he going to think?"

Nick was spared answering; just then they both heard the drone of an engine, and seconds later, the smaller of VDK's two planes, the Beechcraft Bonanza, came into view. As though Darby sensed he was being watched, he set the plane down with a kiss and taxied quickly to the place where Chris and Nick and Max, the silent limo driver, waited. The aircraft had barely rocked to a stop before Chris was striding purposefully toward it.

Darby climbed out. He was a retired airline pilot, tanned and handsome, looking at the moment as though he wanted to be anyplace but where he was. "I'm sorry, Mr. Van Der Kellen," he said. "I went all over that damned airport and couldn't find her. I don't know what happened."

Chris cursed again, colorfully and roundly, at no one in particular. Even so, they all winced. The famous Van Der Kellen temper was very near the surface, and everyone was painfully aware of it.

"I knew I should have sent the jet to New York," Chris said angrily, meaning the sleek Westwind 2. "Damn it all, this is important. What could have gone wrong?"

"I'm not sure," the pilot answered. "But just as I was landing, I got a message from a friend at flight control. He said a G. Sullivan was listed on Flight 414, Key International Lines. Do you think that's her?"

Chris groaned. Despite the grandiose name, Key International was the local commuter airline. If she'd come that way...

"If that's Miss Sullivan, maybe she took the ferry," Nick said helpfully before his boss could explode. "If so, she's probably down at the other end of the island."

Chris didn't want to think what a disaster this was turning into. "Come on," he said abruptly. "We'll go and see—and hope that she's all right. Damn it. How could this have happened?"

No one answered; they all deemed it more prudent to remain silent during the drive across the island and down to the other end. Max pushed the big car to the speed limit. The limo purred quickly along, and everyone left Chris to brood alone. After what seemed an endless drive, they arrived at the empty dock, this one made up of smooth sturdily supported planks. But no ferry was in sight. Chris's boat, a sleek inboard he kept for quick trips back and forth to the mainland, was bobbing in his boat house, but there was nothing—and no one—else around. The only sound was the lapping of the waves around the dock supports.

"She's not here," Chris said flatly, stating the obvious. He got out of the car and glanced around, as though he could conjure Miss Sullivan out of thin air. "Now what?"

It was a rhetorical question, or at least they all hoped it was. Nick sat silently in the car, his expression indicating that he was all too aware he had made the travel arrangements. But since he had already shown Chris the itinerary he'd drawn up, which he had ordered carried out, he couldn't be blamed. Unfortunately, at the moment, Chris didn't care who was at fault; he just wanted to find his missing guest.

"Get Charlie on the phone," he ordered Max abruptly.

Immediately, without a change in expression, Max used the car phone to dial the number of the sheriff. Kellen Key maintained its own police and fire vehicles, staffed if needed by officers from nearby Gulf Port. After a moment, Max said, "He's on the line, sir," and handed over the phone.

"Charlie, I've got a problem," Chris said, and explained what had happened. He was red-faced when he finished, embarrassed and furious all over again.

"How could you lose someone on an island the size of yours?" the police chief asked jovially.

Chris wasn't in the mood to joke. "Just send someone over, all right, Charlie?" he said, tight-lipped.

"I'm on my way. By happy coincidence, I'm in the boat nearby."

"Take one of the cars from the airstrip. I'll meet you at the house."

"You got it," Charlie said, and keyed off.

Chris handed the phone back to Max. "We'll go home and wait there."

"Yes, Mr. Van Der Kellen."

Kellen Key was crescent-shaped, and the Van Der Kellen estate was located in the wide middle sector, which faced the bay. About a dozen families lived on one end of the island, many of them related to Nick and his family. Some were fishermen, but more worked in the mango groves and cashew and macadamia orchards the Van Der Kellens owned and maintained as a sideline.

Usually the drive soothed Chris, but not tonight. With every passing mile, he was aware of twilight approaching, and he was really starting to get worried. Gazing out at the passing lush scenery, he couldn't wait to get home.

He couldn't take care of things from the car, but once he found out what had happened, heads were going to roll.

Hoping she was on the key somewhere, he tried to comfort himself with what Charlie had said in jest. After all, what could happen on an island this size? His mouth tightened. He didn't know, but he was damned sure nothing would. He wasn't without resources, after all. There were fifty people on this island in addition to his household help. When he got back to the house, he'd get on the shortwave and put out an alert at the other end of the island. While Charlie checked passenger manifests, everybody else would go out looking. He was just leaning forward to start issuing instructions to Max when the limo pulled up at the front of the estate. He saw the battered brown car by the big front gates when the others did.

"What the hell?" he muttered, reaching for the door. The idling car was blocking the way, and as he got out, Max put the limo in gear and quickly joined him, holding him back with a deferential hand on his arm.

"Better let me," the chauffeur said. He doubled as Chris's bodyguard at times; in the past, there had been threats.

Chris was too impatient to wait. "No, I—" he started to say, but just then everything started happening at once. In the gathering dusk, a figure appeared at the front of the car, and Max's hand tightened on Chris's arm; he was trying to pull his boss down. They were both distracted by the sound of a siren coming from somewhere behind them—Charlie on his way—followed quickly by a loud report, like a gunshot, rending the air.

Chris's first thought was that someone had fired on them. His second was that the shadowy figure might be responsible. He hadn't seen a gun, but in the growing darkness it was hard to see anything, and Max had cut the car beams. He was no coward, and there wasn't time to think. Max tripped on something when he started forward, so Chris took over and launched himself toward the figure.

"Chris!" someone yelled.

"I got him!" he shouted back, and wrapped his arms around the form, his flying tackle sending them both to the ground. He heard a surprised, indignant exclamation, and in the instant before he realized what he had done, he wondered if that bang had been a gunshot at all. Now that his racing mind had time to sort things out, he realized it had sounded more like . . . a backfire from the idling car.

"Oh, no!" he groaned.

Before he could think what to do next, Charlie came roaring up in the police car, its sirens shrieking, its revolving lights blazing. Pinned in that merciless glare, Chris looked over his shoulder. They all seemed caught in a strobelike tableau: Nick's face was pale in the flickering light, and Max and Darby were frozen in midstep.

"For heaven's sake!"

The angry tone brought him around. Realizing he was still lying on top of whomever he'd taken down—and that the figure he'd assumed was a man seemed suddenly very soft and very feminine—he looked down and blanched. A pair of angry eyes glared up at him.

"Oh, no!" he said again. He'd never been so embarrassed in his life.

"Oh, yes," she said, giving him a push. "Would you *mind*?"

Behind him, Charlie laughed and said, "I see you've found her, Chris. Do you want to let her up now, or is this an island custom I don't know about?"

Galvanized, Chris realized he was still just lying there. Leaping up, he held out a hand to help her, but she ignored him. Getting to her feet, she began brushing grass from her skirt with quick, agitated movements.

Charlie was too engrossed in the scene to remember to cut the revolving lights atop the car. They were still flashing, and Chris felt so tense that he nearly yelled at someone to smash the damned things. In addition to everything else, those quick bursts of harsh light were making everything seem more surreal than it already was.

Oh, Lord, how could this have happened? he wondered, still not quite believing that it had. Everything that could have gone wrong seemed to have done just that, and when he looked at the woman again, he could see she was about ready to explode. Hastily, he stepped forward. He wanted to offer his handkerchief, but he sensed that this was not the time to tell her about the smudge of green she had across one cheek.

Wondering how he was ever going to recover from such an appalling blunder, he said, "I'm so sorry, Ms Sullivan—it is Ms Sullivan, isn't it?"

"It is," she said, glaring at him. "And you must be..."

Wishing he were anyone but, he said bleakly, "Christian Van Der Kellen."

"I see," Gail said coolly. "How nice to meet you, Mr. Van Der Kellen. Do you greet all your guests this way, or did you roll out the red carpet especially for me?"

CHAPTER FOUR

"I CAN'T TELL YOU how sorry I am," Chris kept saying. He had shown Gail to the main house, where he insisted she join him in the living room and at least have a cup of tea. He asked again and again if she really was all right, and seemed so embarrassed and so anxious to make amends that she assured him she was fine. Still a little shaken, but fine.

"You're sure," he said.

"Positive," she answered, trying not to smile. She'd been prepared not to like him, but he was so obviously distressed about what had happened that she had to forgive him. And he had done everything possible to make things right; before she knew what was happening out there, the police car with the revolving lights had gone, as had the limousine with the driver and the other two men. She'd been escorted inside, and now she was sitting on a vast white couch while he paced back and forth, trying to regain his composure.

Almost magically, the battered brown car that had caused all the commotion had disappeared along with everyone else. She didn't know where it had gone, or who had taken it away, and she didn't care. She'd been terrified when that car backfired; the day had been such a strain that for a heart-stopping instant, she'd actually thought someone had taken a shot at her. She hadn't even seen Chris leap at her out of the darkness; she'd been trying to get her bearings when suddenly she was being tackled and thrown to the ground. She hadn't been hurt; she'd fallen on grass. But as she lay there, she'd taken stock, and had wondered if she was right for this assignment after all.

Her host couldn't have been more mortified. Obviously stricken at his mistake, he'd fussed over her all the way up to the house, and as soon as they were inside, he'd summoned a matronly woman who looked to be the housekeeper and asked her to bring Gail a cup of tea. A fragile, hand-decorated cup had been offered within moments, and as she sipped the fragrant beverage, she was glad he had insisted. She must have been a little more shaken then she realized.

But now she felt calmer and she watched while he gave other orders: something about seeing to a meal, and making sure her luggage was brought in and taken care of. Then he went to a bar in one corner of the luxurious room to pour himself a drink. Bringing a graceful brandy snifter back with him, he smiled stiffly at her and sat on the couch opposite.

There were two couches, both overstuffed and soft and blindingly white. Other massive furniture was scattered about the room, all in pastel tones and dwarfed by the vaulted ceiling and two-story picture windows forming a prow at one end of the room. The decor seemed perfectly in tune with the setting and the island itself, and as she glanced around she wondered what the rest of the house looked like.

"I don't usually do this," he said, indicating the brandy. "But believe me, this type of thing doesn't usually happen. I don't know how things could have gone so wrong, but I promise you, I'll find out."

From the look on his face, she didn't doubt that he'd do exactly as he said. Even sitting, he seemed to radiate energy; she wouldn't have been surprised to feel a crackle in the air. Now that she'd actually met him, she couldn't understand how her travel arrangements had become so muddled; the flying tackle aside, he seemed to be so completely in charge that she couldn't imagine a mix-up. The thought flashed briefly through her mind that he'd arranged the mix-up on purpose, but she realized how ridiculous that was. He thought she was Damion's executive vice president; it would be folly to treat her so shabbily when he wanted to do a deal with her boss. It just didn't make sense. But she had to wonder what had happened; according to his bio, the head of VDK Enterprises didn't do things this way at all.

Remembering the file she had on him, she frowned slightly. She'd memorized all the pertinent facts about him, but she realized now that nothing she'd read or learned could possibly have prepared her for Christian Van Der Kellen in person. As young as he was—and she knew he was only thirty-five—he wore power and authority as naturally as if he'd been born to it. Which of course, he had been. But nothing in his file had equipped her to deal with his undeniable magnetism, and she felt herself being drawn to him despite all that had happened. Quickly, she took another sip of tea.

"Please," she said, "it's all right. I'm here and no harm was done."

He looked at her keenly, obviously unconvinced and still clearly upset about what had happened. "I'll make it up to you," he said, his dark eyes holding hers. "I promise you that."

Something about the way he was looking at her made her feel warm and flush again, and suddenly she recalled how it had felt to be lying underneath him. It had happened so quickly, but she still remembered the feel of his strong arms around her, and his powerful body over her. Without even trying, he had evoked potent feelings in her—feelings that Stanley had never been able to arouse—and before she knew it, she was wondering what kind of lover he would be.

Dazzling, she thought, and quickly set aside her cup.

"I'm sorry," she said. "It's been a long day. If you don't mind, I think I'd like to—"

"Of course," he said at once, springing up. "Where are my manners? First I manhandle you outside the gate, then I keep you when you're tired. Again, please forgive me."

How could she not? He seemed so anxious to please, so genuinely apologetic, that any lingering annoyance disappeared—especially when she was shown by another servant to the guest house—a "cottage" that had to be bigger than her parents' home in Albany, New York. Here, everything was of a floral motif; she felt as though she'd wandered into a garden. Even the scent of hibiscus hung in the air.

The servant, a wizened little old man, brown as a nut with a shock of white hair, bowed incessantly and promised to return quickly with a light supper ordered by "Mr. Chris." It arrived shortly on a trolley laid with crystal and linen, accompanied by a huge bouquet of flowers from Chris welcoming her to Kellen Key, with a card tucked inside adding another apology. After the servant had gone, she sampled the consommé and tasted the tiny sandwiches made with home-baked bread, the best she'd ever eaten. Fingering the petals of one of the roses in the huge bouquet, she wondered if the estate had its own greenhouse. She wouldn't have been surprised; it seemed to have everything else.

Suddenly weary, she went into the bedroom, where her clothes had been carefully put away. Her nightgown and robe had been folded at the foot of the big four-poster bed. Sighing with pleasure, she took a long bath and nearly fell asleep in the scented tub.

IN THE MORNING, Gail awoke to the sound of gentle rolling surf and birds singing outside her window. She had promised to meet her host for breakfast, and she dressed quickly in a simple cotton shift. It was a beautiful morning, and when she was shown to an elegantly set table on the terrace at the back of the main house, she stopped to admire the breathtaking view.

The terrace was really a deck, cantilevered out over a sloping lawn that led to a stunning beach, where tiny wavelets lapped against white sand. It looked like something out of a coffee-table book, a picture of the perfect getaway. Even the day seemed made to order, not too hot, with warm sun and the slightest of breezes bringing with it the salty tang of the sea. She'd never seen such a lovely place, and unconsciously, she sighed.

Chris came out onto the terrace while she was admiring the view, and when she sighed, he came anxiously forward. "Good morning. Are you feeling well this morning? No ill effects?"

She'd almost forgotten the fiasco the night before. Besides, now that she was here, and once again being treated royally—a young woman had arrived at the "cottage" this morning with coffee, offering to draw her bath—she was willing to forget yesterday entirely. After meeting Chris, she was sure there was a reason for what had happened, and she was equally positive that he'd take care of it and see that it would never happen again.

"No ill effects whatsoever," she said, smiling. "How could there be, in such a beautiful setting?"

He glanced out at the glorious beach. "Thank you. I'm glad you like it. Please, sit down."

He held her chair, and then sat opposite her. As though it were a signal, the same little man who had brought her supper last night appeared with a silver pot of coffee. She smiled at him in recognition, and he grinned back, his eyes practically disappearing in his brown cheeks.

"How are you this morning, Señorita Sullivan?" he asked.

"Very well, thank you, Mr. Diaz," she said. She'd learned his name last night.

He bowed. "Please, my name is Raphael."

"Then you must call me Gail."

He bowed once more. "As you wish, Señorita Gail."

She noticed that her host was smiling, so she let it go. Nodding his thanks when Raphael moved around to pour his coffee, Chris waited until the old man had gone before he said, "You're certainly taking this well."

"Why not?" she replied, sipping the excellent fresh-grown Kona. "It was a mistake—mistakes happen. You didn't plan it that way, did you?"

He looked appalled. "Absolutely not!"

Smiling at his outraged expression, she shrugged to show she truly had forgiven him, and then tried to remember why she was here. It was harder than she had imagined. Surrounded by all this lush island beauty, attended to by this handsome man, her every wish seemingly anticipated, she was tempted to enjoy herself and forget business for a while. Sternly, she reminded herself that she wasn't here to do that, and she said, "Then we'll just forget it. And I won't mention it to Mr. Damion, so it won't affect any transactions, I promise."

Chris leaned back, his dark eyes on her face. "I'm glad to hear you say that. In your place, I might not be so gracious."

She had to smile at that; she didn't doubt it was true. But again she said, "I'm not here to be gracious. I'm here because of Kalliste International."

He was still looking at her. What was he seeing? Uncomfortable under his scrutiny, she was about to say something when he said, "You'll pardon my saying so, but you seem so young to be an executive vice president."

She had to struggle with her expression. Had he seen through her already? Then she told herself she was being ridiculous; that couldn't be. If he wasn't just making conversation, he was obviously trying to probe politely to determine how much influence she had with her supposed employer.

"How kind of you to say so," she said. "I was just thinking the same thing about you, heading a company the size of VDK."

He grinned. "Touché."

She decided to press him a little. He had to be convinced she was legitimate, or he'd never trust her, so she said, "If you're not satisfied with my qualifications, Mr. Van Der Kellen—"

He interrupted quickly. "Please, call me Chris. And I didn't mean to imply that you weren't qualified. Quite the contrary. I intended to express my admiration for your success."

She'd jumped the gun. Hoping her expression didn't betray her, she sat back. "As I did mine for yours," she said as smoothly as she was able. Then she had an idea.

"I'm sorry if I sounded defensive. I suppose that's the result of coming from a family of overachievers."

"You, too?" he said ironically. "Well, I can understand that."

Familiar with his background—the demanding father, the expectation that he would grow up to run the family company—she knew he understood it very well. Hoping she could use that as a jumping-off point so that he'd start talking about himself, she was dismayed when he leaned forward and said, "Tell me about your family."

She was here to learn what she could about him; she didn't want to talk about herself. Wondering if she was a little out of her depth after all, she gestured weakly. "There's really not that much to tell."

"I can't believe that. Go on—please."

She couldn't think of a graceful way to refuse. Trying to be as brief as possible, she said, "Well, before he retired, my father owned his own civil engineering firm in Washington, and my mother had worked her way up to school principal. One of my brothers is a designer at Lockheed, and the other is an architect in Los Angeles."

"And you're executive vice president at Kalliste International," he said thoughtfully. "I see what you mean about achievers."

"Yes, well..." She really didn't want to discuss this further. "But we're not here to talk about my personal life, are we? I came because you might have questions about Mr. Damion's resorts."

"Let's not talk business yet," Chris said.

Disconcerted, she began, "Oh, but—"

"I never discuss business before breakfast," he said. "It's bad for the digestion, haven't you heard?"

"No, I . . . hadn't," she said, faltering. He was sitting there smiling at her, a smile that for some reason made her treacherous heart skip a beat. Why was that? She couldn't deny that he was a handsome man, but she reminded herself firmly again that she was here on assignment. That was all she should have her mind on—all. She didn't care how handsome he was, or how intently his dark eyes rested on her, or how charmingly his mouth quirked when he smiled. She didn't care about any of those things; the only thing that mattered was getting her job done.

"Well," she said. "If that's what you prefer . . ."

"I do," he said calmly. "And after we finish, I'll show you around the estate."

She didn't want to be shown around the estate. Already she felt as though she were floundering, and she hadn't been here a full day yet. She'd been drawn to this man last night; this morning the feeling was even stronger. She'd better just do her job and get out of here before—

Before what?

"I'd like that very much," she said quickly, stifling *that* thought. She looked away so that she wouldn't have to look into those dark, intense eyes. "This is such a lovely place."

That much was true. Tall trees flanking the beautifully curving bay swayed gently in the wind, and far out on the water, she saw a sailboat skimming by. Chris followed the direction of her glance before he looked back at her again.

"Yes, it is," he said, his voice low. "I wish I could be here more often. I grew up here. . . ."

His voice trailed away, and when he saw her looking at him curiously, he gave an embarrassed shrug. "Happier times then, I guess."

She wasn't sure what he meant. Was he referring to the more innocent times of childhood—or was that an oblique reference to the company problem Damion had suspected, and which had brought her here? Remembering that this was just the kind of information she was supposed to get, she asked casually, "Is that nostalgia, or regret?"

"Both, I suppose," he said, and seemed to give himself a mental shake. Laughing shortly, he changed the subject. "Now, which would you like—an omelet or a Continental breakfast?"

She chose the Continental and was served a croissant that was so light she thought it might float away. Having decided to play the guest for the time being, she sat back with a sigh when she finished. "That was delicious."

Chris pushed the last of his omelet away. "I'll tell Hana you appreciated her efforts."

"Hana?"

"Raphael's wife. She's my cook and—" he smiled fondly "—my surrogate mother. Or she thinks she is, anyway. You met her last night."

"Oh, yes, the woman who brought the tea," Gail said, and looked at him curiously. "Why does Raphael call me *Señorita* Gail, and you *Mr.* Chris?"

A shadow passed quickly over Chris's face and then was gone. "There was only one *Señor*," he said, "and that was my father."

"I see," she said. Obviously she'd stumbled onto sensitive ground.

Her host shrugged, as though it didn't matter, and then asked a personal question of his own. "You haven't said anything about your husband. What does he do?"

"Oh, I'm not married," she said, and pictured Stanley, who was definitely suffering in the comparison with Chris. And then, even though she already knew it from the file, she asked, "How about you?"

"Divorced," Chris said.

"Oh. What a shame."

"Yes," he replied. "Celeste accused me of being more married to the company than I was to her. She was right. I couldn't blame her for leaving. The surprise was that she stayed as long as she did."

"I'm sorry," Gail said. It seemed the safest thing to say.

"So was I." Chris stirred his coffee. "But that was a long time ago."

Two years, she thought, and reached quickly for her own cup, telling herself she'd have to be more careful. She'd almost blurted that out without thinking, and while he could rightly suppose that she had a file on him, it might be best just to play things by ear. She could learn more that way.

But she was still curious that he hadn't become involved with any woman again. Two years was a long time, and although he'd been photographed at different functions with some of the more highly visible names in entertainment and society, none of those relationships seemed to have led to anything serious and she wondered why. Chris Van Der Kellen was not only good-looking, but extremely eligible as well. He should have been snapped up long ago.

"Well, I guess we'd better—" he started to say just then, and glanced beyond her with a small start of recognition. "What are you doing here?"

Gail turned to look over her shoulder. She hadn't heard anyone come out to the terrace, and she was surprised to see Chris's assistant standing behind her. She'd been introduced to him the previous night, just after the fracas and before Chris had spirited her away.

When he saw her looking at him, he smiled. "Hello, Miss Sullivan."

"Hello—Nick, isn't it?"

Chris gestured. "Nick, you don't have to stand in the doorway. Join us. Gail, you obviously remember my assistant, Nick Sierra."

"Yes, of course," she said. "How are you, Nick?"

"I'm fine. But I suppose the more pertinent question is how you are this morning. Have you recovered from your . . . ordeal?"

"It's as though it never happened," she said, watching as he came to the table. She hadn't had much time to notice the night before, but now, in daylight, she saw that he had black, straight hair, deep brown eyes and a complexion that indicated his Latin heritage. Her file had indicated he was Chris's age, but the difference between the two men was almost palpable. Chris exuded an aura of confidence and power and wealth; beside him, Nick seemed a pale imitation. Remembering that they had grown up together, she studied him as he and Chris began to discuss something, wondering if that difference had ever bothered him.

It didn't seem to this morning. He had some papers that he handed to his boss. "I tracked down the problem with the travel arrangements, Chris."

Instantly, Chris turned grim. "And?"

"And...I don't know," Nick said with an apologetic, unhappy glance in her direction before he turned back. "This is a copy of the itinerary I sent out, with instructions to the secretary. Apparently, something got garbled."

Chris's eyes darkened even more. "How could that happen?" he demanded. "It was simple enough—book the flight to Tampa, and then have Darby and Max take over from there."

Nick looked even more unhappy. "I know, Chris. I can't explain it. You see the copy—"

"Who was the secretary who made the arrangements?" Chris interrupted.

Both men were ignoring her, and as she watched silently, Gail had a glimpse of the man who ran VDK. An edge had crept into Chris's tone; even his face had changed, his expression sharpening along with his voice. Gone was the affable host he'd been only moments ago; in his place was a man who had earned his reputation as a tough businessman. Remembering the file she had on Kerstan, Chris's father, she shivered inwardly. Chris was supposed to resemble the founder of VDK; in this moment, she could almost believe they were the same man. The image disturbed her. She'd read about Kerstan, and she didn't want to think Chris was like him—ruthless and cruel and demanding.

"I'm sorry, Chris—"

"Chris, it doesn't matter," Gail said, interrupting Nick. "I'm here, and we've both agreed that sometimes these things happen."

Chris flashed her a glance that made her wish she hadn't spoken. "I told you, these things don't happen in my company."

She should have heeded the warning, but she saw the unhappy expression on Nick's face, and she wanted to help. If she'd forgiven and forgotten, why couldn't Chris?

"It's not important, really..." she started to say.

His expression darkened. "It is to me. Now, please, let's drop it."

"But—"

He looked at her again. "Please," he said with cutting finality. "There are things you don't understand."

What things? she wondered. What was he talking about? Sure there was more to it than she had previously imagined, she sat back. "As you wish."

He heard her tone and was immediately contrite. "I didn't mean to be so abrupt. It's just—" He stopped. "I'm sorry. I can't explain."

"I understand," she said, and wished she did. Positive now that his obsession with the mix-up last night had another cause, most probably the rumored troubles at VDK, she longed to stay and listen, but knew she should excuse herself. "Would you prefer if I left you alone?" she asked.

He got to his feet instead. "No, that won't be necessary. I'm afraid I'm the one who has to leave. Some business at the mainland office. You'll forgive me?" Without waiting for an answer, he gestured to Nick, who took the cue and said goodbye before he quietly went out to wait for his boss. Chris paused a moment. "I'm sorry, I hope you understand. I'm sure you'll be all right here."

She didn't understand at all. Surely, he wasn't going to leave her alone after all the trouble she'd had getting here! What about the tour of the estate, or the discussions they were scheduled to have about the Kalliste deal? He saw her expression and said quickly, "It's only for a few hours. Please, my home is yours. Make yourself comfortable, rest." He gestured toward the water. "The beach is private. No one will disturb you there."

He was gone before she could object, leaving her to stare after his departing figure with an expression of dismay. Things had been going so well. What had happened?

"More coffee, Señorita Gail?"

Startled again, she turned and looked up into Raphael's kind brown eyes. He was holding the silver pot, but she shook her head. "No, thank you, Raphael. I've had enough."

The little man bowed. "Mr. Chris say the beach very beautiful this morning, *señorita*."

Gail glanced again in that direction. Indeed it was. The sand was so white, the water a deep blue. It certainly looked inviting, but another idea had occurred to her, and she scraped back her chair. "Yes, it is. I think I'll change and explore."

"Very good, *señorita*," Raphael said with a crinkle of his eyes. "We have lunch served for your pleasure at twelve-thirty. Do you care for anything specially prepared? Mr. Chris say to give you whatever you like."

Her mind was already on other things, but she smiled at the little man. If she didn't have a job to do, she could definitely get into this, she thought, and said, "Whatever Hana fixes is fine. Please, tell her she's a wonderful cook. I've never had such delicious croissants."

Raphael bowed again, clearly delighted. "I'll tell. She will be happy to know that she has pleased you."

Two minutes later, her heart in her throat, Gail was tiptoeing down a hallway she had glimpsed while coming through the main house. She hoped it led to the office she was sure Chris must have here at home. As she crept along, she thought about what she was doing and couldn't believe it. If she were caught . . .

She wouldn't think of that. She had a job to do, and she was going to do it. Part of that job was collecting information for her client, and to do that, she had to invade Chris's privacy by going through his desk. She winced at the thought. It had sounded so simple and straightforward in New York, but now that she knew Chris, it seemed like snooping. Quickening her steps so that she wouldn't have to think about it, she hurried down the hallway. Open doors led off either side, and as she peered into each room, she began to think she'd taken a wrong turn. This was obviously the bedroom wing; maybe she had miscalculated.

Pausing, she tried to think. The house was laid out in a shortened and elongated U shape, with the arms of the U shorter than the bar across. She'd studied the main house from the guest cottage earlier in the morning, and when she remembered the direction Hana had come from with the tea last night, she was sure the kitchen and laundry room and other service areas had to be on the other side. That left this part of the house for the other rooms, with the huge living room acting as the central and focal point—very sensible, since it was the area with the best view of the bay and the beach. Glancing over her shoulder again with a frown, she wondered if she'd somehow gotten turned around. Maybe Chris had his office off the kitchen area, she thought, and hoped not. If that were true, she hadn't the faintest idea how she'd get around Hana, who was sure to be there. She could hardly say she was just exploring; what sort of guest would be fascinated by the service wing?

Hoping she wouldn't have to face that difficulty, she continued down the hall. She saw two more doors at the end, and that was all. Praying one of them would yield what she was looking for, she reached for the doorknob of the closer one. Keenly aware that the longer she stayed in the house, the likelier she was to be discovered, she quietly pulled it open and peered inside. This was another bedroom; she knew instantly it belonged to Chris.

Telling herself she should shut the door again and go on her way, she couldn't resist the impulse to step inside instead. It was definitely a man's room, she thought when she saw the king-size bed with the heavy, carved oak headboard and matching furniture. There was a deep blue carpet on the floor and lighter blue curtains at the big windows. A clothes valet by the foot of the bed had a jacket carefully hung over it, and she ran her fingers over the luxurious material, enjoying the nubby feel of the raw linen and the faint scent of the after-shave she already recognized as Chris's wafting up from it at her touch.

A beige leather recliner was positioned at the end of the room by the plate-glass window and was flanked by a floor lamp over a low table. A book was on the table, facedown to mark a page. Moving closer, she glanced at the title and raised an eyebrow. The book was *Great Expectations*, by Charles Dickens. It was a long time since she'd read it herself, but she remembered the story about the coming of age of a young man named Pip, who became a man of character after a life of disillusionment and sadness. She frowned. Was the theme of the book significant? Why would Chris be reading it?

She didn't have time to decide. Hearing a noise, she spun around. Was that a footstep in the hall? She thought she heard a cough, a laugh—she didn't know what she heard; she only knew she had to get out. Glancing wildly around for a place to hide, she looked at the big walk-in closet, and dismissed the idea as soon as she thought of it. *All right, then, how about under the bed?* She looked in that direction. No, that was absurd—the first place anyone would look.

She had to do something; now she was sure she heard someone in the hall. One of the maids, coming to clean? She had to get out—how could she possibly explain being here?

Then she noticed that the plate-glass window was really a sliding glass door that led out to the deck. She didn't stop to think if she'd be able to get off the deck once she was out there. Pulling the door open, she slipped through just as the bedroom door opened.

Just in time! Outside, breathing heavily, but screened from whoever was inside by the heavy curtains, she quickly looked around for an escape route. If she had to, she'd jump to the ground, she thought, but that proved unnecessary. A series of steps led down to the grass, and she took them by twos, disappearing into the trees at the edge of the wide lawn just as she heard the sliding glass door open again.

Letting out a sigh of relief at her escape, she ran all the way to the guest cottage and practically fell in the door. Maybe she wasn't cut out for this cloak-and-dagger stuff after all, she thought, pressing one hand to her chest as she gasped for breath. Even though she was safe now, her heart was thundering in her ears and her legs felt weak. She had to sit down.

Clinging to the chair, she wondered what she would have done if she'd been caught. How would she ever have explained what she was doing there? She cringed. Worse yet, what would she have said to Roger when she was forced to return ignominiously to New York, admitting that she'd failed on her very first day undercover?

Grimacing at the thought, she dragged herself up. She couldn't just sit all day. By the time Chris returned, she had to look as though she'd lain out on the beach the entire time he'd been gone. But her expression was sour when she went to change into her swimsuit; for all she'd learned, she might as well have spent her time lounging on the sand. All that stress and strain—not to mention her terror at the thought of being caught—and she'd come up with exactly nothing. If this was the way things were going to go, she might as well leave right now....

IF NICK HAD BEEN SURPRISED at Chris's insistence on a quick visit to the mainland, he gave no sign of it. Chris knew his assistant had been startled this morning by his sudden decision to go into the office; the plan had been for him to stay at Kellen Key today and show Damion's representative around.

But after meeting Gail, he'd had to get away for a while to restore his equilibrium. Now, as the plane whisked them back to the island after a morning at VDK, Chris gazed out the window, brooding, wondering what was happening to him. Down the aisle, Nick went over some papers, leaving him alone. At times like this, he was glad of Nick's almost uncanny ability to read his mind; he didn't want to sit and chat, not when he felt he'd made a fool of himself ever since Gail had arrived.

The problem was that he hadn't expected her to be so attractive. And he certainly hadn't expected what had happened last night. Christ! Just thinking of it made him want to cringe, and he could feel himself getting red all over again when he remembered that flying tackle. How could he have done such a thing? Even though she'd assured him that the incident was forgotten, he was sure it couldn't be, and he didn't see how her report to Damion could possibly be favorable under the circumstances. If he'd been in her position, he would have wired back his recommendation to forget the whole thing and would have gotten away from Kellen Key as quickly as possible, before some other catastrophe occurred.

Maybe he should send her away, he thought. It seemed now that this deal had been cursed from the start. Despite Nick's reassurances, and his secretary's horror this morning when she found out what had happened, he still wasn't convinced that the mix-up in those travel arrangements had been a series of misunderstandings, as everyone had insisted. He couldn't rid himself of the thought that it had been planned, even though Pat insisted he didn't know anything, and Dan had clearly been appalled. Nick had been so apologetic, and the secretary had seemed ready for the ax to fall. They had all *looked* sincere, but...

In the end, he'd decided to let it go. He had used the incident as an excuse to stay away from Kellen Key, but things were bad enough without him being a coward into the bargain. He couldn't avoid Gail forever, no matter how confused and uncertain his feelings were, and so he had called for the plane to be ready. Now he was on his way. Darby would set down soon but Chris didn't feel under any better control now than he had that morning. Why couldn't Damion have sent a man? Was that a ruse, too?

No, he knew he was being ridiculous. Gail could never be part of a deception; the expression in those marvelous eyes told him that—as did that attractive tilt of her chin. That thought reminded him of the attraction he felt to her, and he felt grim again. Why did he react so strongly to her? She wasn't the most beautiful woman he'd ever met, but she was certainly the most interesting.

Every time he thought of how she had felt last night, how soft her body had been under his, he was aware of a tightening in his loins. This morning at breakfast, he'd had to keep reminding himself who she was. He wanted to take her in his arms all over again.

He felt hot. What was the matter with him? He never thought such things. He'd better remember who he was, what he was about. He had had much better control over himself until he'd met Gail Sullivan.

Maybe he *should* send her away, pretend that he'd decided against buying the resorts. He could say he'd changed his mind; it was as simple as that.

But then, as Darby began the descent, Chris knew it wasn't that simple. He'd set plans in motion—other plans that were intimately connected with the purchase of Kalliste International. He'd designed this elaborate scheme not only to buy those resorts, but to catch VDK's traitor, and he couldn't back out now because of an adolescent attraction to a woman he'd just met. No, he'd have to go through with it. He could, if he wanted to; he'd done things much more difficult.

THE CALLER CHOSE a different pay phone this time, just to be on the safe side. Chris had been tense this morning; he was sure his boss suspected something, but just didn't have proof. He was determined not to give him any. Lighting a cigarette, he took a drag while he waited for an answer. Wade Sutton picked up the phone on the third ring.

"I've been expecting you to call," Sutton said in his gravelly distinctive voice. "What happened?"

"Nothing," the caller said disappointedly. "I did what you said and screwed up the travel arrangements, but he must have convinced her it was all a mistake. Have you found out anything on your end?''

Sutton's voice was a rasp. ''You take care of your business—I'll handle mine.''

The caller wouldn't be baited. Sutton needed him, and he smiled nastily. ''I take it that means you haven't found out anything.''

''It's just a matter of time,'' Sutton said harshly. ''In the meantime, keep a sharp eye out. I don't like it that she's still there. It means—''

''I know what it means,'' the caller said, and felt confident enough to push a little. ''As you say, you handle your end. I'll take care of mine.''

Sutton was more than equal to him. ''See that you do,'' he said, and broke the connection.

CHAPTER FIVE

CHRIS HAD SCHEDULED a dinner party that second night to introduce Gail. Fortunately for her, he reminded her of it when he got back to the island. Even though it was afternoon by then, she was still feeling breathless from almost being discovered snooping around the house, and had completely forgotten about the party. It seemed that she'd just settled herself on the beach, trying to look as though she'd been there for hours, when he came out; she was so flustered that she couldn't tell if he suspected anything or not.

But then, why should he suspect anything? she wondered later while she was getting ready for the evening. For all he knew, she was exactly who she'd said she was. She hadn't given him any reason to think otherwise—not yet, anyway.

Trying not to think of that, she undressed for her bath, and then looked at herself, horrified. Gingerly, she touched the strap marks her swimsuit had left on her shoulders. It hadn't hurt until now, but as the burn started to sting a little, she cursed herself for not remembering she hadn't been thinking too clearly after almost being caught in Chris's bedroom, and now she was paying the price. She looked like a lobster: her nose was red and she had white circles around her eyes from her sunglasses.

"Boy, you're going to make a hit tonight," she muttered, and held her breath as she climbed into the tub, anticipating a scream from her sunburn. But one of the maids—bless her heart! Gail thought blissfully as she sank into the scented water—had obviously seen her condition. A bottle of bath oil was placed conspicuously on the side of the tub, and whatever was in it did wonders for her burn. By the time she emerged from her bath, she felt almost human again. The worst of the redness had faded, and as she carefully toweled herself dry, she began to hope that once she was dressed, she wouldn't look as though she'd been parboiled.

Miraculously, once she'd put on her makeup and zipped up the dress with the beaded jacket Suzanne had loaned her, she looked...like herself, but better. Most of the burn had turned into a healthy-looking glow, and after she rubbed in some lotion that had also been left for her, the stinging sensation was almost bearable. Since this was a party, she decided to put her hair up, and for once it behaved as it should. Hoping it was an omen for the evening, she stepped into high-heeled sandals and was ready.

Or at least, she hoped she was. She took a deep breath before setting out on the path that meandered toward the main house where the party was being held, trying to gear herself up for what she suspected was going to be another ordeal. After nearly getting caught that morning in Chris's bedroom, of all places, she couldn't afford to forget even for a minute why she was here. The party wasn't a social event for her, but an intelligence-gathering opportunity. Roger was depending on her, and she couldn't let him down.

Chris was standing by the doorway when Raphael let her in. The appreciative look on his face when he saw her nearly made her forget her resolve. He looked even more handsome tonight than he had earlier; his white jacket made his hair look so black it seemed almost blue, and his eyes had that intense look as he gazed at her, making her feel...

Hastily, she smiled and came forward. "I hope I'm not late."

"Not at all," he said with a smile that made her heart thud. Gallantly, he added, "But if you had been, it still would have been worth the wait. You look beautiful."

Wishing he would stop looking at her that way, she tried to laugh. "You're very kind. But I think I spent too much time on the beach today. I got a little sunburned."

He looked instantly concerned. "Oh, yes, I should have warned you. The sun in this latitude can be very intense. I'll have Cecilia bring you some lotion."

"She already did—or someone did, anyway. It worked wonders."

"Good. It's a local concoction—aloe, and something else that's a closely guarded secret."

"Well, I certainly hope they market it," she said, and became aware of the scent of his after-shave again. She couldn't identify it; it was an unusual fragrance, lemony and spicy at the same time—clean and...sexy. Trying to keep her mind on the conversation, she added hastily, "A product like that would sell like hotcakes to vacationing tourists."

He laughed. No problem for him carrying on the conversation. "Oh they market it, all right," he said. "On the big keys. But in tantalizingly small amounts, so there's always a demand."

Wondering why she was suddenly having to fight this sudden, powerful attraction to him, she tried to marshal her thoughts. "The big keys?"

Looking amused, he said, "Right. The islands have become major tourist attractions. But come, I've monopolized you long enough. I'd like you to meet the others."

"Yes, that would be nice," a new voice said at Gail's elbow. "We've all been waiting discreetly in the background to be introduced."

Gail turned, and looked up. Standing behind her was a big man with sandy hair, blue eyes and freckles. Chris laughed. "You never just stand discreetly in the background, Pat," he said, and introduced Gail to his vice president, Patrick Delaney.

"Hello," she said, offering her hand. "How nice to meet you."

Delaney bowed. "You're kind indeed if you can say that after the fiasco last night. Please believe me—that's not a proper introduction to VDK." His blue eyes studied her. "I do hope you've recovered from our... warm reception."

"It was original, I agree," she said, not looking at Chris because she was afraid she'd start to laugh. Then she sobered. "But really, I'm fine. No ill effects at all. And Chris has done everything possible to apologize and make me comfortable."

"I certainly hope so," Delaney said, giving her an appreciative glance. "Might I say you look beautiful tonight?"

"Why, thank you," she said, and glanced covertly in Chris's direction. She was surprised to see that he was watching Delaney with a strange expression she couldn't interpret. Her instincts alerted, she pretended not to see and turned back to Delaney instead. "Are all the men at VDK so complimentary?"

"I don't know," he said, chivalrously offering his arm. "Why don't I show you around and you can discover for yourself? You mind, Chris?"

If Chris minded, he didn't show it. "Not at all," he said easily. "Go ahead."

The big living room seemed filled with people at first, but after Patrick finished introducing Gail to them, she realized that not so many were here after all. There was Delaney's wife, Betty, a large, comfortable-looking woman with a wonderful smile, and the Harrises—Daniel, who was VDK's comptroller, and his petite Asian wife, Su-lin, who had the most beautiful, graceful hands Gail had ever seen. Nick came forward to greet her with a smile, bringing his date for the evening, Tania something-or-other, a tall, striking blonde who was obviously more interested in her host than she was in her escort. Tania's expertly made-up blue eyes, complete with a fringe of false eyelashes, followed Chris wherever he went, and as Gail watched this little byplay, she was shocked at the stab of jealousy she felt.

Telling herself that was ridiculous, she let Patrick introduce her to the other couples, who had come from neighboring islands for the party, but it was difficult to keep her mind on small talk when she kept covertly glancing around to see where Tania was. By the time Gail had met everyone and Patrick went to get her a glass of wine, Tania had left Nick and had closed in on Chris.

Having dismissed Raphael, Chris was doing duty by the bar when the leggy blonde in her skintight sapphire-blue sheath perched on one of the bar stools to gaze soulfully into his eyes. Across the room, Gail noticed that Tania had also propped her generous bosom on top of the bar to make sure that Chris wouldn't miss a thing. Trying to be amused at this obvious ploy, Gail noticed that whether Chris had been taken in or not, Patrick had been caught. He seemed to have forgotten his errand entirely; her wine in hand, he was standing by the blonde, staring at her as raptly as she was looking at Chris. Wondering what Tania was saying that was so fascinating, Gail decided that if she wanted something to drink she'd have to get it herself. Hoping she wasn't being as conspicuous as Tania was, she headed casually in the direction of the bar and arrived in time to listen to one of the most outrageous Southern drawls she'd ever heard.

"Well, ah jus' doan know *whut* to do about this li'l ol' 'heritage ah got from mah *Daddy*, Chris," Tania was saying when Gail sat down. "D'yew think yew kin *possibly* help me t'de*cide*? Ah mean, yew know how *women* are! We jus' doan have a *head* for finances, do we?"

Speak for yourself, honey, Gail thought, and wondered why she felt so annoyed. Why should it matter to her if Nick's date was making a play for Chris; it wasn't any business of hers. In fact, she thought, glancing covertly around, if anyone should be offended, it should be Nick. But when she saw him, deep in conversation with someone in a corner, she realized he hadn't noticed—or didn't care—what was going on over here. That seemed odd to Gail. Why bring a gorgeous woman like Tania to the party and then ignore her?

Tania seemed to realize then that she had company, and gave Gail a dirty look as she reluctantly removed her assets from atop the bar. The accent disappearing like smoke, she said petulantly, "Do you *mind*? We were trying to have a conversation here."

Gail gave her a sweet smile. "Oh, I'm terribly sorry. I didn't realize I was interrupting."

"Oh, you weren't," Chris said, and came around the end of the bar. He took her arm, much to Tania's disgust. "I'm sorry Tania," he said. "But I've neglected my guest of honor too long. Will you excuse us?"

"But Chris," Tania said, pouting, "what am I going to do about my investments?"

Chris had already started pulling the amused Gail away. "I'll send Dan over to talk to you about that. He's much more knowledgeable than I am."

Now that they were halfway across the room, Gail couldn't resist. "Is that true?"

His mind obviously still on escape, he gave her a blank look. "What?" he said, and then laughed. "Oh . . . no. I mean, Dan does know what he's doing in the market, but it seemed the safest thing to say. Look, why don't we go out onto the terrace for a few minutes? It seems awfully warm in here."

"I agree," Gail said innocently. "That Tania seems like a pretty hot number."

"Tania is Nick's date," he said firmly. "*He* can handle her."

"I wonder if anyone can handle her," Gail said, and smiled when he sighed in relief as they escaped to the deck outside. Was this the suave, sophisticated Christian Van Der Kellen she'd read about who escorted the most polished of socialites to all those distinguished affairs? Thinking that he seemed to have many more sides than the file on him revealed, she found herself wondering what else she might discover, and quickly leaned against the deck's rail. Now *she* felt warm.

Joining her, Chris shook his head and muttered, "For the life of me, I don't understand what Nick sees in women like that."

Gail certainly agreed with that, but she didn't feel it was her place to say. Instead, she said cautiously, "Tania is certainly beautiful."

Chris looked at her as though she had to be joking. "I'm sure he thinks so." He turned away again. "I'm sorry. I didn't mean to drag you away from the party."

"Oh, I don't mind," she said, and didn't. It was so beautiful out here; by listening carefully, she could hear the gentle lapping of waves against the shore, and the moonlight on the water was very romantic. Realizing where her thoughts were heading, she straightened abruptly. "But perhaps I should go back inside," she said. "I'm sure your people have some questions for me. That's why they're here, isn't it?"

"Yes, but they can wait," Chris said, dismissing his guests with the unconscious arrogance of someone for whom everyone else waited, not the other way around. He'd been leaning looking out toward the water; now he turned and rested his elbows on the rail. He regarded her with such a strange expression that after a moment she began to feel uncomfortable. She wanted to look away from him, but she couldn't. To her dismay, she seemed mesmerized by his dark glance.

This is a mistake, she thought, and wanted to insist that they go back in. Something in his face stopped her, and suddenly she knew that he wanted to kiss her. When she realized that she wanted to kiss him, too, she was annoyed with herself. What was wrong with her? Only an hour or so ago she'd given herself a stern talking-to, resolving to keep her mind on business, no matter what. Now she told herself firmly again. Chris Van Der Kellen was the object of an investigation, *not*, by any stretch of the imagination, a love interest. The job she was supposed to do required that she keep all her wits about her, not drift off into some romantic fantasy about how much she'd like to kiss, and be kissed by, this man. Roger was relying on her, so was Harlan Damion. Everything depended on her success, not the least of which was a promotion—something she'd better remember if she didn't want to spend the rest of her life going over expense reports, or analyzing data everyone else brought in.

That distasteful thought brought her up short, and she was about to suggest they return to the party when Chris said thoughtfully, "We haven't had much chance to talk about the Kalliste resorts themselves, have we?"

This seemed a subject she could safely discuss, so she said, "No, we haven't. But I'll certainly be glad to tell you anything you want to know."

He surprised her by asking, "Have you been to all the resorts yourself?"

It was a logical question, so she wasn't sure why she was surprised. Trying not to think that her familiarity with Kalliste International was due to her intense studying of the file on the resorts, she nodded. "Certainly. I've been to all four—many times."

"I haven't."

"No?" She sounded surprised because she genuinely was. If he was thinking of buying the chain, why hadn't he visited them first?

"I haven't had time," he said, and glanced at her as though he'd suddenly made up his mind about something. "Until recently."

She wasn't sure she liked the sound of that. "Oh?" she said cautiously.

It seemed that he'd come to some decision—which one, she wasn't sure. As she watched warily, he straightened from his casual position at the rail. "It's really i prudent of me to buy something I haven't seen, don't you think?''

Trying to hide her relief, she nodded. "Well, it does seem more logical to visit before you buy," she agreed, thinking that if he planned to make a personal tour of the four resorts, that would give her more opportunity to investigate—safely, from New York.

"And things are a little slack at the office right now, so I could squeeze in a few days.''

Thinking of all the extra time that would give her, she smiled encouragingly. "You're the boss," she pointed out. "You can be gone as long as you like.''

"I'm afraid that isn't true," he said. "I haven't had a vacation in . . . I can't remember when.''

This was getting better and better. "Then it's time you had one," she said firmly. "And when you get back, we can—''

"I'd like you to go with me.''

Caught up in encouraging him to go, she rattled on for a few seconds, until she realized what he'd said. "I'm sure you . . . *what*?''

"Oh, don't misunderstand me," he said quickly. "Of course I mean as an official escort. As Kalliste's representative, you could provide so many more details about the resorts than I could glean from a report.'' Now he was the one to smile encouragingly. "Don't you think that's true?''

It would be true if she was who she'd said she was, but not now! Starting to feel anxious, she told herself to be calm and rational. She was trained to deal with emergencies; all she had to do was . . . think.

"Yes, it's true," she said, making herself give an apologetic shrug. "But I'm afraid I didn't plan on being

away from the office more than a few days at this point."
She gestured helplessly. "I'm sorry."

Chris wasn't accustomed to having people refuse a request—any request, no matter how inconvenient. "Oh, I'm sure we can arrange things," he said smoothly, and then gave her a keen look. "Unless you have an objection?"

Now what was she to say to that? *Anything!* she thought in panic. *Just don't agree to go!* Oh, she never should have said she'd visited the resorts many times; if she went with him, he'd know she was a fraud the instant they walked inside the first lobby. For one thing, she wouldn't know any of the people; for another... No, it was impossible. It would *never* work. Even with advance preparation, someone was sure to say something that would blow her cover, and even if that didn't happen, she could do something herself. She might make some awful mistake, like turning left when she should go right, or walking into a closet when she meant to go out the door. She'd make a fool of herself, and just as bad, she'd blow the whole case. He'd find out who she was, and once that happened, she'd be fired... or worse.

"It's not that," she said hastily, trying to think. Her brain felt like a hamster furiously running the wheel in its cage, racing like mad, but going nowhere.

He was silent for a moment, not nearly long enough for her to come up with an alternate plan. "Oh," he said, comprehending—or thinking he was. "It's Harlan, isn't it? Well, don't worry. I'll take care of him."

"Take care of him?" she echoed stupidly.

"Of course," he said, as though it were already done. "I'll just say that I can't make up my mind until I've had a personally escorted tour of all the resorts. And who better to provide the tour, but Kalliste's representative herself? I'm sure he won't object—not with the sale at stake.''

She didn't have to think about that. They'd all be caught in this web of lies if Damion refused. "No," she said faintly. "I'm sure he won't."

"Then . . ."

At last, a feeble idea. It seemed to swim up through the fog of her beleaguered brain like an exhausted tadpole, trying for the surface. She seized it like a lifeline, hoping it would buy her a few days' grace, at least.

"Well, I really have to make some arrangements of my own first," she said, wondering if he'd notice if she jumped the rail and ran hysterically back to the guest cottage to put in a panic call to Roger.

"I understand," Chris said. "I realize how sudden this is."

Her laugh sounded shrill to her own ears. "Yes, I really didn't plan to be gone so long, you see. I know you'll think it's a silly excuse, but I really don't have anything to wear."

He dismissed that obstacle with a wave of his hand. "That's easily taken care of."

Weakly, she said, "It is?"

"Sure. I'll have Max take you in the boat to the mainland tomorrow and you can do whatever shopping you like. Charge it to me, of course."

That wasn't going to give her enough time. Trying to protest, she said, "Oh, I couldn't possibly—"

"Nonsense. This was my idea, and it would be a pleasure. If you like, I can have Darby fly you to Miami—"

What she'd like was to have Darby fly her across the world. "Oh, Miami isn't necessary," she said helplessly. "I'm sure some . . . shopping center nearby will suffice."

It would have to, she thought bleakly. If Roger couldn't

think of a way to get her out of this, she could fly to Paris and it wouldn't make any difference.

"Then you'll make arrangements?"

She gave him a sickly smile. "I'll do what I can."

"Well, if you need help convincing Damion, just let me know."

"Yes, I will."

"Great," he said, and smiled. Lucky him, he could afford to be happy. He wasn't heading into disaster. "Maybe we should get back to the party then."

"Yes," she said, wondering how soon she could escape so she could call Roger and tell him to *get her out of this!* "Maybe we should."

Then he went in and announced to everyone that, when Gail had made her arrangements, he and she would be making a business sweep of all the Kalliste resorts. They would leave almost immediately.

Everyone seemed pleased but Gail. She was so preoccupied with how she was going to handle the situation that she didn't notice for some time that one or two of Chris's guests seemed a little *too* pleased that he planned to be gone for a while. When she did notice, she filed the observation away to be examined at a later time. At the moment, she had her own problems to worry about.

It was after midnight before she was able to excuse herself gracefully. She hadn't realized it was so late, and she glanced nervously at the clock when she let herself into the guest house. Roger would have a fit if she woke him up, and she wondered if she should just wait until tomorrow to call him.

No, no, what was she thinking of? That would be too late! Now that he'd decided to do this thing, Chris was eager to be on his way. She had exactly one day before departure, and she'd only managed that much of a grace period because of the shopping trip. She couldn't squeeze any more time out of him, or he'd be suspicious. Making up her mind, she sat down and dialed.

As she'd feared, she did wake Roger up. He sounded so groggy when he answered that she wasn't sure it was he, and she said hesitantly, "Roger?"

He recognized her voice. "This better be damned good, Gail!" he growled. "Do you know what time it is?"

Now that she was on the phone, she was so upset at the idea of having to take Chris on the tour that she hardly knew what she was saying. "Yes, it's very late—"

"I know that!" he exclaimed. "Now, what the hell do you want?"

She told him, as briefly as she could, ending despite herself with a weak-sounding "Roger, he wants me to go with him! What am I going to do?"

He'd apparently come to full alert during her recital, for without pause, he said, "Go with him, of course."

She was appalled. She had hoped he'd come up with something to get her out of this. "What? But I can't do that!"

"Why not?"

"Why *not*? Because I'm not prepared for it, that's why! Because I didn't anticipate having to take him on a tour of the Kalliste resorts, which, I might remind you, I've only visited in pictures! That's why not!"

"You're an operative now, Gail," Roger said flatly. "You've got to be flexible."

"Flexible! But he's going to expect me to know those places intimately, Roger! I'd already said I'd been to all of them many times. Many times! You know as well as I do that seeing them in advertising promos is *not* the same as being there yourself!"

To her relief, Roger was silent a moment. "Yes," he said finally. "I see your point."

She felt reprieved. "Then—"

Her stay was short-lived. "I'll just have to send a courier down with additional information, that's all," he said thoughtfully. "We'll get names of people who work at the various places, more detailed layouts, that kind of thing. You can find time to memorize them, can't you?"

"It's not a problem of memorization, Roger!" she cried, and then tried to get hold of herself. She wasn't acting professionally, and she tried again. Her voice lower, she said very carefully, "He expects me to be totally familiar with these places, Roger. He'll *know* I'm a fraud."

"Not if you don't make any mistakes," her boss said cheerfully. "And who knows? Maybe he'll get tired after just one."

"Oh, if I could only believe that were true!"

"Well, you'll just have to handle that when the time comes," he said. "Now, is there any way you can get off the island for a few minutes tomorrow? I can't very well land a courier there in plain sight."

She was still wondering how this could have happened. Distractedly, she said, "Chris is going to have someone take me shopping tomorrow on the mainland. He mentioned a shopping center called..." She told him the name and he wrote it down.

"Okay," he said. "I'll have someone meet you there. Outside the biggest department store, whatever that is."

That was vague enough, but whom was he sending down? "Someone!" she repeated. "Who?"

"I don't know yet. Look for a man with a big manila envelope."

"Oh, great!" she said. It was getting worse and worse!

"I don't know what you're so upset about," Roger said. "In fact, the more I think about it, the better it sounds."

"Oh, yes, you can say that," she said bitterly. "You're safe in New York."

"Look at it this way. The more time you spend with him, the more time you—we—have to get the goods. This could be a blessing in disguise."

It sounded like a nightmare to Gail, who just knew something was going to go wrong. She was about to say she couldn't do it when her pride came belatedly to her rescue and she realized how she sounded. What was the matter with her? Safe in Manhattan, she had assured Roger—and anyone else who would listen—that she was fully capable of going out into the field. In fact, she'd eagerly accepted the assignment even before she knew what it was about. She'd been confident then; what had happened now? Just because she'd hit a snag was no reason to call it quits. After all, wasn't she the one who had said she craved excitement and adventure and travel? How could she complain when in one fell swoop, she'd just gotten all three?

"You're right," she said, finding her backbone at last. "I'll plan to be at the shopping center as close to…eleven as possible tomorrow morning. Will that give you enough time?"

"Good girl," he said, sounding proud of her. "That should be okay. Oh, and good luck."

Thinking she was going to need it, she managed a civil goodbye. Then she went into the bedroom and undressed. But after she'd put on a nightgown and climbed into the big, wide bed with the ironed sheets, she couldn't sleep. In addition to everything else, her sunburn was stinging again, and this time even lotion didn't help.

TIRED BUT UNABLE TO SLEEP, Chris tried to read until he felt drowsy. But even Dickens couldn't lull him into nodding off, and finally he tossed aside the book. Wide-awake and dressed in shorts and a T-shirt, he went to the sliding doors in the master bedroom. The party to introduce Gail was long since over, and his guests were probably abed themselves, sound asleep, as he should be. The estate was big enough to accommodate everyone who had been at the party, so he'd invited them all to stay over; now he wished he hadn't. He didn't want so many people around when he was in this mood, whether they were dead to the world or not.

Frowning, he looked in the direction of the main guest house, where Gail was staying. He couldn't see much of the cottage from here; vegetation screened it from view, as it had been intended to. Certain she was slumbering, too, he grumbled something and went outside, thinking a walk would help his restlessness.

The night was warm, and he padded barefoot down the steps and along the path toward the beach. A moonlight stroll on the sand usually soothed him, but tonight it didn't seem to help. After a few steps, he stopped and looked back at the guest cottage again, then he sighed. What was he doing? He had no business taking off on a pleasure trip, not now, when he was supposed to stay at the office to catch a crook. What ever had possessed him to ask Gail to take him on this ridiculous tour?

Ah, but you know what possessed you, a little voice said. *It was that look in her eye, the tilt of her head....*

"Or maybe the perfume she was wearing—or the way that dress fit," he muttered aloud to still that badgering voice inside his head. Impatiently, he bent down and picked up a flat little stone that shone at his feet. As he'd done when he was a kid, he fixed it between his thumb and his forefinger and sent it spinning out over the water, where it bounced once...twice...three...four times before it disappeared. A faint smile flickered across his face. He still had the knack; he'd always been able to beat Nick at the stone skipping game.

The thought of Nick made his smile disappear and he began to trudge along the sand again. How could he have become so...so mesmerized by Gail that he'd forgotten what the objective was here? Oh, sure, buying the resorts was important to him, but even more vital was catching the saboteur in his organization. And how did he expect to do that from afar? No, he had no business flying off on this little tour. He'd cancel the arrangements in the morning, say he'd made a mistake, tell her he couldn't go after all.

He shook his head impatiently again. What was he thinking? He didn't have to explain anything to anyone. If he'd changed his mind, that was his business. Besides, from the dismayed way she'd reacted tonight, he didn't think she'd mind all that much calling off the tour. When he first presented the idea, she'd looked as though he'd just grown fangs. His reputation—either as a businessman or a bachelor, he thought with a wince—couldn't be that bad. Didn't she like him? Why should it matter if she didn't?

It doesn't, he told himself irritably, and because he was so annoyed, he picked up another stone and sent it spinning. When it sank this time without a trace, he smiled grimly. He wasn't surprised; somehow that suited his present mood perfectly. This walk hadn't helped at all; he was more indecisive now than when he'd come out. What was it about Gail Sullivan that made him feel like a kid about to go on his first date? He'd squired all sorts of women, both before and since Celeste—blue bloods and socialites and entertainment figures; none of them had affected him like Gail. Not even Celeste.

"Now what?" he muttered. Should he go or not? He really did have no business flying off at a time like this, and yet...

He hated being indecisive; he'd been trained practically from birth to make quick decisions based on available data. Remembering all those ordeals at the dinner table, when out of the blue, Kerstan would present him with some problem and expect him to answer in the allotted few seconds, Chris wondered what decision his father would make now. But he knew already: there would be no contest. Kerstan Van Der Kellen would have stayed home and taken care of business.

Thinking about it, Chris's expression became even more grim. Well, that settled it. As Kerstan himself had so often drummed into his head, he wasn't like his father, and he never would be. That decided, he turned back and headed toward the house. He'd worked things out, as far as they went; if he and Gail were leaving soon, he'd better get some sleep.

CHAPTER SIX

By MORNING, Gail was convinced her moment of weakness had passed. Roger was sure she could handle the assignment; there was no reason why she couldn't. She had the training, and she was the one who had insisted she was ready for more responsibility. It was ridiculous for her boss to have more faith in her abilities than she did, and she was resolute when she went up to the main house for coffee and a quick breakfast before she started out.

She was just fine—until Max brought the boat around to take her shopping, and she learned that Chris had detailed his driver to escort her the entire trip. She had assumed up to that point that he'd take her to the mainland, and she'd be on her own from there. Dismayed at this unexpected complication, she tried to convince Chris that she'd be better off by herself. He wouldn't hear of it.

"Don't be silly," Chris said. "Max will enjoy it—won't you, Max?"

The driver smiled and touched a finger to his cap. "Can't think of anything I'd rather do," he said.

She didn't believe that for a minute. "That's very kind of you, Max," she said, and turned once more to Chris, trying to hide her anxiety. She couldn't have that man accompanying her wherever she went; how would she explain him to the courier? Worse, how would she explain the courier to *him*? Wincing at the thought, she tried again, hoping she didn't sound as desperate as she was beginning to feel. "Chris, please. It's really not necessary. Max will be bored to death following me around, and—" necessity called for it, so she fell back on a detested cliché "—you know how we women are when we're shopping. This could take all day."

"Fine," Chris replied, unperturbed. "I'm going to be working here in the office at home, so I won't need him anyway."

That distracted her for a moment. *He has an office here?* she thought. She hadn't found it yesterday when she looked. But she couldn't afford to be sidetracked; this other business was too important.

"Honestly, Chris, I'd feel as though I were taking him away from something important—"

Max answered this time. "The only thing I have to do today is wax the limo, Ms Sullivan. I'd be glad to go to town, really."

At first Chris looked amused when he glanced down at her again, but then as he gazed at her, his expression changed, and she wasn't sure why. His sudden scrutiny made her feel off balance, and she wondered if she'd protested a little too much. Nervously smoothing the skirt of the print sundress she was wearing, she tried to smile.

"I'm sorry," he said. "Forgive me for staring, but you look—"

That was it, she thought with relief. She wasn't dressed right. Because the day was warm, and she was traveling by boat, she hadn't wanted to fuss, so she'd just put on this dress and tied back her hair. Her makeup was minimal—mascara and lipstick, but as she looked at Chris, in his white slacks, brown loafers and yellow sport shirt, she definitely felt underdressed. Remembering that Suzanne would have died before putting a nose outside her apartment without heels and hose and full makeup, she suspected she'd made a mistake. Maybe women here dressed up to go shopping, she thought, and said quickly, "A little too casual? That's easily fixed. I'll just go and change."

"No, please," he said. "I like the way you look."

She'd started off, but he put a hand on her arm to detain her. Despite herself, his touch sent a little thrill up her entire arm, and she was so unnerved by the effect that simple physical contact with him had on her that she nearly said she'd been thinking the same thing about him. Horrified, she confined herself to a simple, "Thank you."

To her relief, Chris left it at that. For a moment he looked as though he wanted to say something more, but finally he said, "Well, I'd better let you and Max get going. If possible, I'd like to leave late this afternoon. Do you think that will give you enough time?"

She felt a stab of alarm. So soon? She'd thought she'd worked it all out last night, but in the light of a new day, she wasn't quite as confident as she had been. How could she be, when the slightest casual touch from this man made her heart skip a beat and her skin feel on fire?

"I'm sure it will," she managed.

"Are you ready, then?"

As ready as I'll ever be, she thought, and reached for her bag. She'd deliberately brought a big one so she could stuff the information from the courier inside without detection, and she summoned a bright smile she hoped wasn't too blatantly false. "I'm in Max's hands."

"You couldn't be in better care," Chris said, and walked with her to a little dock half-hidden by a tree leaning out over the water. Max had tied up the boat there, and he was already inside, checking...whatever it was that boat drivers checked.

Gail didn't know anything about sailing, but as she glanced at this boat, she felt a thrill despite herself. As different from that dilapidated old ferry as a racehorse was from a shaggy old pony, this craft was long and sleek and painted white with a sporty red stripe. Written in gold lettering inside the stripe was the name *Kellen Two*.

"When you said boat, I thought it would be a little speedboat," she said. "You know, like they have for rent at lake resorts?"

Chris and Max both laughed. "You're in Florida now, Gail," Chris said. "Besides, this little baby is as safe as can be."

She looked down. "But where's the engine?"

Grinning, Max pointed to a bump with an air-scoop affair toward the back. "Under there."

She was fascinated. "How fast does it go?"

Max's grin widened. "I promise I won't go over ninety."

"Ninety!"

"He's teasing," Chris said, gazing solemnly at her, as though to gauge her reaction. "He has strict orders not to go a knot over seventy-five."

"Well, I'm glad to hear that," she said, and put her hand in Max's outstretched one and jumped inside. He steadied her for a moment until she got her balance, then went to the front.

"You can swim, can't you?" Chris asked from the catwalk.

"Why, do you think I'll have to?" she called back.

He looked indignant. "Not a chance. I was just asking. Besides, this baby won't sink."

She grinned. "Isn't that what they said about the *Titanic*?"

He laughed and pointed. "Just in case, there are the life jackets. Now, have a good time, and remember, just charge what you like to the estate."

"Oh, I can't—"

He raised a hand. "I insist. You won't have any problem—Max will verify that you're my guest. Just sign everything over to Kellen Key. The shop owners will know where to send the bills."

She had no doubt of that. Thinking that if this was how the other half lived, she could definitely get used to it, she waved as Chris started back to the house. She was just settling back when Max started the engine with a roar that nearly brought her to her feet again in fright. He looked at her over his shoulder and grinned. Obviously enjoying the driving, rumbling din, he shouted, "You ready?"

"Let her rip!" she shouted back, and gave a thumbs-up sign to show she was game. But the instant he turned to the wheel again, she sat back and held on for dear life. The boat seemed to actually lift out of the water as they started out, and before she knew it, they were . . . flying.

She'd never experienced such a sensation. Before they were out of the bay, the wind had whipped her hair free, blowing it straight back from her head, and even under her sunglasses, she had to squint. There was a windshield at the front, but still a fine mist was wetting her face, and when she looked behind them, she saw two foaming white plumes roiling out from the back. Ahead, the water was sapphire blue, the sun was warm despite the stiff breeze, and as the boat bounced over the waves, she laughed in delight. Max heard her and smiled again over his shoulder. Carefully, holding on, she made her way forward until she was standing beside him. They grinned at each other.

"This is really somethin', isn't it?" he shouted over the noise.

"Can you go faster?" she shouted back, holding her hair out of her eyes.

Max obliged and the front of the boat lifted like a spirited stallion being given full rein. Throwing her head back, Gail laughed again. This was living!

"Does Chris ever drive this boat?" she shouted.

"Are you kidding?" Max yelled. "He's won the Gulf Coast race the past three years running!"

"I can see why! This boat is fantastic!"

"Oh, not with this!" Max shouted. He shook his head, his grin widening. "With the *real* boat, the *Kellen One*!"

Thinking how much she'd give to ride in that one, Gail laughed again and looked forward. Deep blue ocean stretched out in front and to the side and behind them. The only thing that would have made this ride better was if Chris were here, standing beside her.

That thought sobered her, and as she shaded her eyes with her hand and looked out over the water, she wondered if she was more attracted to Chris than she had believed. If so, she was in real trouble, for she couldn't fight that appeal and do her job, too.

Biting her lip, she glanced behind her; already the island was just a dot on the water. When she thought of Chris standing on the dock, she had to admit that he was one of the most attractive men she'd ever met. And he was certainly eligible, and exciting and magnetic—

With an effort, she reined in such thoughts. What was the matter with her? She'd met handsome, attractive, compelling men before.

Yes, but not like Chris.

Abruptly, she signaled to Max that she was going to go back and sit down. Busy with piloting the boat, he nodded and kept his eyes straight ahead, leaving her to feel her way carefully to one of the seats. When she got there, she fell into it with a plop, feeling suddenly depressed. This attraction she felt to Chris—and she couldn't deny that was exactly what it was—couldn't interfere with what she had to do. Somehow she had to find a way to handle it.

Her mouth tightened. She wasn't helpless. She was a trained agent; she knew what she was doing. That was why Roger had sent her on this assignment, why she had insisted on coming. She had only herself to blame if, in her eagerness to get going, she hadn't wondered if this would happen. But she'd never dreamed of becoming attracted to the subject. Did such a thing happen to other agents?

Straightening again, she told herself firmly that it wasn't going to happen to her. She was a professional; that was all she had to remember.

Just then Max turned from the wheel and pointed, shouting that they were almost there. Half-standing, she looked ahead to the shoreline coming up quickly on the horizon. There wasn't much time. She'd spent most of this glorious ride either completely forgetting why she was here, or trying to convince herself that she wasn't getting emotionally involved with Chris when she knew damned well she was. That was a problem she'd deal with later; right now she had something else to do. Her immediate concern was deciding how to get rid of Max long enough to meet her courier and get that vital information.

One problem at a time, she told herself. That was what Roger was always telling everyone at the office. But that reminded her of something else: whom had Roger sent to meet her? If it wasn't someone from the office, how would she recognize him?

Look for a man with a big manila envelope, Roger had said. Well, that was just great. What kind of help was that?

It was too late to worry about it now. While she'd been trying to prioritize her difficulties, Max had guided the sleek boat into a slip at a marina, cutting the powerful engine at exactly the right moment so that the side of the craft just kissed the catwalk. Impressed despite her inner turmoil, Gail started to shout, "That was—" Then she realized how quiet it was. Without that powerful throbbing of the engine, the silence seemed loud to her ears. Shaking her head to clear the inner ringing, she said more normally, "That was fantastic!"

"Glad you enjoyed it, Ms Sullivan," Max said, obviously delighted. "Mr. Van Der Kellen will be pleased."

Hearing something in his tone, she looked at him suspiciously. "Did he tell you to give me a ride like that?" she asked.

"Well..."

"The truth now."

Trying to hide his smile, Max said, "He told me that if you looked like you were enjoying yourself to...to open it up a little."

"And that's what you did—opened it up a little?"

At her stern expression, he looked faintly anxious. "Well—"

She couldn't pretend any longer. Grinning suddenly, she said, "Then in that case, on the way home, I want you to open it up a *lot*! And if Mr. Van Der Kellen minds—"

"Oh, Chris won't mind, Ms Sullivan!" Max said delightedly. "I guarantee!"

After tying up the boat, he jumped out to help her. As she put her hand in his and was lifted effortlessly to the dock, she said, "And call me Gail, please, will you, Max?"

He hesitated. "Oh, I don't know if Mr. Van Der Kellen would like that—"

"Don't worry about Mr. Van Der Kellen," she said, thinking of Chris and his instructions to his driver. How had he known that she'd love a fast boat ride like that? She smiled conspiratorially at Max. "I'll take care of him."

But her problem a while later was how to take care of Max. Like a faithful puppy, he accompanied her to the shopping mall near the marina, and was never far from her heels even when she stopped a dozen times in a pretense of looking at something that caught her eye—a ploy he was sure to suspect sooner or later, since what she was really doing was taking a furtive look around for her man with the manila envelope.

She was just thinking that this was never going to work when she had an idea. They'd just gone into another boutique, this one conveniently featuring resort clothes, and she gave a little cry as though she'd found exactly what she wanted. Grabbing up armfuls of clothes without even looking at what she was taking off the racks, she staggered with the garments to where her escort was waiting by the door.

"Max," she said with what she hoped was a convincing smile, "why don't you go get some coffee? I thought I saw a little coffee shop down the way, and this—" she lifted the heavy stack of clothes and pretended to look self-conscious "—is going to take me a while, as you can see. I hate to keep you waiting."

"Oh, that's no problem," he said, and pulled out a paperback he'd stuffed in a back pocket. "You just take your time. I'll be glad to sit here and read."

She fought to hide her dismay. She'd been so sure this was a great idea! "But...don't you think you'd be more comfortable in that coffee shop?"

"Oh, no. There's a couch right over there. I'll be just fine."

Why had she chosen one of those boutiques that provided comfortable seating and even magazines for long-suffering men who came shopping with their girlfriends or wives? Well, it was too late now. With a determined-looking saleswoman bearing down on her again, she was forced to give Max a strained smile and promise to be as quick as she could.

"No problem," he said again, as the saleswoman quickly took most of the clothing from her arms and tottered with clanging hangers toward what was presumably the dressing room area. "Take all the time you like. I'll be here."

Hoping she could count on that, she quickly followed the clerk, who was trying to push the big load through a too-small dressing room door. Smiling apologetically, Gail helped her shove the giant stack through, and then asked if the store had a rest room.

"Oh, yes," the woman said, panting. "It's right over there."

"Oh, good," Gail said. "I'll just be a minute, then I'll come back and start trying on." Glancing at the clothes hanging over the chair, on the hooks and over the doors, she gave an apologetic shrug. "Sometimes I have the hardest time finding just what I want."

The woman had recovered. "I know just how you feel. If you want different sizes, I'll be right outside."

"Oh, that won't be necessary," Gail said quickly. The last thing she wanted was someone fluttering around, checking on her progress. "I'll be just fine. Why don't I just call you if I need something?"

Hoping the woman would take the hint, Gail started toward the ladies' room. Praying that the place had a window, she held her breath when she pushed the door open, and then wanted to cheer at how clever she'd been. Miraculously, the place not only had a window, but it was one that cranked open. She hadn't allowed herself to think what she'd do if the window had been the slatted kind; she never would have gotten through. But this one would do perfectly—if she could just get up there.

Quickly checking both stalls to make sure they were empty and she was alone, she climbed up on the counter. What she would do if someone came in and saw her awkwardly hanging from the sill while she tried to force her leg over, she didn't know. She couldn't think about it right now; she...had...to...lift...herself up and...

With a grunt and a scraped shin that made her wince, she managed to pull herself up onto the sill from the counter. Now she could open the window as far as it would go; all she had to do was slip through. Balancing precariously while she considered how best to accomplish all this, she held on and shakily looked outside. If anyone saw her crouching here, she'd die of embarrassment.

But the gods were still being kind. As she'd hoped, the bathroom faced a sort of alley between two shops, and the alley was miraculously empty right now. A Dumpster outside the window provided a good climbing-down place, but it was a little out of her reach. Thinking she'd have to try to reach it anyway—that, or risk breaking an ankle from the ten foot drop the ground—she debated how best to start. Finally she decided she'd just have to go for it, and so, holding onto the window frame, she gently eased herself down, searching with her foot for purchase on the Dumpster. Her skirt rode up, exposing a lot of thigh, and the thought flashed through her mind that she must have made a ridiculous picture, hanging from some store's bathroom window, like a shoplifter trying to escape. The thought of trying to explain her situation spurred her on, and she flailed around with her foot, unable to see where the damned Dumpster had gone. Her arms were getting numb, and she scraped her elbow as she swung there in midair, wondering how long she could hang on.

"How do people *do* this?" she muttered to herself, picturing Roger or any of her colleagues at work in such an ignominious position. If she didn't find that trash can soon, she would fall, and then how would she ever explain herself to Chris?

Galvanized by the thought, she tried one last flail and had the satisfaction of cracking her ankle on the edge of the Dumpster. Tears of pain sprang into her eyes, and she bit back a cry, but at least she had found what she was looking for. Taking a deep breath, she pushed off from the window ledge and dropped with a bang onto the top of the Dumpster. The noise she made sounded loud enough to wake the dead, and she crouched instinctively and looked around, expecting people to come running. When nothing happened after a moment or two, she grabbed the edge of the lid and swung down.

Well, that wasn't too bad, she thought: one scraped shin, one scuffed elbow and one cracked ankle. It could have been worse. Trying not to to think how she was ever going to get back in again, she dusted off her hands and went to look for her courier. She didn't have much time; even a man as tolerant as Max would soon start to wonder what had happened to her.

When she emerged from the alley, she saw that the mall was relatively crowded, which made it easier for her to blend in. After quickly brushing herself off, she joined the throng, wondering how she was ever going to find a man with a manila envelope in this crowd. Aware of the minutes racing by, and Max back in the boutique, hopefully unsuspecting, she began racing up and down, looking for the person she was supposed to meet. Just when she was sure they'd missed each other, she thought she spied someone up ahead. Yes, he was carrying a big envelope! He must be the one!

Intent, she increased her pace trying not to be too obvious. He had his back to her, and he seemed vaguely familiar, but she was so glad to have found him at last that she didn't care who it was.

As if he sensed her approach, the man turned just as she reached him. She was so shocked when she saw him that she actually skidded to a stop. *"Stanley?"*

"Hi, Gail," he said, as though it were the most natural thing in the world to meet here, miles away from New York, while she was on an assignment he was supposed to know nothing about. She couldn't believe her eyes.

"Stanley, what are you doing here?" she cried, and then realized they were in a very public place. Grabbing his arm, she hustled him out of the thoroughfare and into the shelter of a telephone bay. She still couldn't believe this was happening. How could Stanley, of all people, possibly be here?

Stanley looked disappointed. "You're not glad to see me," he said.

"Glad to see you! What are you doing here? Stanley, if this is some kind of...some kind of..." She couldn't even imagine what had brought him here. Realizing she was stammering, she took a breath. He held out the envelope.

"I brought you this," he said. "It's the information you wanted."

She looked at the envelope in renewed disbelief and grabbed it from his outstretched hand. Until she saw the telltale Brenner and Company address, she'd hoped it was some kind of joke. But now she had to accept his presence, and she grabbed his arm again, giving it a little shake. "How do you know what information I wanted? Where did you get it? *How* did you get it?" Despite herself, her voice rose again. "Stanley, why is this happening?"

He was starting to look a little alarmed himself. Whatever he had thought, showing up like this obviously wasn't working, and he tried ineffectually to pat her hand. She snatched her arm back, protectively cradling the precious envelope. Although she didn't know why; heaven knew what it contained. How had he gotten it?

"Calm down, Gail," he said. "I can explain."

"Fine!" she cried, aware of the passing minutes, and Max waiting in that shop. Suppose he got restless and sent the saleswoman back to check on her? What would he do if they found her gone? Oh, this wasn't the way it was supposed to be! Things like this never happened to James Bond! Drawing herself up to her full height, she glared at Stanley. "Go ahead, explain!"

He seemed eager to do so, proud of himself now that he had the floor. "Gail, I missed you so much, I just had to find a way to apologize—"

"Apologize!" Whatever he wanted, now wasn't the time!

He dug in his pocket. "And I wanted to bring you back this."

Incredulously, she looked down. He was holding her engagement ring—what used to be her engagement ring. She closed his hand around it. "Stanley, we talked about that!"

He startled her by grabbing both her arms. She was so surprised that she nearly dropped the envelope, and they did an awkward little dance while she tried to retrieve it. Aware of several passersby giving them strange looks, she cried, "Stanley, stop!"

He released her, but said anxiously, "Gail, please, just listen. I . . . I really went through a lot finding you—"

"I can imagine! What did you do—bribe someone at work?" She was horrified at the thought. Oh, wouldn't Roger be pleased about that!

He flushed. "Of course not. One of the secretaries there is . . . is a little sweet on me—"

"*What?*" Shocked, she looked at him. "Who?" she demanded. She'd tell Roger about this as soon as she got back!

"I'm not going to tell you," he said indignantly. "What kind of man do you think I am?"

"One who's in a lot of trouble!" she shot back. "I can't imagine how you could have done such a thing—or why!"

"Because I love you, Gail," he said plaintively. "And when Dar—when she told me about having to call the courier service early this morning for you, I told her I'd bring the information."

"*What?*"

Grabbing her arm again, he said urgently, "I know it's not very nice to admit, using such a sweet girl like that, but I was desperate, Gail. Until Dar—until she told me, I didn't know where you were, or when you were coming back, and I *had* to see you again to tell you how sorry I was, and how much I loved you, and how much I wanted you back! Can you forgive me? Will you take your ring back so we can go on as before? Please, Gail, I'll die if you say no! I'll just shrivel up right here!"

This isn't happening, Gail thought, attempting to disengage herself from Stanley's desperate grip. Embarrassed at the way he was clinging to her, she tried to pry his fingers off her arm, and smiled weakly at some woman passing by who gave her a disapproving look.

"Stanley!" she hissed. "People are looking!"

"I don't care!" he practically sobbed. "I'll do anything, humiliate myself in any way to get you back! If you want me to go down on my knees, I will!"

To her horror, he dropped dramatically to the ground in front of her. "Stanley! Get up this instant!" she cried, and pulled him to his feet.

"You see?" he said plaintively. "I mean it, Gail! What can I do to convince you?"

She didn't want to be convinced; she wanted him to disappear. Sure that Max was going to show up at any moment, demanding to know what the hell was going on, she said hastily, "I'm sorry, Stanley. We agreed it wouldn't work—"

"But I've changed my mind!" he said pitifully.

"But I haven't," she said. The minutes were racing by, and she was getting more tense by the second. Certain her blood pressure was about to go through the roof from sheer anxiety, she tried to be as gentle as she could. She didn't want to hurt Stanley; she just wanted him to go away!

"Please, Stanley, listen to me," she said. "We want different things—that hasn't changed. We'll always want different things. Don't you see, it will never work. It's best this way. You'll find someone else—"

"No!" he cried in panic. "I won't!"

"Yes, you will," she said firmly. "I know it. You're a kind and decent man, Stanley. Any girl would be—"

"If I'm so kind and decent, why won't you take me back?"

She fought an impulse to glance at her watch. "Because I'm not the right woman for you, Stanley, and I'm sure that once you think about it, you'll agree. Now, please, I've got to get back. People are depending on me. You'll be all right, I promise."

She didn't give him a chance to argue this time, but started moving away quickly. She hadn't gone two steps before his mournful voice floated after her, "I won't give up, Gail! I won't!"

Praying no one was looking at her, she didn't look behind, but raced back to the boutique, coming to a stop about two stores before it. She'd wasted so much time with Stanley that she couldn't afford to squander any more trying to figure out how to climb back in the bathroom window. Fortunately, a group of girls were heading in the direction of the store, and when she realized they were going inside, she joined them, keeping her head down and peeping through elbows and arms to see if Max was still sitting on the couch. To her relief, he seemed absorbed in his book, but she didn't want to take any more chances.

Streaking to the back of the shop, she flung herself headfirst into the dressing room, grabbed her bag and stuffed the—unopened, thank God—envelope inside. Then, hoping they were the right size and fit and style, she snatched up an armful of clothes that she hadn't had time to try on, and came out just as the saleswoman was coming toward her.

"Oh, there you are!" the woman trilled. "I thought you'd gotten lost!"

Hoping the clerk wouldn't notice that she was trying not to gasp from being out of breath, she handed over the clothes. "I'll take these, if you please."

"Certainly," the woman said, and wrote up a sales ticket that made Gail blanch. Well, it served her right, she thought, and was starting to write a check when Max appeared by her elbow.

"I'll sign for that," he said. "Just send the bill to Kellen Key."

"Certainly, sir!" the saleswoman said, sounding awed and impressed. Then she gave Gail a strange look. Gail knew exactly what the look implied, and she felt herself flush.

"I'm a guest," she said.

Obviously wondering what kind of guest would allow her host to outfit her with an entire new wardrobe, the woman smirked. "Of course," she murmured.

To the red-faced Gail, it seemed a fitting end to the trip.

CHAPTER SEVEN

THEY DIDN'T LEAVE until the next morning. Gail found out when she got back to Kellen Key after her shopping trip that Chris had decided to take the jet because of its greater range, and they had to wait to locate his second pilot, Jack, who didn't know about the tour, and who was off somewhere fishing.

Gail was just as glad; she needed the extra hours to study the file Roger had sent down. Thankful that Chris seemed preoccupied as well, she excused herself after dinner and then spent half the night memorizing details about Kalliste Bahama—the first stop on the list—and the other half hoping that Chris would decide he'd seen enough after visiting the Bahama resort and forgo the rest.

Bleary-eyed and fuzzy-headed, she was up early the next morning, going over everything again. Roger had thoughtfully included pictures of the administration and managerial staff members so she wouldn't have to fumble putting faces to names when she arrived, and he'd written a note assuring her that everyone knew she was coming and what her supposed function was.

But knowing all this and acting it out were two different things, and despite her extensive preparation, she still felt anxious in the morning before the maid, Cecilia, came to help her pack. Preoccupied, she thought that one of her biggest problems—in addition to the fact that she'd never actually visited the resort—was that there were so many details to remember. If she'd truly been who she said she was, she would not only have been familiar with all the front-of-house staff, but she'd have a nodding acquaintance with the manager and the clerks and the security people—not to mention those who worked in housekeeping and in the food and beverage service, she thought grimly—and of course, the accountants, none of whom she had ever seen. As she finished her coffee, she realized it would be a miracle if she didn't make some awful gaffe the instant she walked into the lobby.

But it was too late for doubts now, she decided, and told herself that as long as she remained calm, everything would be all right. She had been trained for this, and she had a quick mind. If worst came to worst, she could talk her way out of a jam.

That decided, she was about to take a shower when there was a diffident little knock on the door. Cecilia had arrived. When she saw all the packages and bags that Gail had just dropped on the chaise and them promptly forgotten about, she clucked her tongue in dismay.

"Oh, miss," she said worriedly, shaking out a mint-green shift Gail was sure she'd never seen before. "If I had known, I would have taken all this to be pressed."

Embarrassed, Gail just waved her hand. She'd been so busy memorizing the file that she'd forgotten all about her clothes. "I'm sure everything will be all right," she said. "You know how wrinkled things get in a suitcase anyway."

"Oh, but not if I pack them very carefully," Cecilia said, wide-eyed, shaking out another garment, this one an expensive-looking white cotton-knit sweater with a nautical design.

Gail looked at the garment in dismay. Had she really put that on Chris's charge account? The item must have cost a fortune. Her face reddened. What was he going to think? Wishing she'd paid more attention to the clothes she'd just scooped up in the boutique, she made a vague gesture. "Well, just do what you can, Cecilia. This is my fault. I should have called you sooner."

Smiling shyly in response, the maid quickly gathered up the bags of clothes. "I'll just take these back to the house and give them all a quick press," she said. "It won't take but a moment."

"Oh, but you don't have to—" Gail started to protest. But the little maid had already gone. Feeling guiltier than ever, she decided there was nothing else to do but continue with her shower.

An hour later, her new clothes carefully pressed and packed, and the bags out on the front porch to be picked up by Max, Gail gave the cottage a last inspection to make sure she hadn't forgotten anything. Although how she could have, she thought, she didn't know. She was getting so spoiled with being waited on hand and foot that it was going to be a rude adjustment when she got back to her own apartment.

Grimacing at the thought, she checked her appearance. Since she had all these new clothes, it had seemed a shame not to wear a new outfit, but it had taken her a while to decide. What did one wear when one arrived by private jet at a posh and exclusive Bahama resort? A business suit seemed as wildly inappropriate under the circumstances as a string bikini, so she had opted for white linen slacks topped by the nautical-design sweater Cecilia had aired earlier. Her single accessory was a yellow scarf, the color of which matched the stripe in the sweater. She'd knotted it casually around her hair, which was loose to her shoulders. With flats and some make-up, she felt she looked the picture of casual elegance, and struck a pose in front of the mirror to prove it. She stared at herself for a few seconds, and then burst into laughter. Wouldn't Suzanne be surprised to see her now!

Still smiling, she turned away from the mirror. Her glance fell on her purse by the door, and the tip of Roger's file sticking out from it, and her smile faded. Reminded abruptly of the reason she was really here, her expression was more serious as she gathered up the rest of her things and closed the door behind her.

By the time she followed the meandering path from the guest cottage up to the main house, Chris was standing on the front porch, watching Max load bags into the trunk of the limousine parked outside. The efficient chauffeur had already fetched her luggage, she noticed, and turned her attention to Chris. Dressed in tan slacks and loafers, with a cream-colored sport coat and a blue open-necked shirt, the master of Kellen Key looked so handsome that her breath caught. She knew she was staring, but she couldn't help herself. *Why does he have to be so good-looking?* she wondered bleakly. *Or have such a wonderful smile? Or wear his clothes so well?* She was starting to admire everything about him, and even in her befuddled state, she knew how dangerous that could be.

The subject is dressed casually today, she told herself in a sort of mental essay style designed to bring her thoughts sternly back into line. *He looks calm and confident, with no trace of uneasiness. We are proceeding to Kalliste Bahama by private jet. Will advise upon arrival. End of report.*

Composed and sure of herself again—or as sure as she was going to feel, she amended grimly—she came around the side of the house just as Chris turned to look in her direction. Her heart banged again when she saw his eyes light up, and she managed to give a gay little wave.

"Good morning," she said, thinking that was innocuous enough.

"Good morning. You look wonderful."

Her treacherous heart thudded again, but she refused to be affected by that smile. Or maybe she was more affected than she wanted to admit, because she blurted without thinking, "Thank you, I'm glad you approve. But I really can't take any credit, since this is all your doing. Please let me pay—"

He interrupted her with a lift of his hand. "I thought we agreed. The shopping trip was my responsibility."

"No, we didn't exactly *agree*," she said. "You told me—"

"Besides, you didn't spend nearly enough. Since this was my idea, I wanted you to have a good time."

Thinking of the time she'd had, she smiled wryly. "I did have a good time. And how can you say I didn't spend enough? That bill was outrageous. Which is why I—"

To her surprise, he laughed aloud. When she looked at him curiously, he shook his head. "I'm sorry," he said. "I'm not laughing at you. It's just that Celeste would have spent that on Cyrano without a second's thought."

"Cyrano?"

He spread both hands. "Her Pekinese."

"Your wife named a Pekinese Cyrano?"

"It just goes to show you what a twisted sense of humor she had, doesn't it?"

Gail wasn't sure what to say to that, so she got into the car. She'd ridden in limousines before—not often; once or twice—but never one like this. The seats were tan, made of butter-soft leather, and the bar-console in front of her was polished mahogany. Even the beige rugs on the floor were plush. A crystal vase she was sure was Baccarat on the console held a single red rose, and a bottle of champagne rested in a crushed-ice nest. There was also a television, a complicated-looking phone system, an intercom to Max, a compact disc player, a cassette player and even a small library of books. Amazed, she looked at Chris as he got in beside her.

"Do you live here when you're not at the house?"

"It used to feel like it," he said wryly. "I got so tired of it that I had it brought over from the mainland so I wouldn't be tempted. But now we have another one over there, so I save this for VIPs."

Flattered despite herself, she said, "I would have been just as comfortable in a regular car."

His mouth quirked. "I doubt it," he said, and punched the intercom button. "Ready when you are, Max."

"On our way," came the reply. "Shall I take the scenic route?"

Since even Gail knew by now that the island had only one main road, she laughed. Smiling at her, Chris shook his head and said to the driver, "Just make sure Darby and Jack are waiting for us."

"They've been there since dawn."

"Good," Chris said, and keyed off as Max started the car and they pulled smoothly away. Settling back, he looked at Gail again. "Champagne or coffee?"

Reveling in all this luxury, Gail had put her head back against the seat. A tinted sunroof right over her head let in just enough light; it was like looking through air. Without lifting her head, she said, "Champagne? Isn't a celebration a little premature?"

"Celebrations are never premature," he said, reaching for two delicate crystal flutes he'd placed on the bar. The car was so perfectly sprung that he didn't spill a drop when he poured. Holding out one glass to her, he held up the other, adding, "But if you like, we can celebrate the beginning of this little tour. May it be fruitful for both of us."

Suddenly nervous without really knowing why—perhaps it was the look in his eye—she took the glass he held out. The car was spacious, so there no hint of confinement, but without warning, it was difficult to get her breath. Chris was sitting at the other end of the seat; nevertheless, he seemed much too close, and she had to make an effort to answer casually. "In that case, cheers."

They clinked glasses, and Gail had to restrain herself from tossing back the entire flute of champagne. Horrified at her sudden desire to move closer to him, to touch the hand that rested so casually on his knee and to run her fingers through his thick, black hair, she moved next to the window on her side. If she was starting to feel like this already, how much worse would things be when they were *really* alone?

Cringing at the thought, she turned toward the tinted window and pretended to be absorbed in the passing scenery outside while she reminded herself firmly of the real reason she was here.

"Gail, is something wrong?" Chris asked.

She turned jerkily from the window. "No, of course not," she said. "Why do you ask?"

"Well, you seem very tense this morning," he said, and hesitated. "Perhaps I shouldn't have insisted that you take me on this tour. I know how hectic things can get at the office, and if I've put you in a difficult position, I'm sorry."

He looked so apologetic that she had to reassure him. "No, no, please, don't think that. Nothing is wrong, believe me." *But that isn't true,* she thought, and hurried on. "I'm looking forward to this, honestly. I...I haven't had a vacation in quite some time, and I—" another lie; how easily they come to her now "—I've always enjoyed Kalliste Bahama. It's very restful."

"Oh?" Chris said, eyeing her carefully. Too carefully, she thought. Had she made a mistake? Then she realized to her horror that she might have when he added, "I thought from the reports that there was a lot of activity there."

She suppressed a groan. *Get your mind on business,* she ordered herself, and made a quick mental rundown of the file. How could she have said such a stupid thing? she wondered, and tried to fix it without being obvious. "Oh, there is. After all, it is known for its water sports. But that doesn't mean that everyone who goes there runs around with scuba gear on all the time. There are landlubbers like me who enjoy spreading out a towel and reading a good novel, you know."

"Oh, I see," Chris said, and to her relief looked amused. "Then you didn't mean it when you told Max how much you enjoyed the boat ride yesterday?"

Wondering what trap she'd stumbled into now, she tried to remember the conversation she'd had with Max. It was no good; with Chris looking at her like that, she was having trouble remembering her own name. "What do you mean?" she said.

Clearly enjoying himself, Chris shrugged. "Max told me he thought you had a good time on the boat. But I see that you were just trying not to hurt his feelings."

"Oh, no, that's not true!" she protested at once, thinking of the glorious ride. She could live to be a hundred and never forget how it felt to have the wind in her hair, or that fine mist of spray on her face. And the speed! She'd felt as if she was flying across water. Just thinking about it made her heart race all over again, and she said fervently, "No, that was wonderful!"

"Then you enjoy sailing," Chris said innocently.

"Oh, yes, it's—" She stopped suddenly, alerted by something in his eyes that made her finish suspiciously, "Why?"

"Well, I've read that one of the most popular sports at Kalliste Bahama is parasailing, and after Max told me how much you enjoyed the boat, I was sure you'd want to show me how."

"Parasailing?" she repeated. She wasn't sure she even knew what that meant. Whatever it was, it didn't sound like something she wanted to do. Ever.

But before she had a chance to think of an excuse, they had arrived at the airstrip. Max stopped the car and came around to open the door and she stepped out on the tarmac and ... stopped.

A fantasy plane was waiting—a beautiful, sleek, gleaming jet, with a pointed nose and upturned wing tips. It seemed to be poised on the runway like a falcon just waiting for the command to soar, and when she saw it, she forgot all about parasailing, and everything else. Her eyes glowing, she looked from the plane to Chris. She hadn't realized until then that he was watching her, waiting for her reaction.

"Chris—" she started to say, and felt suddenly choked. He was smiling at her, and in that smile was something special—a look that made her realize he'd done this for her, not because he was rich enough to do it, or arrogant enough to show her he could, but simply because he wanted to please her. No man had ever looked at her like that, and she knew in that moment that she was falling in love.

Then Darby said something, and the spell was broken. Still feeling bemused, she allowed Chris to take her arm and lead her to the plane.

The jet had a range of nearly three thousand nautical miles, accommodations for twelve and an interior that would have done a decorator proud. The cabin featured a crimson couch and matching seats on one side, and a galley toward the back. The floor was carpeted in gold throughout, with the VDK logo outlined in crimson down the center aisle. With the two engines nestled at the rear and a wingspan of almost forty-five feet, the plane was so impressive that Gail took one look around and said helplessly, "Chris, this is . . . I'm impressed."

He looked pleased and embarrassed at the same time. "Another of my homes away from home," he said. "I travel a lot."

"If you travel like this, I can see why," she said, taking a seat on the couch and sinking into it. "This is beautiful."

"I'm glad you like it," he said, and then Darby checked back, introducing his copilot for the trip, a tanned man named Jack. Gail didn't learn until much later that Chris had insisted on two pilots; even though he was licensed himself, he'd decided to leave the flying to the others, and keep her company in the main cabin.

"You ready, boss?" Darby asked as Jack went forward and took the right seat.

"When you are."

Darby grinned. "Hang on to your hats."

Gail was so excited by this time that she nearly missed the takeoff. Unable to help contrasting this vehicle with that horrible commuter plane, she was busy staring at the swiftly passing scenery outside her window when all of a sudden they were in the air. The lift-off was so smooth and powerful and quick that she laughed in delight. Beside her, Chris just smiled as she craned her neck to look down.

Already they were far above the ocean's surface. Thinking this was about as close to heaven as she was going to get, she finally tore herself away from the window long enough to look at Chris. She'd intended saying something, but this feeling was beyond words. Her eyes sparkling, she just shook her head, speechless. Laughing, he reached for her hand, and suddenly the air between them became charged.

Later, she didn't know what had really happened. One minute she was delighting in the flight, and in the next... She looked down. Without realizing it, she had turned her palm up and laced her fingers with his; the sight of their hands together made her feel . . .

She didn't know what she felt, and slowly, she lifted her eyes. Chris had stopped smiling; he looked just as confused and uncertain as she felt. She knew he wanted to kiss her, and against her will, she could feel herself being drawn to him. Just for an instant, before she caught herself, she actually asked herself if it would matter. It would be so easy just to lean forward, to close her eyes...

Then reason took over, and with a supreme effort, she removed her hand from his. She wanted to say something bright and inconsequential to prove how sophisticated she was; some clever remark would show that she was used to handling such awkward situations with ease. But everything she could think of seemed superficial and shallow, and Chris didn't deserve that.

"I'm sorry," she said softly.

Those dark eyes held hers. "So am I."

Had she made a mistake? Part of her moaned yes, but another, more rational part of her mind told her that the bigger mistake would have been giving in. Even if she wanted to get involved with this man, which, of course, she did not, she didn't have that option. She had a job to do, people depending on her, a career to think of. She loved her new career, but as she'd already learned with Stanley, it wasn't something she could share. So if she wanted to continue with Brenner and Company—and she did—she had to go it alone, at least until she figured out a way to combine her work and a love life, too. The solution seemed increasingly remote. If Stanley disliked the secrecy involved in her job, how much more would a man like Chris hate it? He was the kind who would be impatient with not knowing where she was or what she was doing, and if she persisted, everything between them would be destroyed.

Appalled by her thoughts, she gave herself a mental shake. What was she doing? Where was her objectivity? One of the first things she had learned in this business was how important it was to separate her feelings and emotions from her assignments. It was time to start remembering that now. Chris was undeniably handsome and attractive and everything she ever could have asked for in a man—but he wasn't the first charmer she'd met in this line of work, and he certainly wouldn't be the last. If she hoped to make a name for herself in the business, she had to learn how to handle situations like this. It would be her first acid test.

Hoping it wasn't going to be her last, she turned and looked out the window again. Directly ahead, a startling contrast to the vast expanse of sapphire-blue ocean was an island, a long, vibrant patch of green surrounded by pinkish-white sand. It was so beautiful in the middle of all that blue that without knowing it, she exclaimed. Hearing her, Chris half rose from his seat and looked over her shoulder.

"Good," he said. "I see we've arrived."

They obviously had. Just then, Gail felt the plane begin a wide banking turn and descent at the same time, and then before she knew it, they were skimming low over the water again with a long ribbon of runway stretching dead ahead. Darby set the plane down without a twitch, and as they came to a stop, Gail looked at Chris. She felt she ought at least to try to explain.

"Chris, I—" she started to say.

He shook his head, as though reading her mind. "Forget it," he said. "I understand."

Do you? she wondered, but didn't reply. Maybe it was best just to leave things as they were, she thought. Under the pretense of looking around for her bag, she glanced out the window at the resort and caught her breath. The pictures she'd seen of the place certainly hadn't done it justice, but she didn't have time to gawk. A sleek limousine, this one cream-colored, was speeding up to greet them, and as they emerged from the plane and the two men inside the car leaped out to greet them, she felt herself tense. She didn't recognize either of them at all, and she wondered if she was supposed to know them. It seemed not, for one of them immediately turned and opened the car door to let a third man out. Gail recognized him right away from the picture Roger had sent. He was the manager, Arthur Zambodji.

"Mr. Zambodji," she said warmly as he came up to them. "How nice of you to greet us like this. You do remember me—Gail—"

To her relief, he didn't miss a beat. "Certainly, Ms Sullivan," he said smoothly. "What a pleasure it is to see you again."

"And you," Gail said, wanting to sink to the ground and give thanks that she'd passed this first test. She turned immediately to Chris. "Chris, I'd like you to meet the manager of Kalliste Bahama, Mr. Arthur Zambodji. Mr. Zambodji, Christian Van Der Kellen."

Chris held out his hand. "A pleasure."

Zambodji took it. "Welcome to Kalliste Bahama, Mr. Van Der Kellen," he said. "I and the entire staff are at your service. This way, please."

And that was how simple it was. Another car came for Darby and Jack, but Gail and Chris were whisked away by the limousine, and before she could blink they were installed in the best rooms in the house—the interconnecting Ambassador suites.

"I'm sure you want to freshen up," Zambodji murmured, after bustling around making sure everything was in order. Vases of flowers were perched on tables; a huge basket of fruit rested on the coffee table in the living room. Over the cellophane, his eyes briefly met Gail's. "If you require anything—anything at all," he repeated, "please just dial 1701. As you are aware, Ms Sullivan, that is my private extension. I will have the phone manned night and day."

Blessing Roger for his advance preparation, and for the tact of this man, who was subtly letting her know where he could be reached if she needed help, she smiled warmly. "I'm sure we won't need assistance twenty-four hours a day, Mr. Zambodji, but thank you. I'll remember that."

The manager bowed, preparing to go out. But Chris, who had been standing by the huge expanse of windows that looked directly down on what Gail was sure was one of the most beautiful beaches in the world—with turquoise water and pink-white sand—turned to look at him.

"I see the parasailers are out," he said. "Is there any way to get a boat to take us out to the launch?"

Zambodji didn't blink. "I've already designated one to be at your disposal, Mr. Van Der Kellen. The driver is standing by. What time shall I tell him you want to leave?"

"Oh, in about half an hour, don't you think, Gail?" Chris said, and then saw her appalled expression. He seemed puzzled. "What's the matter?"

"Well..." She hesitated, waiting for Zambodji to take his cue and disappear, which he did, quietly closing the door behind him. She'd been sure that Chris was teasing her about this parasailing business, and as soon as the manager was gone, she said, "I thought you would want to see the hotel first—"

Chris dismissed that technicality with a wave of his hand. "There'll be time for that later. The place isn't going anywhere, and it's a beautiful day. I thought you liked the water."

"Oh, I...I do," she said, and looked nervously out at the people on the parasailing platform. Should she tell him that she'd never been parasailing in her life?

"Great," he said. "Then get into your swimsuit, and let's go."

"Now?"

"Unless you want to try it in the dark."

She wasn't sure she wanted to try it at all, and she was about to remind him that they'd come all this way because he was supposed to be checking out the hotel. She had thought that meant he'd be visiting the various departments, asking questions, talking to employees. She'd never dreamed that he'd been thinking of—her eyes went to that platform again, out on the ocean. Someone was being lifted high into the air under a colorful billowing parachute-type of thing, pulled along by a towline behind a speeding boat. Everyone looked as though they were having a wonderful time, and she looked back at Chris. He was watching her watch the parasailers, and in his eyes was a glint of—what? Amusement? Challenge?

That decided her. "Now's as good a time as any," she said, and went to her own suite to unpack her swimsuit.

Her determination to show Chris how game she was lasted until they took the boat out over a sparkling expanse of sea and joined the half dozen or so people on the platform. Someone had just finished a ride, and had arrived back safely. His eyes were sparkling, his face flushed with excitement and ruddy from the breeze.

"God, that was great!" the sailor cried, struggling out of his harness. "I can't wait to go back up!"

Gail was just thinking that he could certainly take her place when he turned to her and thrust out the harness. "Here, you try."

"Me!" she exclaimed, trying not to show her alarm. If she had to do this, she'd at least hoped she'd have some time to observe how it was done. "Oh, no," she said quickly. "Someone else can try. They've all been waiting, and we just got here."

"No, no, that's okay!" came the chorus. "We've all been up at least once. Come on, you've got to try! It's like nothing in this world!"

Gail was certain that was true. Hastily, she thrust the harness in Chris's direction. He was the one who'd wanted to do this; let him go. "Here, you do it."

His eyes had that maddening twinkle in them again. If she hadn't been so upset at the thought of her impending doom, she would have been better able to appreciate what he looked like in that brief suit. *With a body like that, no wonder he wears clothes so well,* she thought, and blushed despite herself, even though it was true. With his broad shoulders and trim waist and long legs, he looked as though he worked out with weights frequently, and his coloring was naturally dark so already he looked tanned. He was wearing an unbuttoned shirt, and with his dark hair blowing in the breeze and that devastating smile of his, he looked like every fantasy she'd ever had. She realized she wasn't alone thinking that. There were several other women on the platform, and they were staring at Chris, too. Surprised by the stab of protective jealousy she felt, she wanted to step closer and proclaim—

What? *This man is mine?*

Hastily, she thrust the harness out to him again. "Here."

"Oh, no. Ladies first," he said, and before she knew it, he was buckling her into the thing. Suddenly panicked, she turned and looked into his amused dark eyes. Pride was one thing; killing herself was another.

"I don't know how!" she said, feeling it was better to humiliate herself than to take a headlong dive into the sea from six hundred feet up.

He gave her a quick look. "You've really never done this before?"

"No!" she wailed, reaching in relief for one of the buckles that held her in. He put his hand over hers.

"Hey, don't panic. There's nothing to it. You don't have to do a thing but enjoy the ride."

"But—"

"Just remember the signals."

"What signals?"

"They're written on this little card." He pointed to a plastic-enclosed card that was tied to one of the lines. Until then, she hadn't even noticed it. "Both arms straight out means you're doing okay. Swinging your right arm down means to slow down, swinging the left arm up means to speed up. Your left arm straight out means you want to be lowered, your right arm straight out means to lift you. Got that?"

"No!" she said in panic.

"Well, don't worry about it. If you forget, just read the card."

"Oh, but—" she started to exclaim.

He leaned forward abruptly and kissed her briefly on the lips. "People are waiting. Up you go."

Blinking at the suddenness of the kiss, and bemused at how firm his lips had felt in that brief instant, she was still trying to get herself together when he signaled the driver.

"Wait!" she cried, but she was too late. The driver of the boat that had been idling some distance from the platform saw Chris's signal and opened the throttle. In a split second, the wind caught and filled the canopy that several helpful souls behind her were holding aloft. Like a brilliant white and red and green umbrella, the sail billowed—and lifted. She was off the platform before she even knew it, her feet flailing in the thin air.

"Chris!" she shouted, but he was already far below her. In three seconds, she was high overhead, the boat speeding full throttle into the wind, towing her. In five seconds more, with the wind giving her an added boost, she was literally at the rope's end, maximum altitude. Clutching tightly to the lines, she tried to remember. The line was three hundred feet, someone had said, so that meant she was... *two hundred feet in the air!*

"Oh, God!" she moaned, and shut her eyes tightly. But after a few seconds, when she didn't feel herself plummeting to the waves below, she opened her eyes cautiously. She could feel the vibration in the towline; it seemed to sing in the wind. And overhead the chute, catching and losing the wind, snapped like laundry on a clothesline. That high, she could hardly hear the boat's motor, or any other sound, except that of the wind spilling through the lift-boosting slots in the canopy.

Cautiously, she glanced around, and then... smiled. This wasn't so bad, she thought. In fact, it was wonderful! Now that she wasn't so scared, she decided to experiment. What were the signals Chris had told her about? Without thinking, she thrust her left arm straight out. Instantly, the towboat slowed and she began descending. She was so fascinated that she forgot to bring her arm in, and she plunged lower...and lower...taking less than ten seconds to drop from her previous height to a mere twenty feet. Sure that she was going to crash into the ocean after all, she hastily brought her left arm in and jabbed the right one out. Gleefully, it seemed to her, her driver saw her signal and throttled up the boat. Her heart in her throat, she soared straight up. When she hit the apex, she laughed aloud. This was *almost* as good as riding in Chris's boat!

After that, she experimented a few more times with the arm signals, once dropping so low to the water that her feet got wet, then giving the signal to go higher and faster. She was having a ball. All too soon, it was time to head back and give others a chance. Practiced by now, she landed back on the platform with nary a stumble, and laughingly gave the boatman an exuberant thumbs-up.

Chris was there to help with the harness, and she was so elated and excited that she flung herself into his arms.

"That was wonderful!" she cried. "Oh, Chris, you've got to try!"

And he held her tightly and laughed and kissed her once more—a real kiss this time, his lips warm from the sun and salty from the sea. No man had ever tasted so good; no arms had ever felt so right.

"I knew you'd like it," he said, his eyes sparkling, and kissed her again.

CHAPTER EIGHT

HOURS AFTER her parasailing experience, Gail was still in a daze. She and Chris had agreed to meet later for dinner—only because, by the time they got back to the hotel, she was so tired she could hardly keep her eyes open. Embarrassed, she had excused herself to take a nap, and had been asleep almost before her head touched the pillow. She might have slept through the entire night if a snatch of music from the pool cabana below hadn't impinged on her consciousness and dragged her awake. Shocked to realize that she'd slept two hours, she took a shower and, wearing a short terry-cloth robe, went out to the balcony to enjoy the sunset.

Everything was so beautiful here, she thought, looking out. The breeze that had earlier lifted her to such heights had died down to a whisper, bringing with it the scent of tropical flowers. Below the balcony, the pinkish-white sand stretched out before her; all the sunbathers and sailors and water-skiers had gone in for the day. Out on the water, only a single boat traveled serenely across the path of the setting sun, its sail tinted copper by the sun's fading rays. The light around her had taken on a gold tint; when she looked down at her crossed arms, she saw that even her skin looked bronzed.

Sighing happily, she leaned against the rail and thought about the wonderful day she'd had. From the time she and Chris had left Kellen Key until now, it had all seemed like a dream. Everything had been just perfect—including that all-too-brief kiss.

Frowning, she told herself not to make a big deal about that kiss. It had been a spur-of-the moment thing; she and Chris had both been happy and excited. It didn't mean anything, nothing at all. She should just forget it.

She couldn't forget it. Despite everything, she kept dwelling on that moment, reliving it over and over again. She could still remember how right his arms had felt around her, and how sheltered she'd felt in that circle. And she could still taste his lips, and feel the pressure of his mouth against hers. She hadn't even had time to unbuckle the harness; the lines from the billowing chute had tugged at them both as they had stood there wrapped up in each other. Only the good-natured shouting of the other people on the platform had brought them back to earth. As excited and elated as she was over that incredible sail, the look on Chris's face in that instant had made everything else unreal. If they hadn't been interrupted, she knew she could have gazed into those dark eyes forever.

Forever? That was a little melodramatic, wasn't it? *Forever* meant commitment, a pledge, eternal devotion...marriage. She frowned. When had she started thinking in those terms?

Quickly, she shook her head in denial. She hadn't started thinking that way at all. But who wouldn't wonder what it would be like to be married to Chris Van Der Kellen? Look what he had done for her so far: the limousine, the plane, that beautiful guest house on Kellen Key. It was all like something out of a dream.

And maybe it was, she thought, straightening suddenly as she wondered if she'd been meant to romanticize this entire scene. Maybe it all was a ploy, something

Chris had planned to impress her so that she'd report favourably to Harlan Damion and he would sell the resorts to VDK. Maybe all this had been part of some design to sway her to his side.

Firmly, she shook her head again. No, she wouldn't believe that. Chris didn't have to impress her, even if he did think she was Harlan Damion's executive vice president. The limo, the planes—everything—that was how he lived; he hadn't pulled out all the stops just because he wanted a favorable report. In fact, she suspected that he hadn't treated her any differently than he would have any other guest. It wasn't his fault that she'd been bowled over by such lavish treatment.

And remember his file, she argued with herself further. She knew that he could be tough, shrewd and demanding in business, and that he expected the most from all his employees. But she'd also seen how loyal his people were to him, how kind and generous he was, how much he enjoyed pleasing those around him. That type of loyalty couldn't be bought; it had to be earned, and from what she'd seen, Chris deserved it.

So Chris hadn't done anything for her that he wouldn't have done for anyone else, she thought, and felt suddenly depressed. *She* was the one who was making a big deal out of it, thinking...

She didn't know what she'd been thinking, but from now on, she'd refuse to be bowled over by all these treats. Somehow, she'd accept them as her due—as she would if she were really Damion's executive vice president, and she had the key to something Chris wanted. It was as simple as that. No more mooning over what seemed to be romantic gestures; no more feeling thrilled and singled out at his treatment of her. She was here to find out just how committed he was to buying Damion's resorts. It was time to stop being so impressed with the trappings and get to work.

Newly resolved, she left the balcony and went inside to get dressed for dinner. But as she stood at the closet debating what to wear, she felt let-down and depressed once more. Now that she had reminded herself—again—just why she was here, her elation at the thought of seeing Chris tonight had vanished along with her zest for this trip. Listlessly, she chose a turquoise silk shift from the closet—another item that had been billed to Chris, she remembered glumly. She resolved right then to write a check for the entire amount spent at the boutique before she went back to New York. It would deplete her already meager savings, but that would be better than feeling indebted.

It was the thought of going back to New York that made her pause. Clearly she wasn't learning anything significant on this tour, so before she made a terrible blunder and did something really foolish—such as thinking she was falling in love with Chris—she had to find a way to cut this short. Hoping that she could convince him it was silly to visit *all* the resorts, she finished dressing.

When she and Chris had agreed to meet for dinner, she had asked him if they shouldn't invite Darby and Jack as well, since they were here on their own. But Chris had just looked at her in genuine amusement and assured her that his pilots were perfectly capable of taking care of themselves. The last thing they would want, he told her, was to be invited to have dinner with the boss when they were surrounded by such...beautiful surroundings. Wishing she had insisted because of the way she felt—she really didn't want to be alone with Chris tonight—Gail added the final touches to her hair and makeup, then looked at her reflection. With all the exercise and the sun, her skin had taken on a healthy glow. *Wouldn't you know it?* she thought glumly. She'd never looked better.

WHILE GAIL WAS STARING at herself in her bathroom, Chris was standing in his with a towel wrapped around his waist and a razor in his hand. The six-inch-screen television mounted on the counter was turned to the news, and when he heard the announcer give the time, he blinked and came back from wherever he'd gone. Realizing that he'd been standing like this for at least five minutes, he started to shave, muttering to himself. What was wrong with him? He never just . . . blanked out.

Rinsing the razor in the sink, he decided he had an excuse to dream. He'd never had a day quite like this; just remembering how thrilled Gail had been by her parasailing experience made him feel good all over again. He could still see her, only a few seconds up, already acting as though she'd been sailing all her life. She hadn't been afraid, had even delighted in the sudden swoops and lifts, coming low enough to dip those beautiful toes in the waves—just like a pro. Smiling, he shook his head. What a woman!

Maybe that was the problem, he thought suddenly: she was too *much* woman. He'd never known anyone like Gail. She brought such zest and excitement, such a sense of wonder to everything she did, that he'd begun to feel rejuvenated, too. Just watching her made him want to laugh from sheer enjoyment. He hadn't felt like that in a long, long time.

Somberly, watching the water run over the razor, he thought that until he'd met Gail, he hadn't realized how dull his personal life had become. She was so different from Celeste, or from any other woman he'd known, that it was no wonder he was entranced.

Max felt the same way, he recalled. When his driver had related that story about the boat ride to the mainland, they'd both laughed. It seemed that they hadn't been out two minutes before Gail was asking if the boat could go faster. Faster! Other women might have been worried about mussing their hair, or if the boat would turn over, but not Gail. She'd been eager for more—just as she had been today. Why hadn't he realized he'd been looking for a woman like this all his life?

His hand froze in the act of putting the razor away. Where had that thought come from? he wondered, and looked at himself with dismay. He didn't want to get involved in a new relationship; he'd spent a good deal of energy since his divorce avoiding just that. And even if he wanted to get involved, he didn't have time; he had too many other problems to deal with. Celeste had accused him of being more interested in the company than he ever would be in a woman—any woman. Nothing had changed since that time. In fact, with this current situation, things were even worse. Until he met Gail, he'd been totally occupied at the office, as he should be. So what was he thinking about now?

He was thinking that he was starting to fall in love with her. At that thought, he felt even more dismayed. Grabbing the after-shave, he splashed some on—a little more roughly than necessary. He was being ridiculous. These flights of fancy were getting out of hand. He wasn't falling in love; it was just that Gail was a beautiful, intelligent, desirable woman. What man wouldn't be...attracted?

Distracted again, he remembered how she'd looked in that swimsuit today, all long legs and slim torso and full, rounded breasts, and he felt a stirring inside himself. With her hair wet and slicked back, her eyes with those thick dark lashes seemed even bigger, almost luminous. She'd been laughing with excitement as she had come in for that beautiful landing on the platform, and she'd looked so beautiful that he hadn't been able to stop himself from kissing her. What man could have resisted? He'd have to have been made out of stone not to feel *something*. But that didn't mean he was falling in love. For God's sake, he hardly knew her.

Ah, but he'd like to, wouldn't he? he thought before he could help it. Just remembering the way she'd felt in his arms, unwieldy harness and all, sent an ache up his loins that made him close his eyes in longing. Picturing that beautiful face again, he wasn't sorry he'd given in to impulse and kissed her; he was only sorry that they hadn't been alone on that platform.

Deciding he'd better abandon that line of thought before he really got into trouble, he tightened the towel around his waist and went into the bedroom. Now he felt unsettled. Wishing he hadn't given up smoking, he debated about a drink, but he didn't want that, either. Finally, hoping some air would bring order to his chaotic thoughts, he went out to the private balcony and watched the last of the sunset. The sky turned from mauve and gold to purple and copper as he stood there, but the glorious sight failed to calm him. Without volition, his glance went to the parasailing platform far out on the water, and before he knew it, he was hearing an echo of Gail's delighted laughter when she landed—right in his arms.

Feeling that ache rising in him again, he told himself it was better to deny it. He had serious problems in the company that he'd left behind—problems that weren't going to go away of their own accord. If he'd hoped or tried to convince himself that getting away would give him new perspective, it wasn't working. But then, how could it? From the moment he'd conceived this foolish trip, he hadn't been thinking of anything but Gail and how to please her. It was such a delight watching her expressive face—she was completely unable to hide her reactions—that he found himself continually thinking of things that would make her happy. He'd been so involved in that pursuit that he'd completely forgotten his priorities.

He sighed. It was a long time since he'd enjoyed himself like this—especially with a woman, and especially with someone who attracted him as much as Gail. But as pleasurable as this interlude had been, it was time to return to the real world. The problems at VDK wouldn't go away if he ignored them; things would only get worse. Whether he wanted to or not, it was time to cut short the trip and get back. He'd tell Gail that tonight, over dinner. He'd say that he didn't need to see the other resorts himself. He had enough information to make up his mind.

But he felt depressed as he went in to finish dressing, and it was an effort to feel upbeat—until he knocked on the door of Gail's suite. As soon as he saw her, everything else went out of his mind.

THE MAIN RESTAURANT at the hotel was one known throughout the islands because it was so romantic and so impressive. The structure had been built around a man-made minilagoon and was covered by a vaulted glass dome. At one end was a muted, backlit waterfall, and in the middle, the free-form pool, surrounded by misted vegetation and native rock. A curved bridge led to a sizable dance floor at the opposite end of the restaurant. Each table was screened for privacy by a profusion of real flowers and vines, and the scent of frangipani was tantalizingly evident on the air.

The maître d' greeted Gail by name, and privately thankful, she responded as though she knew him well, when in fact neither of them had seen the other before. He led them to the best table, but she didn't notice until she was seated how serious Chris looked.

"Is...everything all right?" she asked hesitantly. She'd thought until she saw him again that she had herself in hand. But her first glimpse of him when he came to fetch her had made her realize the folly of that. He was dressed tonight in a tan suit that made his dark looks even more attractive. Just seeing him made her heart beat faster, and her knees feel weak, and she was glad the restaurant lighting was dim, for she knew her face was flushed.

He seemed preoccupied. "What? Oh, no...everything is fine."

She wasn't sure it was. "If you don't like the restaurant," she said, "we can go somewhere else."

"No, it isn't that." He looked down. "It's these table-cloths."

"Tablecloths?" she repeated, and followed his glance. The table was covered by a pale green cloth, presumably in an attempt to enhance the surrounding verdant decor. She'd been so distracted by him that she hadn't noticed, but now that she thought about it, the green was definitely unappetizing. Remembering her supposed position here, she raised a hand to summon the waiter. "I'm sorry," she said. "I'll have it changed at once."

To her surprise—and dismay, since his touch instantly set up a clamor within her—Chris reached out and gently pulled down her hand. "It's all right," he said. "It doesn't matter."

She forced herself to keep her eyes on his face. He hadn't taken his hand off hers, and she was so attuned to him that she felt the warmth of his fingers even on the back of her hand. Trying to remember what they'd been talking about, she said, "If you don't like it, we'll change it, Chris. It's not a problem."

He withdrew his hand. "If I buy this place, I promise you, the first thing I'll do is order white linen." He smiled. "So don't worry about it."

The last thing she was worried about were the table-cloths. "If you buy this place," she forced herself to say lightly, "you can have grass mats on the tables, if that's your choice."

He laughed. "I doubt I'll go that far."

She was starting to feel out of control again, admiring the way the flickering candle in the little bowl on the table caught the highlights in his hair, noticing the wing-like set of his thick eyebrows, which gave his face a slightly devilish cast in this faint light. Forcing herself to remember why she was here, she decided that Damion's representative would have to ask him what he was thinking about the Kalliste deal, now that he'd seen a little of one resort.

"*Have* you decided to buy?"

"I don't know," he said, looking around. "I haven't seen much of it."

That certainly wasn't her fault, she thought, remembering how she had at least tried to show him around when they first got here. That seemed such a long time ago; so much had happened since then.

Nothing happened, except that you went parasailing, she told herself firmly, and said, "We could take a tour after dinner, if you like."

He brought his glance back to her face. "That won't be necessary. You tell me about it."

Was he testing her? She couldn't be sure. She was so confused about him now that she didn't know what to think. She'd hoped after her private pep talk upstairs that she had everything under control, but she knew now that wasn't true at all. With a sinking feeling, she doubted it ever would be, where he was concerned. The awful truth was that the harder she tried to keep things on a professional level, the more difficult it was to remember why she was here. She found herself thinking about everything else but business; with his dark eyes on her, she didn't want to discuss the Kalliste resorts, or anything else related to Harlan Damion. Instead, she wanted to know everything she possibly could about Chris Van Der Kellen.

But that wasn't why she was here, she reminded herself sternly. She said, "I'll be glad to tell you whatever you want to know."

"Good, then we'll discuss it over wine," Chris said. He barely glanced up, and as if by magic, the sommelier appeared, gliding up to their table as though he'd been lurking nearby just for this purpose.

"Good evening, Ms Sullivan," the man said. "It's a pleasure to see you again."

Another test. Quickly, she ran down her mental file of pictures and names and hoped she had fixed on the right one. "And you, John," she said, smiling when she saw the approval flash briefly in his eyes. Relieved, she turned to Chris. "Chris, this is John Sturges, Kalliste Bahama's chief wine steward. John has been with us for—what is it now, John? Ten years?''

He bowed. ''You have such a memory, Ms Sullivan,'' he said admiringly. ''It will be ten years in June.''

Whether it was or not, Gail silently blessed Roger's advance preparation. It was certainly making things easier for her to have all the employees play along. Now that her part was done for a few minutes, she sat back and let the men discuss the wine cellar. Only when she realized that Chris had ordered champagne in addition to what they might have with the meal, did she look up.

Smiling at her expression, he shrugged. ''You seemed to enjoy it in the car.''

''And on the plane,'' she reminded him, thinking that she'd enjoyed all this attention a little too much. Reminding herself again to stick to business, she waited until they were alone, and then resumed their interrupted conversation. ''As John mentioned,'' she said, leaning forward, ''Kalliste Bahama has an exceptional wine cellar. If you like, I can arrange for him to give you a tour.''

''That won't be necessary. I got a good idea of what's there from talking to him just now.''

''Oh,'' she said, wondering why he was staring at her like that. His scrutiny made her nervous, and she said the first thing that came into her head. ''Well, in that case, we could discuss . . . the security department.''

''Fine,'' he said absently, still staring at her. He made a little gesture for her to go ahead, leaning slightly forward, as though he didn't want to miss a single word.

Why was he looking at her like that? Nervously, she picked up her water glass and took a sip. Fortunately she was well versed in this part, from her former work in hotels. Trying to avoid that intent stare, she started to rattle on. "Well, as with most hotels, the security department at Kalliste Bahama is considered as part of the front-of-house staff because of their contact with guests. Not that the resort has a real problem with security," she added hastily. "We have stringent hiring requirements, and of course the guests are the highest caliber. As I'm sure you've noticed, this resort—the entire Kalliste chain, in fact—has just had new computerized locks installed on all the rooms, along with secondary automatic door-locks. The front office is instructed to strongly encourage all guests to leave valuables in the safe—or the safe deposit boxes in the security department itself. So you see we have the most modern, up-to-date security system devised—"

Realizing she sounded like a teacher of hotel management, she stopped abruptly. Chris was still staring at her, his chin on his hand. "Go on," he said, looking amused.

Go on? With what? Why was he making her go through all this? she wondered suddenly. He had the same files as she did. Did he suspect something? She felt a stab of panic. Had he finally figured out she was a fraud and wanted to see just how far she'd play out the charade?

"Maybe we should discuss another department," she said hastily. "The kitchen staff is extremely competent here. Basil is the executive chef, and I'm sure—"

"I'll judge the staff over dinner," Chris said.

Feeling more desperate by the minute, she said, "Then perhaps we should talk about the business side. The accounting department—"

"I've reviewed all the figures."

What was he leading up to? Deciding maybe she didn't want to find out, she said, "Then, how about advertising and PR?"

"I've seen the brochure."

She'd come to the end of her rope. Starting to get irritated now, she asked a little sharply, "All right, then, what do you want?"

"I want to dance," he said. "Will you join me?"

She'd been so intent on not digging herself into a hole that she hadn't noticed the band had appeared. After tuning up, they'd begun a slow, languid tune from the forties. She glanced in their direction, and then at Chris. "Oh, I don't think so...."

"You don't dance?"

It was a long time since she'd been out on a dance floor. Stanley had hated making an exhibition of himself, as he called it, so on the rare occasions they'd gone out, she'd had to tap her toe on the sidelines. She loved to dance. But not with this man. If just touching her hand a while ago had sent her into an emotional tizzy, how much worse would it be in his arms again?

"Of course I dance," she started to say. "But—"

"Then may I?" Chris said, and before she knew it, he was leading her across the arched bridge and onto the dance floor. As though on cue, the band segued into a very romantic version of "Begin the Beguine," and when Chris's arms went around her, Gail was lost.

She'd known that he would be a wonderful dancer, and of course he was. With the music winding like a silvery ribbon around them, and Chris whirling her over the dance floor, she forgot everything but the pleasure of being in his arms once more. She'd always loved to dance, and he was such a sure leader and so light on his feet himself that they danced as though they'd been born to it. It was magical. As though everyone else sensed that something special was happening out on the floor, they cleared away so that she and Chris had the area to themselves. He used the entire surface, gliding and swaying and even dipping her in time to the music, so that by the time the song ended, she was breathless—and more in love than ever.

"That was . . . wonderful," she murmured, still dazed by the incredible experience.

Chris held her tightly and stared into her eyes. "Do you do everything well—or does it just seem like it?" he asked, his voice as husky as hers.

They heard the smattering of applause just then, and looked around bemusedly as other diners gave them a hand. Gail was embarrassed, but Chris took it all in stride, grasping her hand and gesturing with the other in her direction, acknowledging her beauty and grace.

"Stop," she protested, her face flushed.

"Why?" he said, looking down at her. "You're the most beautiful woman here."

And you're the most handsome man, she thought, leading the way firmly back to the table. The champagne had arrived in the meantime, and after that, the rest of the evening passed in a daze. They had just finished—or tried to finish—a dessert of flaming cherries jubilee, when Gail sat back.

"I couldn't eat another bite. That was wonderful."

"Yes, I have to admit it was," Chris said, smiling. "Almost as good as what Hana can do at home, when she sets her mind to it. How about a nightcap?"

She groaned. "I couldn't possibly!"

"Then let's go for a walk on the beach."

"What! Now?"

"What better time?"

What better time indeed? Telling herself that she'd decided to do this mad thing because it was part of her job, and not because she wanted to prolong the evening, she allowed him to help her with her chair.

Wizardlike, the maître d' appeared. "Was everything to your satisfaction?" he asked anxiously.

"Absolutely perfect, Pierre," Gail said.

"Please convey my compliments to the chef," Chris said. "And to the rest of the staff."

"I'll be happy to do that, sir," Pierre assured him, and after bowing, he went with them to the door.

Shining over the beach was moonlight from a crescent moon that seemed to smile at them. Tiny waves lapped at the shore and the water was as clear as dark glass. It was late enough that they were the only ones out and so quiet that they could hear the breeze rustling through the trees around the resort. Pausing on the last step of the terraced deck that led to the sand, Gail held on to Chris's arm while she took off her high heels.

"Hey," she said, noticing that he was making no move to remove his own shoes. "This was your idea, remember? You can't go walking on the sand in your shoes! What will people think?"

"I don't think this crowd will notice, do you?" he replied, indicating the empty deck chairs, lined up around the pool like silent sentinels. "But since you insist . . ."

His shoes and socks in hand, they went down to the beach. The sand was still warm from the heat of the afternoon, and Gail buried her stockinged toes luxuriously. "I haven't done this since I . . . I can't remember when," she said.

"What? Walk on the beach at night?"

The words were out before she thought. "Walk on the beach at night . . . in the moonlight . . . with a man. . . ."

"It is romantic, isn't it?" he said softly, and took her hand, bringing her around to him. "Very romantic," he added, looking down into her eyes.

She knew he was going to kiss her; knew too, that she should disengage her hand and just back away, making some innocuous remark, or better yet, a little joke, to show she was in complete command of the situation, and herself. But she couldn't seem to do that. Her breath caught as his gaze held hers, and she couldn't seem to do anything but watch helplessly as he slowly lowered his head to hers.

Just before his lips touched hers, she murmured, "This isn't right...."

"I know," he murmured back, and then he kissed her.

He had kissed her before, but not like this—not with such passion and intensity, and a yearning that communicated itself to her very soul. Desire leaped inside her like a white heat, and she wrapped her arms around his neck just as he pulled her closer. They fit so well together, she thought dazedly; no awkward positioning of arms and legs, just body against body, chest to breast, heart to heart. His lips were hot and demanding, and when he probed with his tongue, she opened her mouth and welcomed him. The fire rose, igniting to heated life, and she could feel the heat spreading through her as his hands dropped lower, cupping her into him.

"Oh, Gail," he murmured. He was trembling, as was she. For a wild instant, she wanted to sink down on the sand, in full view of the entire hotel.

But just then, like the banging of a hammer against the lid of a pan, they heard a cacophonous eruption of singing and shouting and music that sounded as though it were rising from the ocean. It crashed in on them like surf on the sand, and Chris lifted his head and looked around.

"What the hell? What's that?"

Gail sensed she was supposed to know, but she'd been so lost in sensation that it was an effort to come back. Dazedly she looked around, too. "I don't..." she started to say, and then saw the apparition approaching from the other side of the breakwater to the left of the hotel. The marina was down that way, and this ship had obviously come from that direction. Now, with its sails wrapped in light, and music pouring forth from loudspeakers on the deck, she clearly saw the three-masted *GoodTime* round the bend and start its party journey around the island. College students swarmed over the decks hoisting bottles of beer, yelling and having the time of their lives.

Belatedly, Gail remembered reading about this in her file. "That's—"

"The end to a romantic night," Chris said darkly, giving the noisy, rollicking ship a glare that should have sunk it on sight.

Gail had to agree. The appearance of the party ship had destroyed the mood, and so they just stood there and watched it gaily sailing across the water in front of the hotel. Gail had to laugh when firecrackers suddenly started going off, lighted by some kid hanging high in the rigging of the ship.

Sighing, Chris bent down and retrieved their shoes and his socks. Then, with their arms around each other, they went back inside.

"Now would you like a nightcap?" he asked, at the door to his suite.

Her suite was right here, and she hesitated. Should she accept? She seemed to have no will at all where Chris was concerned. Knowing she should just make some excuse about how late it was and go inside, she rationalized that now would be a good time to tell him that she had to cut short the trip and head home again. It was especially important to tell him in view of what had nearly happened a few minutes ago on the beach. If that ship hadn't come along, interrupting them...

"I'd like that," she said, and added, "because there's something I'd like to talk to you about."

He seemed to have become somber, too. "Good. I've got something to tell you, too."

But neither of them had a chance to say what was on their minds. The message light was blinking when they came into the suite's living room, and when Chris answered, his expression turned so grim that Gail decided he needed privacy. She was edging toward the door when he lifted his hand, commanding her to stay. He listened some more, then replaced the phone.

"I'm sorry," he said. "There's a problem at my Phoenix office. I'm afraid I have to go there tomorrow and straighten it out."

Telling herself she should feel relieved and not disappointed, as she did, Gail said quickly, "I understand. I should be heading back anyway—"

But Chris didn't seem to hear her. "I was just thinking," he said. "Kalliste Scottsdale is right outside Phoenix. I'm sure my... my problem at the office won't take long to fix, and then we could just go on to the next resort." He turned to look at her. "Would that be convenient?"

It wouldn't be convenient at all! She'd just been offered a perfect excuse to cut short this trip; she had to take it. There was no question about that, not after what had just happened out on the beach. If she stayed with him, things could only get worse, more complicated, more involved. No, no; she'd tell him that she had pressing business at her office, too, and then get away before she made a bigger fool of herself than she already had.

But she didn't say any of that. Instead, to her horror, she nodded and said, "I have to get in touch with my office, Chris. But I'm sure that will be fine."

And then she spent the rest of the night wondering what in the world she'd been thinking of. Worse, what she had done.

CHAPTER NINE

GAIL SPENT A RESTLESS NIGHT coming to the realization that she couldn't fool herself any longer. By morning, she had decided that she'd have to call Roger and admit—as much as she hated to do it—that she'd committed the worst sin in the trade: not only had she lost her objectivity, but she'd gotten involved with her subject. Roger was going to have a fit.

But he was so enthusiastic when he found out who was calling so early in the morning that she lost some of her resolve.

"Gail!" he said cheerfully. "You found out anything?"

She took a deep breath. "No, and I don't think I'm going to."

There was a silence. "Oh?" he said finally. "Why not?"

"Well, it's just not working out," she said, hoping she could convince him without telling the whole story. If he didn't agree with her, she didn't know what she'd do. She couldn't go to Phoenix with Chris, but now that she was actually talking to her boss, she couldn't admit what a failure she'd been, either.

"Go on," he said.

"I'm sorry," she said. "But it's just no good. We'll have to try another approach—maybe getting someone else into his Florida office. I can't find out anything this way. Think about it—what's Chris going to tell me? That he's acted interested in buying Kalliste International when he really has no intention of going through with the deal? After all, he knows—or he thinks he does—that I'm Damion's executive vice president. Naturally he's going to be on his best behavior.''

There was that silence again. Going over her little speech in her head, she was sure she'd made sense. In fact, now that she thought about it, she wondered why she hadn't thought of all this before. The points she raised were so very reasonable!

Or did they just seem so reasonable because she wanted out?

Before she had time to decide, Roger asked cautiously, ''What do you suggest?''

Elated that she'd won him over—to this point, at least—she said immediately, ''I want to come home and work on another angle. Chris is heading to his Phoenix office this morning, so it's a good time to—''

''Why is he going there?''

Too late, she saw her mistake. Hastily, she tried to correct it. ''I don't know. There's been some kind of crisis that demands his personal attention. But that's not—''

''And you think *now* is a good time to come home?''

''Well, why not? As I said, I haven't found out anything here, and it doesn't look like I'm going to with this cover. That's why I—''

''I think you should go to Arizona with him.''

''But Roger—''

''No buts. This is a perfect opportunity to check around one of his offices and see what you can find out. You said yourself you weren't learning anything there. What you need is a little time in his files.''

"His files! How do you expect me to do that?"

"I don't know. You're the one in the field—you think of something. And you did say you'd take him on the grand tour. How can you bow out now?"

"I can say something pressing has come up at *my* office!"

"But that wouldn't be true."

"Who cares?" she cried, exasperated, and told herself to calm down. She wouldn't get anywhere shouting at him. More quietly, she said, "If you don't want me to work this from New York, let me try from Florida. Maybe I could talk my way into his office there."

"How?"

"I don't know! I'll think of something!"

"No, that's not going to work," he said stubbornly. "I still think you'd be better off going to Phoenix."

"But—"

He interrupted her shrill protest. "I'm sorry, Gail, but I've got to cut this short. Jean had to go on emergency leave—something about her family, and I have a new temporary secretary. She sort of mixed up appointments. I'm supposed to be somewhere else right now."

Something clicked in the back of her mind at that, but before she could think what it was, she heard a knock on her door. Thinking it was the bellhop for her luggage, she said, "Just a minute, Roger. Someone's at the door—"

"No time," he replied. "Call me when you get to Phoenix. 'Bye."

"Roger!" she cried, but she was already speaking to a dead line. "Damn," she muttered, and slammed down the phone. She went to answer the door.

It wasn't the bellboy. To her dismay, Chris was standing there, and when she saw him, she couldn't prevent sending a guilty look toward the phone. How loud had she been speaking? Had he heard any of that conversation?

"Chris," she said faintly. "Come in."

"No, I just wanted to see if you were ready." He then deflated her quick hope that he'd solved his Phoenix crisis and they didn't have to go to Arizona after all by adding, "Darby and Jack are at the plane right now. Do you need anything before we go?"

Just a suit of emotional armor, she thought, and went with him to her doom.

Because of the time change, they landed at Sky Harbor International in Phoenix early that afternoon, but long before that she was in trouble. When they stopped briefly in Houston to refuel, and for Chris to make a few phone calls, he looked so unhappy when he returned that she couldn't just ignore the fact.

"Chris," she said hesitantly. "Would you like to talk about it?"

He shook his head. "No, I don't want to bore you with business details."

"It wouldn't be a bore!" she exclaimed, and thought how true that was. If she could find out something now instead of waiting until they got to Phoenix... Quickly she added, "I'd like to help."

He smiled. "You already have."

"How?"

He reached for her hand. "Just by being here. If I was alone, I'd just... brood."

Even the casual touch set up that clamor inside her. Wanting to smooth that worried frown from his face, she tried to think of something cheerful to talk about. "Well, since you don't want to discuss business, why don't we talk about Arizona? Have you ever been to the Grand Canyon?"

She was instantly sorry she'd asked the question, for his eyes darkened with remembrance. "Yes, when I was a child," he said. "My father took Nick and me on one of those donkey rides down the rim."

"You don't sound as though you enjoyed it."

He shrugged. "Well, one didn't exactly *enjoy* doing things with my father," he said. "He always seemed to make everything either a competition or an endurance contest."

"How awful!" she exclaimed, and then was embarrassed. "I'm sorry. I didn't mean—"

"No, that's all right. It's the way he was."

She was silent a moment, thinking how different her own experience was. Her father had always encouraged, never demanded.

As though he realized he'd made her uncomfortable, Chris said, "We did enjoy the Petrified Forest, though. All those misshapen trees. It was like something out of a science fiction landscape. I'll never forget my wonder at the thought of that whole area covered with silt so many thousands of years ago. It was amazing to learn that minerals seeping into the pores of the trees could gradually turn them to stone."

Despite his effort to lighten the mood, there was still that shadow in his eyes. She wanted to cradle his head against her breast and stroke his brow to take away those lingering painful memories, but instead, she made herself laugh and say teasingly, "Who told you about the Petrified Forest?"

He looked surprised. "My father."

Deciding it was time to be a little daring, she leaned toward him. "Well, I hate to say it, but your father was misinformed."

He looked so startled that she thought for sure she'd made a terrible mistake. Did one denigrate a legend? She saw him frown.

"Misinformed?" he repeated. "No, I don't think so. According to geologists—"

"Geologists are scientists!" she scoffed. "What do they know? Let me tell you the real story about how the Petrified Forest came into being!"

Looking amused, he sat back. "All right. Go ahead."

She paused dramatically. "Well, according to Indian legend—which is, in many ways, much more accurate than science," she added, "a goddess came to that area long, long ago, after a tiring journey. Weary and very hungry, she killed some game and then tried to cook it using the wood from the surrounding trees. But the trees were too green to burn, and that made the goddess so angry that she turned them all to stone, forever and ever more! And *that's* how the Petrified Forest came into being."

He just looked at her for a moment. Then he threw back his head and laughed. "Where on earth did you hear that?"

"From an old Indian, of course," she said and gave him a sly look. "Don't you believe me?"

He laughed again, genuinely amused. Then, before she knew what he intended, he reached for her and pulled her to him. Kissing her on the nose, he said, "I'd rather believe that than a roomful of geologists—including my father. That was wonderful. Do you have any more stories like that?"

She was having a difficult time catching her breath—but not because he was holding her too tightly. Gazing up into his eyes, so close to hers, she fought to remember what he'd asked her. "I have a complete repertoire," she managed to murmur. "My mind runs to trivia."

His voice suddenly husky, he said, "Then you'll have to tell me more."

Her heart was starting to hammer so loudly she was sure he could hear it. "Any time you like—"

"How about now?" he said, and started to kiss her. He was just pulling her even closer when Darby opened the cockpit door and stuck his head in. "We're starting approach, boss—" he began, and then, seeing what was going on, blushed a bright red. "Oh . . . sorry," he said, and slammed the door shut.

Thinking of his face, Gail burst into laughter. "Poor Darby!"

Chris didn't look so amused. "Poor *Darby*? What about me?"

She looked at him with twinkling eyes. "He's your pilot," she said. "You should teach him about timing."

"I'll bet the trees in the Petrified Forest felt the same way," he said glumly.

She laughed again, but this time after a frown in her direction, he joined her. Then, with his arm around her, they looked out the window as Darby lined up for final approach. Loving the feel of Chris so close to her, Gail looked out the window at the bright patch of green that was Phoenix, rising from the dessert like the mythical bird after which it was named. She pointed to one of the area's famous landmarks, Camelback Mountain, and when Chris glanced over her shoulder and saw it, too, he agreed that the mountain formation really did look like a reclining camel. Then, moments later, they were skimming the runway at Sky Harbor.

Chris had a car waiting for him instead of the limousine Gail had grown to expect, and as he made arrangements with Darby and Jack for a layover, she made her own plans. After a few minutes the pilots went their own way, and Chris held open the passenger door of his car for Gail and said, "We usually stay at the Biltmore when we're here, but since it's so close, I'll just drive you out to Kalliste Scottsdale. That way—"

"Oh, I don't mind going to the office with you," she said quickly. As Roger had insisted, this was her chance to poke around a little, and she couldn't miss it no matter how guilty she was starting to feel.

He shook his head as he started the car. "Thanks, but I'm afraid you'll just be bored. I've got meetings set up back to back to deal with this . . . problem, so I'll be tied up the rest of the day. I'm sure you'll be more comfortable at the resort."

As much as she hated to, she decided to push him a little. Was her comfort the reason he didn't want her around the office—or was there something else?

"Well, to tell you the truth, Chris, I have some work to take care of myself," she said, trying to sound apologetic. It wasn't difficult; already she felt so guilty at deliberately deceiving him that she wanted to justify her actions. "I hoped you'd let me have an unused office for an hour or two. Or, if that's too much trouble, just a desk and a telephone somewhere. Could we manage that?" She smiled. "I promise to stay out of the way."

He looked uncertain. "Well, if you really want to."

"I do," she said, and then added on impulse, "And if there's anything I can do for you—"

"You mean with my current emergency?" he asked. He shook his head again. "Thanks for the offer, but no. I'll work it out." Then he looked at her as though struck by a sudden thought. "If you're wondering whether this problem will affect the Kalliste deal—"

"Oh, no, I wasn't."

"Of course you were. I don't blame you. But please, let me assure you that one has nothing to do with the other. I'll work it out. It'll just take some time."

There seemed nothing more she could say to that, and so she got into the car. As he did everything, Chris drove well, and soon they were turning onto a long curving driveway and passing through open gates bearing the VDK logo. Gail was impressed despite herself with the beautifully landscaped grounds. The gardeners in attendance waved as they drove by. At the end of the driveway was a low building made of gray brick and black-tinted glass.

Chris saw her expression and smiled for the first time since entering the car. "It looks sort of like an army barracks, doesn't it?"

"Not exactly," Gail said dryly, looking at the three-tiered fountain in the front, set in the middle of a round reflecting pool that mirrored the building behind it.

"I mean the gray color. I wanted something else, but the architect assured me that gray was . . . cooler."

"Having been here when it was 112 degrees at midnight, I can see why," Gail said. She added teasingly, "Is that why you have the pool—so the employees can cool off?"

"No. We tell them that's a wishing well, and we sweep it for coins every night. It pays for the upkeep around here," Chris told her, straight-faced.

"You must pay your employees well," she said, pointedly gazing around.

He laughed, took her arm and led her inside. There was a guard at a reception desk who leaped up to get the elevator for them, and when the doors whooshed open again at their floor, Gail saw a wide hallway carpeted in plush beige from one end to the other. Ahead were two huge glass doors that led to a big office. When Chris opened them for her, a blond secretary, who had been working diligently at a word processor, dictation headphones clamped to her head, looked up. When she saw Chris, she smiled and immediately removed the headphones.

"Mr. Van Der Kellen!" she said. "We've been expecting you."

"Good," Chris said, his mind clearly on business now that he was here. "I'd like to get started immediately, so would you have everyone assemble in the conference room in five minutes? Oh, yes. Gail, this is Gloria, my secretary. Gloria, Gail Sullivan, Kalliste International's vice president. Ms Sullivan is going to be using my office while I'm in conference, Gloria. Please see that she has everything she needs."

Gail tried not to look as delighted as she felt. What luck! Still, she was required to protest. Feebly, she said, "Chris, I can't use your office...."

"Don't be silly," he said, and led her inside.

Gail stopped in amazement when she entered the inner office. Another huge expanse of beige carpeting was here, but there was also a black marble slab that was clearly the desk, an array of original oil paintings on the walls, a wet bar on one side, a number of seating groupings, a small round conference table and an impressive ceiling-to-floor window that seemed to look out on the entire city of Phoenix.

"Good Lord," she muttered.

Chris laughed. "See what I mean?"

Trying not to be overwhelmed by all this magnificence, she turned to him again. "Chris, I can't use your office. Really, I wouldn't be comfortable. Don't you have something a little...smaller, perhaps?''

"Yes, but I'm going to be using it," he said. "It's closer to the conference room, and besides...I've never liked this one." His expression turned a little grim, as it seemed to whenever he spoke of Kerstan. "It was my father's, and he enjoyed being ostentatious."

She glanced around again. It was certainly that.

"If you need anything, just buzz Gloria," he said, and handed her the car keys. "I don't know what time you'll be finished here, but take the car when you leave. I'll catch a ride."

He was gone before she could protest further, leaving her alone in all that luxurious space. Blankly, she looked around. Now what? He'd said that he used this office, and since she had no place else to start, she supposed she should begin with the desk. Hoping that Gloria would leave her alone until requested, she'd just started tiptoeing across the acre of carpet when she heard a soft knock on the door.

Her face turning red with guilt, she spun around instantly. "What is it?"

The secretary stuck her head in. "I just wanted to know if you needed anything, Ms Sullivan."

"No, I'm fine, thank you."

"Well, if you change your mind—or you need me to take dictation or a letter or anything—my number is two on the intercom."

Wishing the woman would just go away so she could get on with her intent, Gail thanked her and waited until she withdrew. As soon as the door closed again, she let out the breath she'd unconsciously been holding. Did all undercover operatives feel this way? She was so tense she'd nearly screamed at the sound of that knock.

She made herself continue her journey to the desk. Fortunately, she'd remembered to bring her briefcase, so she set that on the desktop and opened it so that if she were interrupted again, at least it would look as though she was working. The only other things marring the surface were a telephone with a complicated-looking arrangement of buttons and numbers, a leather desk pad and an onyx pen and pencil set with a clock built into it. Six drawers, three on each side, were built into the desk, and she rubbed her hands together nervously as she stared at them. Then, reminding herself that she was only doing her job, she sat down and forced herself to go through the drawers one by one.

Twenty minutes later, standing in the middle of the room, she knew with a sinking feeling that she wasn't going to find anything this way. All she'd found in the desk were stationary supplies, so she'd started in on the bookcase, in case anything was hidden behind the books. Then, feeling increasingly foolish, she'd rifled through the carefully arranged magazines to make sure nothing had been inserted between the pages. She'd examined the wet bar and had even looked behind the paintings. She hadn't found a thing. If Chris had ever worked in this room, no one could prove it. She'd have to look somewhere else.

Grimly, her glance went to the big oak doors. The problem was how to get past the secretary. Maybe she could make up some story about wanting to stretch her legs, or having to find the ladies' room, or needing to look up something in the library. The library! Yes, that was it. Surely the office had a library. She could say she needed some information; she wouldn't have to be specific about what.

Trying not to think what she'd do if she was wrong, she stuffed everything back into her briefcase and locked it. Then she headed for the outer office. Gloria was still working diligently on the word processor; when Gail emerged, she looked up with that bright, helpful little smile.

"Yes, Ms Sullivan?"

"Gloria, I've got to...check some figures. Do you have a library here?"

"Oh, yes," the young woman said, to Gail's relief. "It's just down the hall." She picked up her pad and pencil. "But I'll be glad to look up the information for you. What is it you want to know?"

Gail hadn't expected this; Gloria was too efficient for her own good. "Oh, I...it's too hard to explain," she said vaguely, and waved her hands. "I'd prefer to look it up myself. If you could just point me in the right direction..."

If Gloria thought this odd, she didn't show it. "Certainly, Ms Sullivan," she said. "It's just down the hall. Three doors on your left."

The hallway was long and, fortunately, empty. The deep carpeting muffled any sound her footsteps made, and as she came to the first door, she glanced quickly to the right and left to make sure she was still alone. Then, taking a deep breath, she tried the handle. It opened easily...onto a copy room. Disappointed, she closed that door and went on the next. It occurred to her that she wasn't sure just what she was looking for, but Roger had told her to check around, so that's what she was doing. Feeling increasingly ridiculous, she wondered what her boss expected her to find. After all, Chris would hardly leave valuable documents lying around so that she could take out her trusty little camera and photograph them for evidence.

At least she could say she'd tried. Going to the next door in line, she listened for a moment to see if she could hear anything, and then tried that one, too. It turned out to be a supply closet, filled from floor to ceiling with paper and office goods on racks.

Sighing, she went on to the third, which would lead to the library. Resigned, she was just about to try that door when she heard a murmur inside. Cocking her head, she stopped to listen. Yes, that was definitely a voice—a man's judging by the deep tones. It wasn't Chris—she could tell that much—but she knew she'd heard the voice before. After another quick glance up and down the hall, she stepped closer and put her ear to the door. Frustratingly, she couldn't identify who was talking; the door was so thick, she couldn't tell. All she could hear were snatches of conversation. Whoever it was seemed to be on the phone.

"...told you, he's here..." she heard. Then a short silence. She pressed closer, wondering how in the world she would explain her position if someone came along. Deciding she couldn't worry about that right now, she closed her eyes and concentrated.

"...yes, I know," the man said. "I did what I could.... No, damn it, someone else called him.... After all this trouble to set it up, do you think I—"

The speaker stopped, as though he were listening to whoever was at the other end. Thwarted in her eavesdropping attempt, Gail glanced around. If this call was going through on an outside line, she might be able to pick it up through an empty office. There was a door a little farther on; hoping that led to a desk with an extension, she looked around again, and then quickly slipped inside.

It was an office—mercifully empty. Her eyes went immediately to the phone on the desk, and her heart bounded. One of the call line buttons was lighted, and she was just reaching eagerly for the receiver when the light went out.

"No!" she muttered, and then clapped a hand over her mouth. Had anyone heard her? Some spy she was!

She heard the library door open, and dashed to the door of the office, hoping she was in time to see who came out. Putting her hand tightly around the knob, she pulled the door open as quietly as she could, and nearly exclaimed in disappointment again. She was too late. The tail of a sport coat was just disappearing around the corner. She couldn't see whom it belonged to.

Deciding there was no point going to the library now, she hurried back to Chris's office. But she didn't have time to ponder the meaning of what she'd overheard; Chris was waiting for her when she got there. She nearly fainted when she saw him, wondering how on earth she was going to explain where she'd been.

He didn't seem to notice that she'd been gone. Running a hand through his hair, he said immediately, "Look, Gail, the situation is worse than I thought here. I'm sorry, but it seems as though I'm going to have to spend half the night trying to straighten it out."

She didn't know whether to be relieved or not that he hadn't noticed her absence. Feeling inadequate, she said, "I'm sorry. Is there anything I can do?"

"No, I just feel badly about dragging you all the way here, only to leave you on your own. I had no idea this would take so long."

He looked so frustrated that she decided she should make use of the opportunity. It was for the best, wasn't it?

"I understand," she said. "Maybe we should just forget the rest of the tour, Chris. It doesn't seem to be a good time—"

"No!"

Taken aback, she looked at him. "I'm sorry?"

He was embarrassed by the outburst. "What I meant was that I don't want this . . . this problem of mine to interfere with our plans."

"But—"

He turned suddenly to her, his dark eyes so bleak that her treacherous heart went out to him. It took all her will to stand where she was; she wanted to rush to his side and beg him to let her help.

"You don't understand," he said. "I *want* to check out these resorts." He paused. "I want to see these resorts with you. Can you give me just a little more time to straighten out this mess?"

She wanted to; oh, she did. But she knew what it would mean to stay. Already she could feel herself getting lost in this man—she, who had insisted only a few days ago that her career was uppermost in her life. Her career. She nearly cringed. Her *career* was what was compelling her to spy on this man, to lie to him, to deceive him.

"Oh, Chris," she said helplessly.

"Please?"

That "please" was her undoing. Suddenly she was in his arms and he was holding her tightly, as though he'd never let her go. She could feel the hard, strong beat of his heart, faster and faster, and she looked up at him with swimming eyes. "I don't know," she whispered.

His eyes held hers, filled with as much pain and confusion as she felt. But he didn't let her go. "I don't, either," he said. "But we have to have time to work it out. Will you give it to me?"

And when she should have said *No, this is impossible. It's not right. It can never be right,* she looked up into the face she could no longer deny she loved, and said simply, "Yes."

GAIL WAS EXHAUSTED by the time she got to Kalliste Scottsdale, too emotionally wrung out to appreciate the grandeur of the place, or to notice the figure approaching behind her after she'd checked in and given her bags to the valet. Heading toward the elevator, all she could think of was a long, hot bath, and then falling into bed.

Where she planned to pull the covers over her head. She'd really done it now, she thought glumly. What in the world had possessed her? Now that she was away from Chris's overwhelming presence, she could review her behavior back at the office and cringe. Was she so spineless that one embrace from him could destroy all her willpower? Was she so powerless that she couldn't do what was right?

And just what *was* right? she wondered dismally. Spying on him? Snooping around private offices in the hope that she might pick up some tidbit that would help her client decide whether to sell to him or not? Wanting to be alone, she punched the elevator button again. Where was the stupid thing? If it didn't come soon, she'd take the stairs.

"Gail?"

She was agitated, but not too agitated to recognize that voice. Still, in the few seconds before she made herself turn around, she squeezed her eyes shut, trying to tell herself that this wasn't happening. It couldn't be him, she thought. It couldn't be! Not Stanley, not here, not *now*!

"Gail?"

The hope that he'd go away, or disappear, or turn out to be a feverish illusion vanished when she felt his hand on her arm. Hoping until the last second that she'd made a mistake, she turned. No, it was Stanley, all right, and in a flash her weariness disappeared. She took one look at him and dragged him behind a huge potted palm that was standing near the elevator. Before he had a chance to say anything more, she cried, "This is too much! What are you doing here?"

He gave her a happy smile. "I came to see you, Gail."

This wasn't happening, she told herself. Not again! "How did you know I was here?"

"Oh, I—"

"Never mind! I don't want to know," she said fiercely, and whipped around, pulling aside one of the palm fronds to peer into the lobby. Thank the Lord. Chris had mentioned that since they were all here, he was sending Patrick and Dan and Nick out to view the resort, too. But so far all was clear. If any of them came right now... She shuddered at the idea. How would she explain Stanley? An old friend whom she'd just happened to run into? Nearly groaning at the thought, she whirled around on him again.

"Stanley, why are you *following* me?" she cried. "This has got to stop! Don't you—"

"But Gail," he said, "I love you."

"Oh, Stanley!" She wanted to pull her hair out. "Stanley, Stanley, what am I going to do with you? How can I convince you? I thought we had it all worked out!"

"Yes, but I've thought about it, and I just can't let you go, Gail. Please, I came so far. Won't you listen to me?"

She didn't have time to listen. With every passing second she was sure she was going to be caught, and after all that had happened, she didn't have the strength to explain. Feeling a prickling at the back of her neck, she pulled aside another palm frond and nearly fainted on the spot. Daniel Harris, Patrick Delaney and Nick Sierra had just entered the hotel. They were heading for the reception desk, but it wouldn't be long before they started in her direction, and then what was she going to do? She had to get rid of Stanley, that's all there was to it!

Spinning around, she clutched him by the arm. "Stanley, listen to me," she said urgently. "You have to get out of here, do you understand? You have to get out!"

"But, Gail—"

There was no time for niceties. She'd completely forgotten about the elevator but it finally came, and without ceremony, she pushed Stanley into it. She jabbed the first button she could reach before jumping out again.

"Gail!" Stanley cried, but he was already on his way. The elevator doors had just whooshed to a close when she heard someone else say her name, and she whirled around, trying not to gasp for breath. The three men from VDK were standing behind her, looking at her very strangely.

"Why, hello!" she trilled brightly. "Imagine meeting you here!"

Daniel Harris gave her a curious look. "Didn't Chris tell you we were coming out?"

Certain that any second the elevator was going to come down again and disgorge Stanley, who would cling to her like a limpet until she listened to what he had to say, she gave a nervous high-pitched laugh. "Oh, of course he did," she said. "I must be more tired than I thought. Will you excuse me? I have to go to my room now."

Patrick was looking at her as though she'd lost her mind. "Don't you think you should wait for the elevator?"

She looked at the thing as though she'd never seen it, and laughed again. "Oh, I try to take the stairs whenever I can. It's good exercise, don't you think?"

"But I thought you said you were tired," Nick said.

"I did, didn't I? It must be the altitude. You will excuse me, won't you, gentlemen?"

Without waiting to see what they thought of that ridiculous remark, she turned and headed toward the sign that pointed her to the stairs. Resisting the urge to take them two at a time so that she could quickly escape from sight, she dared a swift glance over her shoulder before she rounded the bend. It was worse than she thought. When she saw all three men staring after her in consternation, she wanted to run back down the stairs again and babble an explanation. She couldn't blame them for wondering if she was all there; she'd made a fool of herself just now, and she still had to deal with Stanley.

Stanley! She'd forgotten all about him! Groaning, she waited until Dan and Pat and Nick disappeared into one elevator while a confused-looking Stanley stumbled off the other. Her expression grim, she collared him and pulled him outside where she told him, as kindly and gently—and as adamantly—as she could, that he had to stop following her. Then she sent him on his dejected way, and dragged herself upstairs to take that bath.

LATE THAT NIGHT, with Chris still safely at VDK, the caller telephoned again from his luxurious hotel room. As he expected, Sutton answered on the second ring.

The caller wasted no time. "We're in Phoenix," he informed Wade Sutton.

"Good," Sutton said approvingly. "Any progress?"

"Chris should have things rolling by tomorrow. But I've made certain it will be too late to pick up that contract. He'll lose a couple mill on this deal."

"It's not enough."

The caller hated to be criticized. "It's only one step!"

Sutton was unperturbed. "I don't want anything to go wrong."

"Nothing will," the caller assured him. "I made certain of that." He hesitated. "There is one thing."

Sutton's voice sharpened. "What?"

"Remember I told you about that woman from Kalliste International—Gail Sullivan?"

"Yes, what about her?"

"She's here, too."

"So?"

"I don't know. I can't put my finger on it. But she's acting really strange. I think we should check her out."

Sutton thought about it. Then he said, "I agree. I don't want anything to go wrong at this stage. I'll put some people on it right away."

"Good," the caller said. "I'm sure there's more here than meets the eye."

Sutton grunted. "If that's so, I'll find out."

"I thought you would."

"Bet on it," Sutton said, and hung up.

CHAPTER TEN

IT WAS TWILIGHT by the time Chris left the Phoenix office. It hadn't taken him as long as he'd anticipated to work things out, but that was small comfort. He knew his solution was only a stopgap until he found out who was betraying him, and why. Just thinking about it made him angry all over again, and his jaw was clenched as he went to the car he'd ordered left for him in the parking lot.

When he thought about the unproductive meeting he'd had with his three most trusted men this afternoon, he wanted to curse. He'd known, when they all protested innocence over this latest mix-up in shipments, that it was time to stop fooling around, waiting for the guilty one to make a mistake. But even so, the decision had been difficult. The spur had been the knowledge that if he didn't take matters into his own hands soon, nothing he did would make any difference. He hadn't been kidding this afternoon when he'd told them about the rumors he'd heard about VDK's growing unreliability, the contracts they'd had to break these past few months because of things like delayed shipments. In business, rumors had a way of solidifying into fact, and when that happened...

That was when he'd made up his mind. After sending them all away, he'd sat down, picked up the phone and called an old friend. He hadn't wanted to burden Matsu Yokomoto with his problems, but some things were necessary. He'd known Matsu for years; the Japanese banker had been a friend of his father's. Matsu was living in Hawaii now. He'd gone there to retire, but had quickly become bored, and at seventy-two had decided to open his own bank. He'd often told Chris to call if he needed anything, and as Chris grimly dialed the number he knew by memory, he thought that if there had ever been a time when he needed help, it was now.

"Yokomoto," Matsu answered when the phone had rung three times.

Chris didn't waste words. After the requisite pleasantries, he simply said, "Matsu, I'm sorry to ask you, but I need your help."

There was a chuckle. "I was wondering when you would call."

"You expected me to?"

"Let us merely say that I hoped you would. I have been following details about your illustrious company in the business news, and wondered if I might be of service."

"You certainly can," Chris said, feeling grim again. "But I have to say, what I'm about to ask is a little... unorthodox."

The old Japanese chuckled again. "Even better," he said. "Tell me what you have in mind."

Since his old friend was probably more enlightened about the situation than he was, Chris didn't insult him with a full explanation. Briefly recapping the problem, he ended with, "And so I've narrowed the leak down to three men: Patrick Delaney, Daniel Harris or my executive assistant, Nick Sierra."

"I am sorry to hear that," Matsu said, sounding as though he truly was. "I've known Mr. Delaney and Mr. Harris for many years. And of course, I remember you and Nick as boys."

"I know, Matsu. So you can see how difficult this is for me."

"Indeed, I can. You are certain—no, never mind. Of course you are. I know you to be a careful man. You would not be saying such things unless you were positive. So. How may I be of assistance?"

Chris took a deep breath. He knew Matsu would do what he asked, but he was also painfully aware that once he set his plan in motion, he wouldn't be able to stop it again. *Do I really want to do it?* he asked himself, and knew he had no choice.

"I have to know which of the three is selling me out, Matsu," he said. "And so I have devised a plan to smoke out the traitor. I've been negotiating to buy a resort chain, Kalliste International—"

"Yes, I have heard of it."

"I imagined you had. My plan is to tell each of my three suspects that I have not only decided to buy the chain, but have plans to expand it immediately—by building a luxurious new resort in Hawaii."

"And do you intend to do so?"

Chris hesitated. "Yes—eventually. But for the moment, I want them to think I intend this right away. In fact, I'm going to tell each of them—separately—that I've already put a bid in for the land. I'll tell Pat that the land is on Kauai, and Dan that I'm going to build in Maui, and...and Nick that the site is on the big island."

"And do you have these three pieces of land in mind?"

"No, that's where you come in, Matsu, if you'll help me. I'm going to give each of them the name of a company that's supposedly looking into this for me, and I'll make sure they know that I've already paid an enormous finder's fee because the land is at a premium. It has to look as though all this is already in effect, you see."

"I do, indeed," the banker said with another chuckle. "And I'm beginning to see where I can help."

Chris smiled for the first time. "I'd hoped you would."

"Well, I do have the resources to set up dummy corporations to smoke out our traitor," Matsu said contentedly. Chris noted the pronoun and sat back, relieved. "And I do have . . . friends throughout the islands who would be more than willing to help another old friend like VDK. You and your father have done much for us, Chris. We do not forget."

"Then you'll take care of it?"

"Give me a few days, and it will be done. Shall I call you in Tampa when all is ready?"

"Yes, that will—" Chris started to say, and then shook his head. "No, Matsu, I think it will be better if I get in touch with you." He glanced at the desk calendar. "I have to be back in Florida by Friday for our island celebration, but since everyone is coming, I'll need to know before then."

"Call me in two days, then, and I will tell you of my progress."

"Matsu, I don't know how to thank—"

"Then please do not," the Japanese broke in. "If I can do this for you, it will be my pleasure."

Chris hesitated. "Two days, then."

"Two days," Matsu agreed, and broke the connection.

Now Chris was standing by the car in VDK's parking lot, keys in hand. Realizing he'd been daydreaming, he unlocked the door and climbed in. Without realizing it, he sighed. It was done. With that phone call to Matsu, he was committed, right or wrong. Now the only thing he could do was wait. Always the hardest part.

Then he thought of Gail, waiting for him at Kalliste Scottsdale, and knew the hard part was yet to come. He didn't want to, but he knew he had to tell her tonight that the trip had been cut short, after all. With Matsu working in Hawaii, he should be back in Florida, preparing things there. Sighing again, he reached forward to start the car. But once more his hand stopped short of the ignition, and he sat back thoughtfully.

Why not continue with the Kalliste tour? Matsu had told him the plan would take a few days to set up, and he couldn't do anything until then. After he'd asked Gail to come all this way, was it really fair of him to turn around now? As he'd told Matsu, he really did intend to buy the resorts; he should see what he was buying before he committed himself. His expression tightened. After all, it might be his last official act as owner of VDK. If his plan didn't succeed, and he failed to smoke out the traitor, he might as well kiss the company goodbye.

But there was another aspect to the situation that he hadn't considered until now. He'd set everything in motion; wouldn't it be better to continue as though he suspected nothing? That way, he wouldn't alert whoever was responsible until—hopefully—it was too late.

Trying not to believe he was rationalizing, he finally started the car and drove out of the lot. He thought he'd feel better once he'd finally set out on a course of action, but as he left the office behind and headed toward Scottsdale, his burden seemed to get heavier. Even the balmy twilight failed to soothe him. He'd planned on phoning Gail once he got in, but he wondered if that was such a good idea. The way he felt tonight, he wouldn't be good company at all.

It was almost dark by the time he arrived at Kalliste Scottsdale, that soft time in the desert when everything seems tinted pink before it abruptly dissolves to inky black. He drove past the ornate wrought-iron gates guarding the resort, thinking that the place looked like an oasis springing up out of the sand. The three-story adobe complex glowed under the floodlights, a rambling stucco structure with arches and tiles and native plants all around. Huge palm trees nodded over a fountain in front, and the driveway curved around under a portico where white-uniformed valets waited. Chris left the car with one of them, glancing around as he entered the huge foyer of the hotel.

The decor was definitely native; the floor was adobe tile, polished to a high degree, so that it gleamed under the recessed lights in the high arched ceiling, and the walls were painted a cool-looking white. Examples of Indian weaving—rugs and serapes and such—were scattered around, as were cacti in big clay pots. One magnificent plant had a printed legend attached to it, identifying it as a rare organ-pipe cactus, similar to the saguaro but with a cluster of many arms. It was nearly twenty feet tall, and was displayed in a place of honor by the door. Furniture groupings were tastefully arranged in the big reception room, low tables fronting rattan furniture covered with colorful fabric. As weary as he was, Chris noted all these details and approved.

An ironwood reception counter ran the length of one wall opposite the door, and Chris headed toward that. Atop the counter was a display of native wildflowers: desert lilies, Arizona poppies, lupine and marigolds, arranged in a beautiful round clay vase. An attractive woman stepped out from behind it and smiled with recognition, even though he'd never seen her before. She had obviously been primed to look for him, for she said immediately, "Good evening, Mr. Van Der Kellen. We've been expecting you."

It seemed that Gail was expecting him, too. After handing the key to his suite to the hovering bellboy, who went to fetch his luggage, the woman gave Chris a message. It was from Gail, who wanted to welcome him officially to Kalliste Scottsdale. The note said she'd wait up until he came in.

Chris thanked the woman, not sure how he felt about Gail's invitation as he followed the eager bellhop to his room. It turned out to connect to the suite Gail had taken, and after the man had gone, Chris glanced toward the door. It was closed, and he debated about leaving it that way. He was tired, preoccupied with his problem at VDK, and he knew he wouldn't be good company.

But then he thought of Gail, with her sympathetic eyes and that beautiful smile, and he wondered if he really wanted to be by himself tonight. Thinking how much he longed to confide everything to her, he went to the door. After a moment, he raised his hand and knocked.

GAIL TURNED when she heard the knock on the connecting door. She was on the balcony of her suite, having come out to watch the sunset, so deep in thought that she hadn't realized until now that twilight had long since come and gone. The sky was an inky black velvet peculiar to the desert night, and in the pools of light cast by the floodlights under the roof, the cacti looked like spectral guardians. She had no idea how long she'd been standing outside, but that soft knock brought her back to the present, and she called, "Come in, Chris. It's not locked."

Despite herself, her heart went out to him when he entered the suite. He looked so tired and drawn that she nearly took his arm and led him gently to the couch. It was on the tip of her tongue to offer him a drink, to ask if she could massage his tight shoulders, rub his temples to smooth that worried frown away, but she wouldn't allow herself to do it. The urge to touch him, to put her arms around him and hold him close was so strong that she knew if she gave in to it, she'd be lost. Instead, she stayed where she was, on the balcony, trying to remember who she was, and why she was at Kalliste Scottsdale.

That wasn't hard to do, not tonight. When she thought of that awful episode with Stanley earlier in the day, she was mortified all over again. She had handled that so badly that she was sure Chris's executives suspected something, and Nick must surely have been alerted. He'd stared at her so strangely while she'd babbled on that the look on his face had made her even more eager to escape. Remembering the embarrassing encounter, she wanted to cringe.

She couldn't afford to have her cover blown, not now, she thought. She couldn't be certain, but she believed she was finally on to something. Ever since she'd had time to calm down, she'd been thinking about that snippet of conversation she'd overheard at the library door, and couldn't get it out of her mind.

After all this trouble to set it up... that unidentified voice had said.

What trouble? Set up what? She couldn't be sure. Had the caller been referring to the current crisis that had called Chris to Phoenix, or—she shivered—was it something more sinister? Had whatever it was happened already, or was something worse planned for the future?

She still didn't know. But she was positive of one thing: whoever had been on that phone had something to do with the problems at VDK. The only question was, who was it? Frustrated, she'd gone over fragments of the conversation a hundred times in her mind since then. She knew she knew that voice; she just couldn't place it. That thick door had prevented her from identifying any distinctive quality.

So what did that leave her with? Some vague assumptions, some unfounded suspicions. She had no proof of anything...yet.

And then there was Chris. Wishing she could say something to him, talk over the problem with him, ask his opinion, she turned as he came out onto the balcony.

"Hi," she said softly. "I wasn't sure you'd even get in tonight."

He gave her a tired smile. "Well, things didn't go quite as badly as I'd anticipated."

"I'm glad to hear that," she said, and then, because she was afraid she'd say something she shouldn't, she turned to look out at the night again. "It's a beautiful evening, isn't it?"

"Yes, it is," he said, lifting his head slightly to the night breeze. After a moment, he said, "What were you looking at?"

She blinked. She'd been staring at him more intently than she realized, feeling that powerful sense of being drawn to him again. It was an effort to stay where she was; she wanted to come up beside him and tuck herself into the curve of his arm. Trying to remember what he'd said, she continued to gaze blankly into the darkness.

"I...I was looking at all the different kinds of cactus," she said.

Smiling, he turned to look at her. Those wonderful eyes of his were still in shadow, so she couldn't quite see his expression, but she knew he was amused. "I suppose you have a story about cacti, too," he said.

She smiled. "As a matter of fact, I do," she said, sensing that he needed a little nonsense right now. "For instance, did you know that the saguaro can live for five years without rain? Or that it has a root system that can spread as much as fifty feet under the surface of the desert in all directions?"

He was amused; she could hear the laughter in his voice when he said solemnly, "No, I didn't know that."

"Well, now you do," she said. Without moving, he seemed suddenly nearer, and her breath caught. *Now isn't the time,* she told herself tensely, and unobtrusively moved back a step. "Would you like to know more?"

"Absolutely," he said. He didn't sound quite so tired now.

She hesitated a moment, unable to look away from him. Why was he looking at her like that? she asked herself. But she knew . . . she knew.

Hastily, she turned and pointed to a squat round cactus just beyond the balcony. "You see that? That's a barrel cactus. When the flutings contract, the whole plant bends southwest, making a . . . a sort of compass." She could feel him staring at her, but she wouldn't look at him. "That way if you're ever lost in the desert without a real compass, at least you know which way is . . ."

Her voice trailed away. She couldn't pretend nothing was wrong, and she said softly, "Chris?"

He was looking out at the little barrel cactus. "I'm sorry," he said. "I guess I'm feeling a little lost myself right now. I was just thinking how nice it would be for something so simple to point the way."

"But I thought you'd solved that problem that brought you here," she said.

"Oh, I did. It's . . . something else."

Again she hesitated. All her senses screamed at her to take him into her confidence. She knew that if they had the chance they could work out the problem together. But she couldn't do it. Remembering Roger, and Harlan Damion and . . . and her own career, she felt like a traitor, but she said, "Would you like to talk about it?"

When he hesitated, too, her heart gave a little leap. But after a moment, he shook his head. "No, it's something I have to deal with myself."

She didn't know whether to be relieved or not that he hadn't told her. Oh, why were things so difficult? If he *had* confided in her, she asked herself, could she really have gone back to New York with the information? Things weren't as simple and clear-cut now as they had been when she'd taken this assignment—not when she felt her loyalty torn two ways. So, when she wanted to say so much more, all she could allow herself to say was a soft, "I understand."

Chris looked out over the desert night again. "I wish I did," he muttered.

He looked so unhappy that she couldn't think of her job, her assignment, what she was supposed to do. This was the man she was falling in love with; she couldn't just pretend she didn't know anything was wrong. Tentatively, she put her hand on his arm. "I wish there was something I could do," she said quietly.

He put his hand over hers and glanced down at her. Smiling slightly, he said, "You already have."

"Oh, no—"

"Yes, you have," he said quietly, pulling her into his arms. "You're here . . ."

She'd known the instant he joined her on the balcony that this would happen. Perhaps she'd known—or hoped—it would when she left the note saying she'd wait for him. Maybe, subconsciously, she'd been aware of the possibility when she agreed to accompany him on this tour. Whatever the reason, it didn't seem to matter now. Something at the back of her mind whispered that she'd be sorry, and she knew she would be, but at the moment she didn't care. The only thing that mattered was the blissful sensation of Chris's arms around her, and his heart pounding hard under her ear. As she raised her eyes to his, she thought fleetingly that the future would just have to take care of itself.

"Gail, I—" he started to say painfully.

She reached up and put a finger over his lips. "Don't say it," she whispered.

Holding her eyes, he took her hand and turned it palm up. His mouth seemed to burn when he kissed her palm, and then the pulse at the inside of her wrist began to pound. She'd never realized what a sensitive spot that was, and she caught her breath. Still holding her to him with one hand, Chris moved his mouth down to kiss the inside of her elbow, and then he put her arm around his neck and effortlessly lifted her off her feet.

"Chris—" she gasped, surprised. He put his mouth on hers, and stopped her protest with a kiss.

She didn't know how they got into the bedroom; she knew he carried her, but she was so lost in swirling sensation by that time that suddenly, they were just...there. Gently, Chris set her on her feet, placing both hands on her waist and drawing her lower body to his. Already she felt the swelling of his erection, and something primitive in her responded, making her press even more tightly against him. He made a low, strangled sound, and put his head back, and she felt a thrill race through her because she could do such things to him, who seemed to be able to evoke all sensations in her.

"Chris, don't you think we should—" she started to say, and then stopped when he put a hand at the back of her neck and gently made her look at him. He moved both hands to frame her face, gazed deep into her eyes and then, very slowly, lowered his head to kiss her again.

This touch of his lips on hers opened the floodgates of passion that she'd been trying to hold back. Without realizing it, only thinking that she wanted more of him, all he had to give, she wrapped her arms around his neck and returned his kiss with a passion that rocked them both. They clung together, swaying, until finally they had to break the contact or be swept away totally.

Gasping, Chris raised his head. He looked as dazed as she felt, his eyes almost black in the dark room, his handsome face etched in shadow and light from the recessed floodlights out on the balcony. "I want you," he said hoarsely. "But—"

She wouldn't allow him to say it. Right or wrong, sorry or not, she had committed herself. "Shh," she whispered, and reached for the buttons on his shirt. Forcing herself to move from one to the other when she wanted to rip the material away, she slowly unbuttoned the garment and spread it apart. His chest was warm and smooth and muscled under her hands, and she put her cheek next to him for a moment, luxuriating in the touch and scent and feel of him. Then she pulled his shirt off and let it drop to the floor.

"No regrets," she whispered again, looking up into his handsome face. "Because I want you, too...."

With a groan, he reached for her. She had changed to a silk blouse and linen slacks, but when he put a hand on her breast, the thin material felt like armor, and she wanted to fling the blouse off so that she could feel his hands on her skin. She reached for the buttons, but he anticipated her, gently pushing away her hand.

"No," he said hoarsely. "Let me...."

As slowly as she had undressed him, he disrobed her. With the release of each button on her blouse, she felt desire mount until she was trembling with the urge to throw herself at him and beg him to make love to her. But every time she lost control and reached for him, he held her gently away, until finally, he had unbuttoned the last button, pulled down the last zipper, unclasped the last hook, and she was standing naked before him.

The look on his face made the excruciating wait worthwhile. Never had a man looked at her like that, and when he finally raised his eyes to her face and murmured, "You...you're so beautiful...." she merely lifted her arms and took him to her. They stood like that for a moment, wrapped tightly together, then with one accord, they moved to the big circular bed.

Chris picked her up again and laid her gently on top of it. He was about to unbuckle his belt when she raised herself on her knees and pushed his hand away. She did it for him, slowly pulling his slacks and shorts down over his lean hips, wrapping her arms around his flat belly, cupping his taut buttocks in her hands, resting her head against him. She could feel him trembling, and she felt out of control herself when she sat back and gestured for him to join her.

The instant he lay beside her on the bed and reached for her, it was as though a storm rose. She wanted to step back, slow down and take her time, but her body seemed not her own. His touch raised an inferno inside her, and she began to touch him, too, hungrily running her hot fingers over his hard, muscled body, exulting in the rising desire she was arousing in him. By the time he entered her, there wasn't time for slow, languorous kisses or gentle caresses; desire had become a throbbing, pulsing living thing, demanding release.

"Oh, Chris," she murmured, her breath hot against his ear. "I can't wait...."

He couldn't seem to delay, either. Hunger was their master, and every ounce of feeling was wrung from them as they clutched at each other, straining for more. His mouth was on her breasts, his tongue on her nipples, his hand moving lower to caress her. She responded by moving in to him, wrapping her legs tightly around him to unite them to the fullest measure.

Without realizing it, they were caught up in that timeless rhythm, and as that pinpoint of pleasure began to spread through Gail and become a mindless scream, she renewed her efforts to bring him with her, until finally, at the same glorious moment, they reached the zenith together and truly became one.

"Oh, Chris!" she cried. And then, with his strong arms trembling around her, she held his head and rocked under him, and they both laughed in utter abandon.

A long time later, he rolled away and put his arm around her waist, drawing her close and snuggling against her. She felt him kiss her lightly on the shoulder and she smiled. "I thought you were asleep," she said.

"I was," he murmured, cupping her breast. "But I thought I was getting too heavy."

She smiled again. "I would have pushed you off."

"Deadweight that I was? What did you do to me, woman? I feel as though I've been through a wringer and come out flat on the other side."

She laughed. "How romantic."

He snuggled closer to her shoulder. "Can't help it," he muttered sleepily. "It's how I feel."

"I don't know how I feel," she said, sighing. "That was wonderful."

He raised his head. "We could do it again."

Her eyes twinkled at him. "So soon?"

He smiled. "That's what you do to me. You want proof?"

She had no time to protest, even if she'd wanted to. Laughing as he reached for her again, she lifted her lips to his. But instead of kissing her, he started whispering of the sensations she caused in him and the ways he wanted her. His hands and mouth began to roam over her tingling body, gently at first, and then with increasing passion as she responded with caresses of her own. Deliberately prolonging the anticipation, he spoke of how soft her breasts were—and kissed them. And how smooth her skin felt under his mouth—and ran his tongue down her torso. He caressed her until she was trembling, but even then he delayed, kissing her eyelids and murmuring how expressive her eyes were; kissing her nose, her cheek, her chin, her neck, whispering how beautiful she was. He said things she had never heard from a man before, and with every word, with every kiss and touch, they both started to quiver until finally neither knew what had ignited such passion, the murmured words or the responses of their own shuddering bodies.

She hadn't thought it could be better the second time, but it was . . . it was. With those murmured whispers, expert touches and adept caresses, Chris took her to heights she'd never dreamed about before, and she cried out first in heedless abandon. He was with her a second later, his own hoarse cry torn from his throat as he buried himself in her, and she laughed as he surrendered, too.

When Gail forced her eyes open, Chris was lying beside her, one arm flung across his face. As though he sensed her looking at him, he muttered, "What happened?"

She laughed, nestling close to him. "You tell me. You're the one who said you had something to prove."

He opened one eye. "And did I?"

"You have to ask?" she said with a sigh, and fell into an exhausted, satiated sleep, a smile on her face.

CHRIS WOKE GAIL the next morning with breakfast rolls and champagne and a cup of the most delicious coffee she'd ever tasted. It wasn't until she sat up sleepily and took her first bite of a flaky cinnamon roll that she realized neither of them had had dinner. She smiled at him, brushing away crumbs.

"I'm starving!" she said.

"I can see that," he said, glancing at the quickly depleted plate. "Would you like another before we leave?"

"Leave?"

He grinned. "As fond as memories of Scottsdale are going to be for me in the future, Darby called this morning to say there's some bad weather between here and California. If we want to miss it, we have to leave for Kalliste Caballero right now—or wait until the storm passes."

She grinned wickedly back. "And how long will that be?"

"Don't look at me like that," he warned her. "If you tempt me, I could keep you here forever."

"That might not be such a bad idea," she said, snuggling back into the pillows.

"I agree. But unfortunately, neither of us have that luxury, so . . . into the shower. We leave in half an hour."

"Half an—" she started to say, and then gave a shriek as he jerked back the covers.

His eyes gleamed at the sight of her naked body, and he licked his lips. "Go," he said. "Before I change my mind."

Delighted at the look on his face, she deliberately struck a seductive pose. "That might not be such a bad idea, either," she said. "You sure we don't have even five minutes . . ."

Groaning, he joined her in bed. He had no choice; the evidence of how much he wanted to prolong this interval was peeking out from beneath the towel he had thrown around his waist, and as she stripped away the terry cloth and revealed him in all his glory, she laughed.

"Aren't you glad I talked you into this?" she said with a wink. "It might have been a little difficult for you to travel like that."

Laughing himself, he reached for her. "We don't have to worry about that now, do we?" he said, and kissed her so thoroughly she was the one who gasped.

An hour later, they were on their way to California. The plane was over Santa Barbara before Gail remembered she hadn't checked in with Roger. Guiltily, she glanced at Chris, who was absorbed in some work he'd brought along. *Oh, what you do to me,* she thought, and decided she'd just have to call New York when they got in.

As though he felt her looking at him, Chris glanced up. "What are you thinking?"

She couldn't possibly tell him how guilty she felt for holding back so much. After what had happened between them, she longed to tell him the truth, but she couldn't—not yet, anyway. Wondering if the time would come soon, she leaned over and kissed him. "I was just thinking that you're about the handsomest man I've ever met.''

He raised an eyebrow. "About?"

Her treacherous heart lurched. He really was so much more than that. Should she tell him? How could she? How could she not? Oh, she didn't know what to do; she felt as though she were increasingly being torn in two ways, her loyalty to both sides being severely tested. Wondering how Solomon would have decided this one, she forced a laugh. "I'm not going to tell you," she said. "It'll only go to your head."

He grinned. "Then be prepared when we get to California," he said.

"I can hardly wait," she replied with a laugh, and tried not to think what she was going to say to Roger.

CHAPTER ELEVEN

LIKE DAMION'S OTHER RESORTS built around a theme—
Kalliste Bahama for water sports, Kalliste Scottsdale for
tennis and golf... *and other things,* Gail thought with a
smile—Kalliste Caballero in Southern California was a
year-round cattle and dude ranch built in the Santa Ynez
Mountains. After flying into Santa Barbara, where once
again they left Darby and Jack to their own devices, Gail
and Chris rented a car to go out to the ranch. It was about
an hour's drive along winding back roads, gentle rolling
hills and trees just starting to turn color with the end of
October.

They were both quiet on the way, Chris occupied with
thoughts of his own, Gail mentally sorting through the
information she was supposed to know about this particular resort. Chastising herself for being so distracted
with Chris that she'd forgotten to go over the file, she
supposed she should be thankful that she'd read it once
in the first place. Since she couldn't very well haul it out
right now, she finally decided that she'd just have to trust
her memory. It had proved reliable so far, and unless
things had changed drastically, she was sure she remembered the names of the California staff, and the general
layout of the place.

But she still felt tense when they finally passed under
a high wooden arch naming the ranch, and she was too
nervous to appreciate Chris's compliment on the logo: a

cowboy riding a bucking horse, his boots thrust far into the stirrups, one arm flung over his head and the other firm on the reins of the determined bronc with all four feet in the air, its mane flying and its head down.

"I forgot to ask," he said. "You do ride, don't you?"

"Ride?" she repeated weakly, and was thankful she didn't have to explain her fainthearted response. Just then they drove around a curve in the road and there was Kalliste Caballero.

As Gail remembered having read, the resort was composed of a series of buildings spread out over several acres, all linked by winding paths. The reception/lounge/office area was located in the center, in a two-story, white-painted edifice made to look like a farmhouse. It was flanked by cottages also painted white, each on its own little separate patch of lawn, with private stone terraces for sitting out. A creek wound through the property; she recalled that in warm weather guests could enjoy swimming in a natural pool created long ago by beavers in the area, who had built a dam above the ranch. The beavers had long since moved to less-populated areas, but the dam was maintained by resort employees, and in summer, barbecues were planned around water activities. Through the foliage, Gail could see the gazebo where dances took place, and in another location, huge barbecue pits. Hastily, she averted her glance to the big oak trees scattered around, some of whose branches were festooned with green moss that she thought she remembered reading someplace was harmful to the trees. A big old barn far to the right had been left in its own natural weathered state. Corrals stood beside and around it. The whole scene looked so pastoral that she expected any minute to hear the ring of the blacksmith's hammer. Trying not to remember that the last time she'd ridden a horse was when she was a young girl, she hastily suggested that they check in.

"You go ahead," Chris said. "I want to check out the barn."

She was too relieved to argue; ever since she'd thought of Roger, waiting for her to report in, she'd been on pins and needles, wondering how to get to a phone without arousing Chris's suspicion.

"Fine," she said hurriedly. "Why don't I get settled, and meet you there?"

Agreeable to that, he waited until two young men dressed as ranch hands—in boots, scarves, jeans and belts with big silver buckles—rushed out to help with the luggage. Then he sauntered off down the path to the barn with his hands in his pockets. Gail couldn't help it; for just a second she paused to watch him, her heart seeming to beat a little faster, as it did whenever she looked at Chris. Even dressed in slacks and a sport shirt, he looked as though he belonged in this setting, and she longed to forget all the intrigue and run after him, linking her arm with his as they wandered down the path to the barn, her head on his shoulder. With a sigh, she went inside.

Fifteen minutes later, installed in one of the connecting cottages, Gail threw her purse and sweater down on the bed and reached for the phone. She and Chris had been assigned adjoining cottages—the best on the place, of course—but she hardly glanced at the luxurious features: genuine Navaho rug on the floor, a fireplace she could have roasted an entire side of beef in, genuine oil paintings depicting scenes of the Old West and a huge carved oak bedstead. A quilt she realized was handmade was on the bed; absently she traced the thousands of tiny, perfect stitches in a shell pattern as she waited for her call to go through. Glancing at her watch, she realized guil-

tily that it was after six in New York; would Roger still be
at the office? She had his home number, of course, but
she was reluctant to call him there. After the fifth ring,
she was just deciding she might have to, when he picked
up his private line.

"Brenner."

"Roger, thank goodness I caught you!" she said.
"What took you so long to answer?"

He recognized her voice right away. "I was down at the
copy room, but never mind that. Where the hell are you?
Is everything all right?"

"Everything is fine," she said, although it wasn't.
"Chris and I are in California—"

"California! I thought you were supposed to be in
Scottsdale!"

"I know, I know. But we...we got finished early in
Arizona, and he wanted to come here."

He didn't sound too happy when he reminded her,
"You were supposed to call me before you decided on the
next stop."

"I know," she said again, wincing. "But...but there
wasn't time—"

"What do you mean, there wasn't time?" he demanded. "What the hell have you been doing? Why
couldn't you get to a phone?"

"It's...sort of complicated, Roger," she said.
"But—"

"You're not getting involved with this guy, are you?"

The question caught her by surprise; denial sprang instantly to her lips, even as she felt her cheeks redden with
guilt. "Of course not! How can you ask me such a
thing?"

To her relief, he let it go. "You're right," he said after a moment. "I'm sorry. I guess I've just been a little worried about you. When you didn't call in . . ."

His voice trailed away, and she felt guiltier than ever. "I'm the one who's sorry," she said, thinking he didn't know just how true that was. She took a deep breath. "Look, why don't we just start over? Chris is exploring, but he'll be back any minute, so we might not have much time."

"Yes, you're right," he said. "But I won't keep you. I've been thinking about what you said about our strategy not working, and I think you're right. I want you to find a way to cut short the tour and come in. We'll re-evaluate the plan then."

She couldn't have been more dismayed. "What! No, no, it's not the right time!"

"But you said—"

"I know what I said, but things have changed. I'm on to something—I'm sure of it!"

"You are? What?" His voice sharpened. "Why didn't you tell me?"

Now she'd done it. Trying to think fast, she said, "Well, it . . . it just happened. I overheard something when we were in Phoenix, Roger. A very strange phone conversation—"

"What, with Chris?"

"No, it wasn't Chris," she said positively. She didn't know who had been on the phone in that library, but there was one thing she *was* sure of, and that was that it wasn't Chris. "There's something going on, all right," she went on. "But I don't know what yet, or who's behind it."

"Well, swell," Roger said sarcastically. "Do you think you could be a little more explicit?"

She reddened. "I'd like to be," she said, her voice a little tight. "But there hasn't been all that much time for me to find out anything, all right? I just heard the conversation yesterday—" Was it really only yesterday? Phoenix already seemed like another lifetime away. "That's why I came to California. I thought that the longer we're together, the more chance there would be—" *forgive me, Chris,* she thought "—of his letting something slip."

Roger was silent, digesting that. She waited tensely, her glance going nervously to the door. Where was Chris? Was he on the other side, listening? She shut her eyes tightly. No, no, she wouldn't think that or she'd be paralyzed completely. Her assignment was difficult enough already; if she thought that she'd made him suspicious...

"Roger?" she said.

He spoke thoughtfully. "Maybe you're right. We've come so far, I guess we should play out the hand."

"Great—"

"But there isn't much time," he warned her. "VDK was in the news again today about a big delayed shipment of lumber that caused no end of problems for a lot of people. Damion called me this morning, nervous as a cat. He's about ready to pull out of this deal."

"No, he can't!" she blurted. "I know Chris wants to buy the resorts."

"Oh, yeah, that's great. When he gets his problems straightened out, right? That might be too late for Damion."

"Why is he in such a rush anyway?" she asked, suddenly annoyed with their impatient client. "He said from the beginning that he wasn't in a hurry to sell."

"That was before someone made him another, very generous offer."

She straightened. "Who?"

"He didn't tell me."

"And you didn't ask?" she demanded hotly. "Has it occurred to you that Chris's problems at VDK might be happening because whoever else is interested in the resorts wants to pull the rug out from under him?"

Roger was sarcastic again. "Well, it might have, if those problems hadn't started *before* Van Der Kellen expressed an interest in Kalliste."

"Oh," Gail said, deflated. Then she sat up straight again. "Well, maybe Damion is just trying to pull our chain a little—have you thought about that? He's already discussed this sale with Chris. It would be unethical for Damion to sell the resorts from under Chris without even giving him a chance to counterbid."

"Not if VDK is as shaky as it's starting to look," Roger reminded her. "That's why you're there, remember? To find out what's going on."

"I haven't forgotten," she snapped back. "But now that you've so kindly reminded me, maybe we had better hang up so I can do my job. In the meantime, you might help, if you're so inclined."

"You can cut the sarcasm, Gail," he said. "We're both on the same side, remember? Maybe you're a little more involved with the subject than you'd like to admit."

"I told you, that's absurd!" she said. But even she could hear how guilty she sounded, and before he could say something more, she went on. "Listen, I know we've got files on Patrick Delaney and Daniel Harris and everybody else, but I want you to dig deeper for me, okay? I need more if I'm going to put this together."

"All right. What else?"

"Find out who else wants to buy Damion's resorts. That might be a help."

"Okay, okay," Roger said. "In the meantime, when do you plan to check in again?"

"Before we leave here, which should be within the next couple of days." She hesitated, not wanting to admit just how much she wanted to finish their tour. *One more resort,* she thought. *That's all....* How was she ever going to leave after that? Shakily, trying not to think of it, she said, "Chris is a little unpredictable, so I sort of have to play this by ear."

"Well, cheer up," Roger said. "You've only got one more resort after this. I know it's been hard, but I can tell you're doing a splendid job."

"Thanks," she said, reddening. *If he only knew,* she thought, feeling even worse. "But I had good training—remember? And all that preparation."

"I'm glad the extra files I sent down were a help."

"Oh, they were—" she started to say, and then was struck by a sudden thought. "Roger, do you still have that new secretary?"

"Yeah—unfortunately. That girl is about to drive me nuts. I can't wait for Jean to get back. Why?"

"Because—"

But just then she realized that she wasn't alone. Whirling around, she saw Chris lounging against the open door between their two cottages, his hands in his pockets, his feet crossed at the ankles. She nearly dropped the phone. How much had he heard?

"Didn't mean to interrupt," Chris said. "I'll wait in here."

"Oh...that's all right," she said, trying frantically to pull herself together. If he was smiling, she thought, he couldn't have overheard too much. Could he have? Realizing Roger was still hanging on the other end, she turned around and hunched over the receiver.

"Thanks, Suzanne," she said, as though she were talking to a friend. "I really appreciate your taking such good care of the plants."

"He just came in, right?" Roger said in her ear. "Okay, call me before you leave California."

"Oh, yes, California is just wonderful—what I've seen of it, that is," she said, and then realized she was supposed to have been here before. Hastily, she added, for Chris's benefit, "You know how much I love this area. And the resort is still as restful as it always was. I'll tell you all about it when I get home. 'Bye now."

With relief, she hung up the phone. She sat there a moment, her eyes closed, trying to pull herself together. What would she do if Chris looked suspicious?

But Chris was sitting on the leather couch in the next room, leafing through a magazine about the Old West when she forced herself to go to him. When he looked up, curious, she tried to shrug casually. "Sorry. I had to call my friend Suzanne. She lives down the hall from me and is taking care of my apartment while I'm gone."

"No problem," Chris said. "I was being entertained down at the barn."

"Oh . . . I'm glad." She was still distracted, breathless from her close call.

"Yes," Chris said, his eyes beginning to gleam with that look she was starting to know so well. Tossing aside the magazine, he got to his feet. "What do you say to a ride before supper?"

"A ride?" she repeated, dismayed. She shook her head. "Oh, I don't think so, Chris. I haven't been on a horse since I was a child."

"Then it's time you got reacquainted," he said. "I've had the wrangler saddle up two broncs. We're hitting the trail."

"But—"

He wouldn't listen to any more objections, even when she tried to tell him she had "forgotten" to bring her boots. "Wear leather shoes, then. Or—" he grinned "—we can borrow some from the boys at the bunkhouse. Maybe one of them has a girl your size."

"No, no, that's all right," she said, wondering how to get out of this. If she went along, she just knew she was going to kill herself. "Chris—"

"Come on, where's your spirit?" he demanded.

It was that look in his eyes that decided her. She never had been able to resist a challenge, and she lifted her chin. "Give me five minutes."

It was closer to fifteen when she emerged from the cottage wearing jeans and a denim jacket and the hiking shoes she'd brought for the desert and hadn't had a chance to wear. Chris was waiting, looking out over the green hills that were shimmering from the recent rain. His expression was somber until he realized she was standing there watching him, then his face cleared and he smiled.

"Ready?"

Now that she was actually faced with the prospect, she tried again. "Chris, I'm not sure riding is a good idea—"

"Nonsense," he said briskly. "You said you'd ridden before."

"But that was when I was younger...*much* younger."

"Well, it's just like—"

"If you're going to tell me that riding horses is like riding a bike, save your breath. It's not like that at all, and we both know it."

"Yes, it is—you'll see," he said. Then, laughing at her expression, he took her hand and led her down the path to the stables, ignoring her rising protests all the way.

As leery as she was of this excursion, she was still impressed by the barn itself, which looked as though it had been built a hundred years ago and hadn't changed since. The wooden siding had weathered so much that it glowed silver, and inside even the floor was wood, worn smooth by countless hooves and cowboy boots. The air was scented with the smell of horses and hay, and all down the length of the structure were stalls on each side, big squares with sides built up to eye level, surmounted by iron bars. The tack room was filled with all kinds of equipment, everything shining with care even though much of it was worn and well-used.

"It looks like nothing has changed since the turn of the century," she commented.

Chris gave her a strange look. "You make it sound as though you've never seen it before."

Belatedly she remembered that she was supposed to be acquainted with the place. Trying to recover, she said, "Well, I have to admit that the stables have never been my favorite part of the resort."

Chris was about to say something when they both heard the ring of spurs on the wooden floor, and when they turned, Gail saw a man coming toward them who could have been an advertisement for the Old West magazine Chris had been looking through earlier. Bowlegged, wearing the chaps she was to learn later were called "shotguns," he looked as if he'd been born in the saddle—and was still sitting in it. He was wizened and whipcord lean, and the silver belt buckle he was wearing looked bigger than he was.

Quickly she searched her memory. Oh, yes, this was Elmo Clay, the head wrangler. Praying that he'd been briefed about who she was supposed to be, she smiled. "Hello, Mr. Clay," she said. "It's nice to see you again."

The man didn't miss a beat. Touching the tip of his weather-beaten hat, he nodded deferentially. "And you, Ms Sullivan."

Gail turned to Chris. "Chris, I'd like you to meet—"

"Oh, we've already met," Chris said, grinning at the man. "Elmo and I had a long talk earlier. It seems that you don't show up around the barn very often."

Wondering just what the wrangler had said, she tried to laugh. "Well, I told you I don't visit the stables when I'm here. Usually, there's so much to do. I have time to fly in and out, not to enjoy myself."

"Well, that's about to change. Elmo has just the horse for you."

"He does?" she said, turning her back on Chris so that she could frantically signal the wrangler to make some excuse.

The cowboy merely grinned in return. "Don't worry, Ms Sullivan," he drawled. "Ol' Hornet will do you just fine."

"Ol' Hornet?" she repeated, drawing back. She didn't like the sound of that at all.

The wrangler gave her what she supposed he thought was a reassuring smile. "You'll see. You'll like him. Come on. I got 'em all saddled out back."

Wondering if she could fake a sudden attack of something, Gail reluctantly followed the two men out of the barn. As they walked down the aisle, Elmo pointing out a stallion in one stall, a mare in another, she was distracted from her predicament long enough to admire the way Chris looked in jeans. With his trim hips and long legs, he looked as though he'd been born to this kind of life; dressed as he was now, he would never have been taken for the head of a Fortune 500 company.

Feeling her heart start to beat a little faster just looking at him, she hurried to catch up, and then saw the three horses tied at the rail outside, obviously waiting for them. One was brown and looked half asleep; another was a big black mare, looking just as placid and bored. But the third—a loud-colored pinto that had a distinct gleam in its eye—turned and looked right at her, and she knew, with a sinking feeling, that this was Ol' Hornet.

"Don't tell me," she said, pointing at the pinto. "That's the one I'm going to ride."

Elmo slapped the horse's flank affectionately. "That's right. This here's Ol' Hornet. A better mount can't be found or bought. He'll take you up or around or over or under anything that gets in the way. He's a dream with cows, the best horse on the place."

She looked at him nervously. "Maybe I should take that brown one," she suggested, pointing to the sleepy one that looked so much more harmless.

"Oh, you don't want Delilah, Miss," Elmo said. "She's a young-un, just bein' broke. I'm going to ride her, give her a little experience on the trail."

"Then how about the black one?" she asked. The more she looked, the less she wanted to get up on Ol' Hornet. She was sure he'd guessed her extreme amateur status and was already planning his strategy. She could just picture them getting out on the trail before he turned and hightailed it for home—with or without her, of course.

"I'm going to ride that one," Chris said. "Elmo tells me she used to be a polo horse, so I should be right at home."

Gail looked back at Ol' Hornet. "Then I guess that leaves me with..."

When her voice trailed dejectedly away, Chris grinned and took her elbow. "Come on, up you go. I'll give you a leg up, if you want."

He had to give her more than a boost. Even though the horse stood quietly—luring her into complacency, she was sure—she had trouble lifting her foot high enough to reach the stirrup. When she finally did plop ungracefully into the saddle and Chris handed her the reins, she looked down and blanched. She felt as though she were ten stories up.

As though he'd read her mind, Chris smiled again as he swung easily into his own saddle. "If you get dizzy, just reach for the saddle horn," he suggested.

For some reason, that got her back up. "Thank you," she said loftily. "But I'm sure I won't need it."

"I'm sure you won't either," he said, and then was preoccupied for a moment with quieting the big black mare, which rolled her eyes and took a sidestep or two, swinging into Gail's mount. Ol' Hornet immediately laid back his ears.

"Chris!" she cried.

"Sorry," he said, his eyes twinkling. "Elmo didn't tell me this mare was a little goosy."

"Figured you could handle her, Mr. Van Der Kellen," the wrangler said from her other side. Elmo's nondescript sleepy-looking horse had burst into life the instant his foot had touched the stirrup. But even though the chestnut mare was humping her back and jumping around, pinning her ears back and trying to get her head down so that she could buck him off, Elmo sat serenely in the saddle as though he were in a rocking chair by the fire. "Let me just get the buck out of this little lady," he said, "and we'll hit the trail."

Chris's horse had decided to try a few spins along with the sidesteps. "Take your time," he said, obviously enjoying his mount's high spirits. "I've got to get this one calmed down."

Gail looked from one to the other, then down at Ol' Hornet, who was placidly standing there, waiting for his ill-mannered stablemates to settle down and get to business. Somewhat smugly, she released her death grip on the saddle horn and patted his neck. Elmo was right, she thought. She and this horse were going to get along just fine.

With the other horses under control, the riders started out a few minutes later on a trail that looked to Gail more like a deer track into the hills. To reach it, they had to cross a big pasture enclosed by a fence, and she was impressed with the way Elmo sidled his mare up to the gate, reached down and opened it, held it for them to go through and then closed it behind him—all without getting off the horse. He looked as if he'd been born to the saddle, and she was envious.

But then, she thought as she glanced at Chris, sitting on his own horse just as easily, Chris seemed just as comfortable. Under his direction, the big black mare had settled into a steady pace, and her beautiful head bobbed with each stride. As they came up beside Gail and the much smaller Hornet, he seemed to tower over her in the saddle, as he did on the ground.

Looking down at her, he smiled. "Now, aren't you enjoying yourself?" he asked.

Her own horse was moving smoothly and steadily, almost without any direction from her. When she realized that Hornet didn't intend to spin around and run back to the barn, throwing her off somewhere in the process, she had found herself relaxing. "Yes," she said, sounding surprised. "I am."

"I knew you would," Chris said, and reached out a hand. Hesitantly, hoping she could keep this fragile balance she had managed to attain, she reached out and put her hand in his. He squeezed her fingers, and then gave a sigh of contentment as he looked around.

"It's really beautiful out here, isn't it?"

Dragging her glance away from his handsome face, she looked around, too. "Yes, it—" she started to say, and then exclaimed, "Look!"

Three deer had come down into the meadow the riders were crossing—a buck and two does. Beautiful creatures with huge, liquid eyes, they raised their heads and looked at the riders and horses, then moved off, gathering speed as the humans came closer. With graceful bounds up the hill, they disappeared with a flick of white-bobbed tails.

Her eyes wide, Gail looked at Chris. "I've never seen anything like that before!" she said, awed.

Elmo, riding slightly ahead, heard her and turned slightly in the saddle. "Oh, we get a lot of deer, Ms Sullivan," he said, and grinned. "Coyotes, too. 'Cept they sound like wolves when they howl. Rings around all through these hills. Some people say that howl is the loneliest sound in the world."

Gail could believe that. Nervously her eyes scanned the horizon. "They don't come down this far, do they, Elmo?"

"Oh, sure. But we just run 'em off. That, or the dogs do." He paused. "'Course pumas are a little different. They're not such cowards."

"Pumas?" Gail repeated. Then she blanched. "You mean *mountain lions*?"

Seeing her horrified expression, Chris winked reassuringly. To the wrangler he said, "I bet you don't see too many of those anymore, do you?"

Elmo regretfully shook his head. "No, I'm afraid not. With all the huntin' that goes on, they're pretty rare. But we do get bobcats now and then."

"And cattle!" Gail exclaimed, startled to see a small group right in front of them as they came over the crest of a hill.

"Well, this is a working cattle ranch, miss, don't forget," Elmo said.

Gail hardly heard him; she was nervously eyeing a steer that had lifted what seemed to her to be a huge head on which sat vicious-looking horns. Although it just stood there, placidly chewing its cud, she wanted to give it a wide berth.

"Can we just move on?" she said anxiously. "I never did get along very well with cows."

"Aw, they won't bother us," Elmo said. "They're more afraid of you than you are of them."

"Don't bet on it," she muttered, trying to guide her horse up close to Elmo's for protection.

But Elmo was having a problem with his mount; it seemed his chestnut mare had decided she didn't like the sight of those cattle. Before Gail's eyes, the brown horse spun around, and while the wrangler tried to get her under control, the herd of cows started to shift nervously. One heifer bawled, causing Ol' Hornet's ears to prick up.

As inexperienced as she was, Gail felt the horse's muscles tense, and she looked fearfully at Chris.

"Just relax," Chris said, having to make an effort to control his own horse. The big black mare didn't like the cows any more than Gail—or her chestnut stablemate—did. "Relax, and it will be all right."

"Are you—"

She never had a chance to complete the sentence. Just then, one of the cows, sensing tension, decided to break away from the herd. It loped off a distance, causing the rest of the group to start milling around. To Gail's horror, Hornet started forward, right into the throng.

"Chris!" she cried. She didn't know what she had done to make Hornet move, but suddenly he was no longer her placid little mount. Before her horrified eyes, he'd turned into a cow horse, ears pricked forward, nostrils flared. Panicked, she looked around. "Chris, what do I do?"

"Don't do anything!" he called, fighting the big black horse, which was turning in circles. "Just sit there!"

The chestnut mare was bucking now, but in the midst of the melee, Elmo looked up and said, "Whatever you do, don't drop the reins!"

"What?" she cried. The anxious lowing of the cattle had drowned out what the wrangler said. She didn't have time to worry about it, for just then one of the heifers bumped against Hornet's flank. The horse spun around, and Gail nearly lost her balance. Dropping the reins, she reached for the saddle horn.

Chris and Elmo saw her at the same time. They both shouted, "Don't drop—"

It was too late. Elmo hadn't exaggerated when he'd said that Hornet was one of the best cow horses on the ranch. The instant the horse felt the rein drop to his neck, instinct and training took over, and because he was facing in the direction of the first cow that had broken from the herd, he lunged after it. Gail was so surprised that she was nearly thrown out of the saddle.

"Chris!" she shrieked, hanging on for dear life.

"Pick up the reins!" he shouted.

She looked down. All she could see was a flying mane as Hornet galloped helter-skelter after the frightened cow. "I can't find them!" she wailed, and realized it wouldn't have mattered if she could: she wouldn't have let go of that saddle horn if her life had depended on it. Hornet in motion was a whirlwind; like generations of cow horses before him, the little quarterhorse seemed to anticipate every move the cow made; if it leaped in one direction, Hornet was there ahead of it, and if it tried to go in another, the horse blocked the escape.

"Please stop, please stop," Gail begged. She didn't realize she was babbling until the stirrup she'd lost in the first lunge banged against her anklebone and she cried out in pain. Instinctively she leaned forward to grasp her ankle, and her fingers came into contact with the reins.

The reins! With a whoop of triumph and relief, she snatched them, crowing as she held them up, "I've got them! I've got them!"

At that instant, the horse stopped. *On a dime and gave you change,* Elmo said proudly later, *just like he's 'sposed to do.*

Gail didn't know anything about that; she was so unprepared for the sudden halt that she sailed right over Hornet's head, turning once in the air and landing, miraculously, on her feet. Dazed, she looked around. To her disbelief, she still had hold of the reins.

"Lordy, Lordy," Elmo groaned, racing up. Throwing himself off the horse, which had finally bucked herself out, he said, "Are you all right?"

Chris had launched himself out of his saddle, too, leaving the black mare to fend for herself. "My God!" he cried, reaching Gail at the same time as Elmo did. "Are you hurt?"

She wasn't sure. Blinking, she tried to take inventory, and realized Chris was anxiously patting her down, like police officers did a suspect they'd caught. Grabbing one of his hands, she laughed. "It's okay, Chris."

He looked stricken. "You could have been killed!"

"But I wasn't," she said, and turned. The steer she and Ol' Hornet had gone after had returned to the herd, and was once again chewing its cud. Looking smug, if a bit pale, she turned back to the men again. "You see? Everything's back to the way it should be. Any more cows you want me and my trusty horse to round up?"

SHE WASN'T SO SMUG by the time they rode back to the ranch. Aware of the anxious glances of her two escorts, she hid her discomfort as well as she could, and kept going only by concentrating on the thought of the hot bath waiting for her at the end of the trail. But she could feel blisters rising on blisters with each stride the once again placid Hornet took, and the inside of her knees felt scraped raw.

"Are you sure you're okay?" Chris kept asking, his face a mask of concern.

"Of course," she'd say brightly, determined to hang on grimly until they reached their destination. At last—at last!—they arrived back at the barn and she could gingerly slide her aching body out of the saddle. She would have landed in a little puddle at the feet of the horse if Chris hadn't caught her.

"I knew it," he said grimly. "You were lying in your teeth the whole time!"

"Only a little," she said, rubbing her hip. Seeing how anxious Elmo still looked, she tried to smile. "Thanks for the ride," she said.

"Any time, miss," he said, worrying the reins of the three horses, all of which couldn't have looked more plodding or docile now that the damage had been done.

"Sorry, Elmo," Chris said. "Would you mind putting my horse up?"

"Sure thing," the wrangler said, and grinned as Chris reached down and literally swept Gail up off her feet.

"You don't have to carry me, Chris!" she protested.

"Oh, yes, I do," he said. "This is all my fault."

"But it's all right."

"We'll see," he said grimly, and he was right. By the time he carried her back to the cottage and gingerly set her on the couch, she was so stiff she couldn't even bend to take off her shoes.

"Here, let me," Chris said, and helped her peel off her jeans as well. Looking horrified at the big red welts on the insides of her knees, he immediately ran her a bath and then rang the main desk for medicine.

"Chris, you don't have to do this," she protested, but weakly, as he gently finished undressing her and lowered her into the foaming tub. It felt so blissful that she gave in. Having a man take care of her was a new experience... and definitely one to be treasured.

Lulled by all this lavish attention, she was almost asleep in the water by the time Chris returned to dry her with a big fluffy towel. She held on to him as he helped her into a nightgown, then carried her to bed.

"Stay with me?" she whispered.

"Only for a while," he said. "You need your rest."

But he was still there in the morning when Gail awoke, leaning awkwardly against the headboard, his arm around her. When she saw how uncomfortable he looked, she knew he hadn't moved because he didn't want to disturb her. Her expression tender, she slipped out of his arms and pulled the covers over his shoulder. Then she crawled out of bed and limped to the bathroom. Looking at herself in the mirror, she smiled at her reflection. She was still in misery, but oh, it had been worth it.

CHAPTER TWELVE

CHRIS DELAYED setting up the conference call to his office in Florida until he was sure Gail was in the shower. He'd gone back to his own room to make the call, and while he waited for Dan and Patrick and Nick to come on the line, he glanced thoughtfully at the closed door between the suites. Remembering the night before, he smiled tenderly before he caught himself. Then he frowned and shifted position, turning away from the door.

He didn't like this; he didn't like it at all. Despite all his warnings to himself, he'd gotten far more involved with Gail than he'd wanted to—than he'd ever intended. Things between them had gone too far, too fast, and now he didn't know if he wanted to stop it.

His frown deepened. He didn't have any choice—he *had* to stop it. He didn't have time for any relationships; this problem at VDK had to take precedence over everything, including his personal life. *Especially* his personal life. Saving the company was paramount; whatever else there was had to wait. Wishing he'd remembered that before Phoenix, he told himself he was sorry about what had happened, but he knew that wasn't true. Remembering that night of glorious lovemaking, he closed his eyes for a moment.

No, he *was* sorry. As wonderful as that experience had been, continuing with the relationship wouldn't be fair to

Gail. He just didn't have the time to devote to her, or to give her the attention she deserved. But every time he decided he'd just come out and tell her that, she'd smile in that way she had, or tilt her head in that endearing manner, and he wouldn't be able to say it.

You've got to, he told himself grimly, and then realized that if he said their... relationship had been a mistake, she would probably think he'd gone so far only because he wanted to cement the Kalliste deal, but had gotten cold feet at the last minute.

That idea hadn't occurred to him previously, and he wanted to put his head in his hands and groan. Having her think he'd taken advantage of her would be a thousand times worse than the truth. Still, he'd have to tell her. Today. He wouldn't let the situation go any further. In fact, he'd cancel their last stop. He'd already decided to buy the resorts, so what would seeing one more prove?

He sighed. Right now, he simply couldn't face the thought of her going back to New York; he wanted just a few more days... just a few more. And then he'd tell her.

Tell her what? That now that he'd had his little fling, it was time to end it?

Just thinking about saying those words made him feel sick. He could never do that to her. But what else could he do? Tell her the truth?

That was a novel thought, he mused, and pondered it for a moment. Yes, it might work—if he wrapped up the situation at VDK as soon as he wanted to. He'd already set things in motion; it was just a matter of time before someone bit. Relieved, he decided that once he caught his traitor, he'd tell Gail everything—everything. She'd understand why he hadn't told her any of it before. After all, what was going on at VDK didn't have anything to do with Kalliste.

Didn't it? If this plan didn't work, he wouldn't have to worry about buying resorts or anything else; VDK would be broke.

One thing at a time, he told himself, and turned his attention to the phone when he heard a series of clicks. Seconds later, Patrick's voice came through, loud and clear.

"Hello, Chris?"

Relieved, he put aside the problem of Gail to deal with something else. "Good morning, Pat. Are Dan and Nick there?"

"Yes, I'm here, Chris," Daniel Harris answered.

Nick spoke up, too. "Right here, Mr. Van Der Kellen."

"Good," Chris said, and got right to business. After having been so indecisive about Gail, it was a relief to plunge into something he knew something about. He'd set up this call as a ruse to rattle a few cages, and he said, "As you know, I don't plan to be back in the Tampa office for a few days yet, but I thought you should know before then some of the details of a new deal I've been thinking about."

"A new deal?" Patrick asked cautiously. "You mean buying Kalliste International?"

"Not exactly. As you're aware, I've almost decided to buy the resorts—"

Daniel Harris broke in. "I've got to repeat, Chris, I think it's foolish to jump into this."

Wondering if his accountant was just exercising his customary fiscal caution, or if his protest sprang from some other factor, Chris said, "I know, but things are about as I expected, and after seeing the resorts in person, I'm more convinced than ever that this is a good move."

"Does that mean I should cancel the request for the research team that was to scout out the economy chain opposition?" Nick asked.

Again, Chris paused. Was Nick just being his usual thorough self, or did he have an ulterior motive for asking that question? Cursing the paranoia that seemed to arise with every conversation he had with his once trusted men, Chris said, "Yes, I never wanted to get involved in that, anyway."

"But I thought you agreed we should look into alternatives," Patrick said.

"No. I didn't say anything like that. I didn't say anything at all. Moreover, after seeing three of Damion's resorts, I've got a much better idea of what I want to do. If I buy the chain, I intend to expand almost immediately."

There was a choked sound over the speaker—almost certainly from Dan, who was more cautious with VDK's money than he was with his own.

"Er...Chris..." Dan said.

"I know what you're thinking, Dan, but—"

Patrick broke in. "I wish to hell I knew what *you* were thinking, Chris!" he exclaimed. "Would you mind telling us what's going on?"

"I don't know what you mean. You were aware that I was interested in the Kalliste deal."

"Interested in the *chain* is one thing!" Patrick said. "But expansion is another!"

"I think what Pat means is that it's not like you to make impulse decisions like this," Daniel Harris said quickly.

"It isn't an impulse decision," Chris said.

"Well, Chris, you *are* committing the company to a large sum here."

Patrick had himself under some control again. "Without discussing it with your top executives, I might add!"

"But I am discussing it with you," Chris pointed out.

"During a conference call from a dude ranch in California—*after* you've already made up your mind?" Patrick demanded.

Daniel interrupted again. He knew the purchase price of the existing resorts; what he wanted to know was how much more Chris intended to commit.

"Chris, this...expansion. Could you tell us a little more about it?"

"Yes," Patrick said heavily, "such as where you intend to find the money to do it? In case you've forgotten, we lost a bundle on that lumber shipment."

Chris turned grim. "I haven't forgotten. But I took care of that yesterday. After you left, I made arrangements to freight the entire shipment to Utah. We'll only lose money on the time it sat in the train yard."

"Well, *that's* good news at least," Patrick said, only partially mollified.

"You didn't know?" Chris said, and spoke to his assistant. "Nick, didn't you send out those memos?"

Nick, nearly silent until now, spoke up. "Yes, Mr. Van Der Kellen. All departments were copied."

"So there are no problems, then."

"No, sir. Not...not with that."

Chris stared at the phone. "Are you saying there's a problem somewhere else?" he asked sharply.

Nick cleared his throat. "I...er...was going to send you a telex this morning, but Mr. Delaney and Mr. Harris thought it would be better to wait."

Chris's tone was ominous. "Wait—for what?"

"It's a problem we can handle from our end," Patrick said. Chris could almost see him glaring in Nick's direction. "Just a little mix-up about some computer components. We'll have it straightened out in no time. I'm more interested in the expansion you just mentioned."

"So am I, in fact," Daniel said. "You were going to fill us in?"

Wondering if they were more interested than they were saying, Chris reminded himself that he had to go ahead, no matter how distasteful it was. All three of these men had been with him for years; one of them, certainly, was betraying the company. He'd set up his elaborate ruse to flush out the traitor, and it didn't matter that he dreaded doing it; it was necessary.

"I'll give you more details in a couple of days when I get back," he said, "but for now, I've thought about looking in Hawaii. The islands are the perfect place for another resort along these lines. After that, maybe we'll look at Tahiti, or perhaps Canada, or even the Virgin Islands."

"Hawaii! Tahiti!" Patrick was nearly apoplectic. "Chris, are you out of your mind? We're trying to keep our heads above water here!"

"Chris, are you sure you've thought about this?" Daniel asked nervously. "I mean, given our current budgetary crisis—"

"I know all about our financial situation," Chris said. "But I'm afraid it's going to get a little tighter, Dan."

He could almost see his accountant blanch. "Wh-what do you mean?"

"Well, you know land is at a premium these days in the islands, and I had to make a decision at once. So I put down a nonrefundable deposit on a choice piece of—"

"You *what*?" Patrick roared.

"How much?" Daniel said faintly.

When Chris told them an outrageous imaginary sum, someone—he was sure it was his accountant—gasped. Even the outspoken Patrick was silent. Only Nick was heard to breathe, almost in a whisper, "Good Lord!"

Chris smiled grimly. *That should keep someone busy,* he thought. Then he added, "I'll give you a more detailed briefing when I get back. Right now I'm on my way to Colorado."

Patrick gathered himself together. "You're going on with the tour?" He sounded outraged and indignant at the same time.

"Yes," Chris said curtly. "And in the meantime, I'd appreciate a full accounting of this latest problem. You can fax the information to me at Kalliste Snowball, in Colorado."

Patrick was still annoyed. "We don't need to fax it," he said. "You might as well know right now that it involves your friend Horst Volker."

Chris muttered a curse. Volker was no friend of his, although their two companies dealt with each other by necessity. Horst ran the American division of the German-based Volker Steel, and VDK had a hospital surgical-supply contract with them that was up at the end of the month. Volker had given him problems before, and he sat tensely forward.

"What is it now?"

"He called yesterday to say he'll be...delayed... shipping that big order."

Thinking he had enough problems right now without having to tread lightly around Volker's giant ego, Chris made an instant decision. "Fine," he snapped. "I'll call and tell him that if he can't make the date, he's in breach of contract. In the meantime, call Allied and see if you can line them up. I'm not going to waste any more time with that temperamental egomaniac."

"But Chris—"

"Do it," Chris said, and broke the connection.

Rubbing his eyes, he sat back. God, he hated this. He wished to hell it was all over. It was small comfort to know that in a few days he'd have the identity of his traitor; at the moment, he felt exhausted, too sick at heart to carry on.

Unfortunately, he had no choice. His glance went to the closed connecting door, and when he remembered that he had to do something about Gail, he sighed heavily. It was too much. Maybe for these few days, he'd put off making a decision about everything and just enjoy this stolen time. He smiled sadly. These few days might be all the time he had left with Gail. He'd make the most of them, because when they got back, he'd have to tell her the truth. And when he did...

Surprised at the pain he felt at the thought of losing her—something he knew was going to happen once he explained, or tried to explain, why he hadn't told her the truth in the beginning—he put his head in his hands. Against all resolve, he'd done just what he hadn't wanted to do. Now it was too late. Wondering when it was that he'd started falling in love with Gail, he put his head back wearily and closed his eyes.

ON THE OTHER SIDE of the door, Gail tiptoed away. She'd listened in on Chris's conference call, and she knew she should have been elated that she had new information for Roger. Instead, she felt guilty and ashamed. She shouldn't have eavesdropped on a private conversation that wasn't any of her business.

"But it *is* your business," she muttered. "It's your job!"

That didn't help, for she felt lower than before. Maybe she just wasn't cut out for this work. Did other agents have the same problem? she wondered. Did other agents fall in love with their subjects? Sighing, she glanced at the connecting door. At least she'd done what she'd been sent to do; the conversation she'd heard just now meant that Chris not only intended to buy Kalliste International, but planned to expand it as well. With that information, Damion could be satisfied that Chris was making his offer in good faith. So she had completed her assignment, come through with, if not flying, then *faltering*, colors, and she could go home. She should really be pleased, she told herself, not feel like bursting into tears.

But it's all over, she thought mournfully. As soon as she called Roger and reported her findings, she could pack up and take the first plane back to New York. She was finished here; there was no need to stay on. Roger wouldn't have to know what a disaster she'd almost made of her assignment—in the end, she had come through. And because she'd done a relatively good job her first time out, she could probably expect a new assignment, perhaps even a permanent promotion. That was something, wasn't it?

Swallowing back tears, she looked at the phone. She had to make the call; there was no use postponing it. The longer she sat here, the more she didn't want the time with Chris to end. She might have been totally unprofessional in getting involved, but she couldn't pretend it hadn't happened. But still, it was over; she couldn't deny that, either. Once Chris found out who she was and what she'd done to him—and he would; he'd have to—he'd never want to see her again. She couldn't blame him; in his place, she'd feel the same way.

Oh, why did this have to happen now? she asked herself tearfully. If only she'd met Chris before she'd taken on this assignment. If only—

But she wouldn't have met Chris under any other circumstances. Their lives were so different their paths would never have crossed if it hadn't been for Damion; it was silly pretending otherwise. She could expect no fairy-tale ending to this story. She simply had to accept that and get on with things.

Unless...

She was just reaching for the phone to make the call when a thought struck her. Chris was packing right now to leave for Colorado; she was supposed to be doing the same thing. Whom would it hurt if she delayed making her call one more day? She'd already found out how committed Chris was to buying Kalliste International; she had done her job. Nothing would change if she just...failed to file her report until they were ready to leave Colorado. If she didn't call Roger, she'd have one more day, at least, with Chris. Who would be the wiser?

She would, she thought, and felt defeated again. She couldn't make herself do it. As tempting as the thought was, she'd been irresponsible enough. If she prolonged the trip for her own selfish reasons, she'd never be able to look herself in the eye again. She'd never be able to look *Roger* in the eye again.

She was just reaching listlessly for the phone again when Chris rapped on the connecting door and opened it.

"You decent?" he asked, poking his head around with a grin.

She was trying to be, she thought, and gave the phone a last glance before she turned to face him. She couldn't very well call Roger with Chris standing right here; she'd just have to wait for another opportunity. The thought occurred to her that she could excuse herself and say she had a business call to make, but she thrust such inconvenient ideas away, saying brightly instead, "Don't tell me you're packed already."

"You know me, I travel light."

She was in the mood to tease, to be frivolous one last time. "With a private plane and two personal pilots?"

He shrugged. "I didn't say I traveled rough, only light. And speaking of planes and pilots, all three are awaiting your command. Say the word, and we're off to Colorado."

Now was the opportunity. She had only to say that something had come up back at her office, and she had to cut the trip short. If he objected, she'd point out that they had only one more resort to visit, and if he was that interested, he could go by himself. Then she could call Roger, make her report and take the next flight home.

The words were right there, but she couldn't make herself say them—not when he was standing so close, looking down at her in that way he had that took her breath away.

"Gail?" he said. "Is something wrong?"

She couldn't stop looking up into those dark, dark eyes. How well she knew him now, she thought dazedly, and how little she knew him still.... Oh, she wanted more time to learn everything about him, to become so close, so intimate, that she would know what he was thinking even before he said it, even before he *thought* it. More, she wanted the time to know his body even better than she already did—that wonderful body of his that fitted so perfectly with hers, so that there was no awkwardness between them.

Even now, just thinking about it, her heart started to beat a little faster, and she could feel a flush come to her cheeks. It took all her willpower not to fling herself into his arms, to raise her lips for his kiss, to wind her fingers in his hair and bring his mouth down to hers, to fall entwined with him on the bed and love the day away.

How could she make up a weak excuse, she asked herself. This was the man she had, without even really knowing how it had happened, come to love. How could she leave him now? They'd only just begun!

Just one more day! she begged her conscience. *Just one!* After that, she'd do all the things she was supposed to; she'd file her report and talk to Roger and go home and make their client happy. And in doing so, she'd destroy whatever chance she and Chris might have had together. If she had to sacrifice so much to do her duty, what harm would come from one more day?

He was still looking at her quizzically. "Gail?"

She'd made up her mind. "Nothing's wrong," she said brightly. "It's just that I'm not . . . packed yet."

He looked instantly concerned. "Still sore from your experience yesterday?"

She'd been so preoccupied with other things that she hadn't noticed until now how stiff and sore she still was. Ruefully, she rubbed a hip. "I don't think I'll ever recover from that ride."

As always, he took charge. "What you need is a massage," he said briskly. "If they don't have a masseuse here, we can fly one in—"

She burst into laughter. Everything was so simple, so easy for him, she thought wonderingly. Fly in a masseuse, indeed!

"Absolutely not!" she declared. "You're spoiling me abominably. Just give me a few more minutes, and I'll be ready."

"You're sure."

"I'm positive," she said, smilingly pushing him toward his own suite. "Now, go on. With you in here, I can't concentrate."

He paused at the connecting door. "You sure you don't want a massage?" he said, his eyes taking on that gleam. "If you don't want me to fly a masseuse in, maybe I could pinch-hit. So to speak."

As tempting as the thought was, she shook her head. "I think a couple of pain tablets will do just fine," she said, and gently shut the door.

TWO HOURS LATER, the tablets having worked their medical miracle, Gail and Chris were on their way. While Gail sat staring pensively out the window as the sleek jet climbed to cruising altitude, Chris went forward to talk to Darby and Jack. She'd told herself that once committed, she couldn't look back. But as the rolling hills of California disappeared, she wondered if she'd done the right thing. Every moment she was with Chris increased her desire to stay with him always. She couldn't bear the thought of leaving him.

But she had to leave him; she knew that. She also knew she had to enjoy what time they had left. *Buck up,* she told herself. It was what her father always told her when she was low. It helped, and she was able to smile naturally at Chris when he emerged again from the cockpit.

"What did Darby have to say?" she asked when he sat down beside her.

Chris grinned. "Just that he hopes you like skiing."

Having grown up in upstate New York, that was something she knew how to do. "Well, we are going to a skiing resort," she said, and glanced out the window. The snowcapped Rockies were below and around them now, but even though clouds were massing in the distance, she could see that far, far below in the valleys, the ground was still clear. Shrugging, she said, "Kalliste Snowball has a snow-making machine, in case—"

"I don't think they'll have to use it," Chris said. "Darby just got a weather update. It looks like the first snowfall of the year is about to come in. Kalliste Snowball should be white by the time we land."

Darby's weather report was right on the money; by the time the jet skimmed to a landing at nearby Snowmass, Colorado, visibility was a scant few miles, and they were one of the last planes in. A blast of frigid air hit them when they opened the door, and Chris laughed as he helped her down the stairs.

"Ah, the wonders of modern civilization," he said, waving the waiting car forward. "Only a few hours ago we were in sunny California. Now we're in the middle of a Rocky Mountains snowstorm. Isn't it great?"

"Wonderful," she said, pulling her coat more tightly around her. She hadn't anticipated the cold; she was still dressed for warm weather. When the car came, she jumped inside, luxuriating in the warm interior while Chris spoke to his pilots, inviting both Darby and Jack to join them.

"No, thanks, boss," Darby said with a grin. "We'll catch the airport shuttle into town, and, well, you know..."

Chris laughed. "Okay, just make sure you know what you're doing with your 'you knows.' I don't want to have to round up two pilots and fly everyone home myself."

"Not to worry, boss," Jack said. "I'll keep an eye on him."

Chris raised an eyebrow. "And that's meant to reassure me?"

Both pilots laughed and waved, and as Chris got into the car with her, Gail watched them walk away.

"What is it?" he asked.

She turned to look at him. "I was just thinking how lucky they are to work for a man like you."

As always when complimented, Chris seemed embarrassed. "I'm the one who's lucky. They're both good at that they do."

"So are you," she said softly.

He looked down at her. "And so are you," he said, kissing her lightly. "I hope you're feeling better."

She was; thanks to the pills, the aches and pains from her wild ride were almost gone. "You mean because we're going skiing?" she asked.

That gleam she was already able to recognize leaped into his eyes. "Skiing? To tell you the truth, I was thinking of something else."

"What?" she said coyly.

He winked. "You know," he said, mimicking Darby.

She looked up innocently, intending to flirt, to make a teasing remark in return. But something in his expression stopped her—that look in his eyes, that endearing quirk to his mouth, that flash of a dimple in his cheek, and without warning she felt a deep pang at the thought that it would be over so soon. *He's everything I ever wanted and didn't know it,* she thought, and turned away quickly so that he wouldn't see the tears well up in her eyes.

"Gail?"

He sounded anxious, and she knew she had to get herself together before he asked her what was wrong. With a supreme effort, she summoned a smile and turned back to him. "I don't know about your 'you knows,'" she said. "But when we get to the hotel, *I'm* going skiing!"

Laughing, he put his arm around her and drew her close. "We'll see about that," he said, and kissed her.

As always, her desire for him was close to the surface. The moment he put his arm around her and held her tight, she lost sight of everything else, and kissed him so passionately in return that she knew he was a little surprised by her reaction.

But not too surprised to take advantage of it. They were both breathing heavily by the time the driver pulled up to Kalliste Snowball, and when Gail realized the car had stopped, she was never so glad for the opaque windows in the limousine—especially the one between the passengers and the driver. Straightening her hair and clothes, she glanced red-faced at Chris.

"I feel like a teenager," she muttered.

He laughed. "So do I. Isn't it wonderful?"

"It's embarrassing," she said, noticing that she'd missed a button on her blouse. Her cheeks burning, she hurriedly did it up, and then pulled her coat closer. "Shall we get out?"

"And continue upstairs?" he asked wickedly.

Laughing, she gave him a push. "Just for that, you're in for another of my stories!"

He pretended dismay. "Oh, no, not that!"

"Hey, you wanted a tour guide," she told him as they emerged, decorously dressed again, from the car. "So that's what you get."

Kalliste Snowball was built hunting lodge style, out of local lodgepole pine and alpine fir. Chris tried to look interested as she pointed out the piñon pines in front of the lodge, making sure he knew that this type was one of the few conifers that bore seeds, the so-called piñon nuts. He was intrigued by one magnificent specimen that had a small sign at the base, giving its estimated age of nearly four thousand years, and then turned to follow her hand when she pointed out a stand of aspen behind the lodge.

The new snow had carpeted everything with a smooth mantel of white, and her breath made a vapor trail in the air, but a few brave leaves had struggled to stay on the trees, and she said, "Do you know why the leaves on the aspen trees tremble whenever anyone looks at them?"

The chauffeur was getting the bags out of the trunks, and since they were standing right beside him, he couldn't help but hear what she was saying. Bags in hand, he glanced where she was pointing.

"No," Chris said. "But I imagine you're going to tell me."

"Yes, I am," she said blithely, and didn't notice the chauffeur leaning closer so he could hear, too.

"Well, the story goes," she said in a whisper, "that once upon a time, the Great Spirit decided to visit the earth. As you can imagine, his coming was such an awesome event that all the creatures of the world trembled at his passing. Except for the vain aspen, which thought itself above such foolish adoration." She stopped and looked around, seeing for the first time the chauffeur's intent expression. She decided to include him, too. "And do you know what happened?" she asked.

With Chris trying not to smile, the driver shook his head.

"I'll tell you what happened," she said, after a dramatic pause. "The Great Spirit was so angry that the aspen didn't bow down and shake like the rest at his passing, that he decreed that henceforth and forever the aspen must tremble whenever anyone, anywhere, looked at it." Pausing theatrically again, she turned and looked at the trees. "And it *does*! Look!"

Obediently, Chris and the driver looked when she pointed. The few remaining leaves on the branches obligingly trembled, and when the two men turned back to her, she solemnly spread her hands. "I told you. It happens every time. Try it, you'll see."

Chris laughed. "You made that up."

"No, I didn't. I swear!"

"You did," he said, and, putting his arm around her, led her into the lobby of the hotel.

Just before they went through the door, she glanced back. The chauffeur was still by the car, alternately turning away from the stand of aspen, and then looking quickly over his shoulder again, trying to catch the trees in default. He looked so comical, turning his back, and then whirling around, that she nearly laughed. But just then someone rushed up to them, and she was instantly thrown back into her role.

"Ms Sullivan!" the man exclaimed. "How good it is to see you again!"

Quickly she searched her memory. Oh, yes, this was Martin Rittenhouse, the manager. With a warm smile, she held out her hand. "A pleasure to be here, as always," she said, and introduced Chris.

"Oh, yes, indeed," Rittenhouse said, enthusiastically pumping Chris's hand. "We've been waiting for your arrival, Mr. Van Der Kellen. I've had the Presidential suites prepared, and of course we've delayed the start of First Run. But now that you're here, delay won't be necessary. You do ski, I presume.''

"Yes, I do,'' Chris said, sounding amused while Gail racked her brain. What in heaven's name was First Run? She didn't remember reading about this!

They both found out soon enough. Barely an hour later, dressed in the gear provided for them, Gail and Chris were on their way up the mountain in the chair lift. All the skiers present at the lodge were waiting for them at the top, poised to take a twilight run down the mountain carrying torches to celebrate the first snowfall. Toting poles and gloves and torches, which would be lighted when they arrived at the top, Gail and Chris had been designated as celebrities to lead the parade.

"Isn't it beautiful?'' Gail sighed, looking around as the chair carried them smoothly up. The sky was turning that lovely shade of mauve and pink that signals snow. The air was crisp and clean, and she had never felt so wonderful in her life. As she glanced at Chris, her breath caught. He looked so handsome beside her in electric blue, his black hair held back by a headband and goggles pushed up on his forehead, that she wanted to lean over and kiss him right there. With one gloved hand he held their poles; with the other he gripped her fingers in her thick glove. As if he sensed her looking at him, he turned with a smile.

"You look beautiful in white,'' he said.

"You're pretty dashing yourself,'' she said, her voice choked.

"You sure you're up to this?''

"Absolutely,'' she said, glancing around at the utterly breathtaking scenery. She turned back to him with a grin.

"Besides, if we had refused, Rittenhouse would have been devastated. It was as though he'd planned the first snowfall to coincide with our arrival."

"That, or the Great Spirit was looking down," Chris said with a wicked smile. "Maybe he got together with the Indian goddess from Arizona. Those spirits seem to have a thing about trees."

Laughing, she was about to say something when the lift gave a lurch. They had arrived at the top, and as they left the chair and skied over to where the others waited, Gail wanted this moment, as she'd wanted so many others with Chris, to last forever. She was so proud to be with him; every time she glanced his way, her heart seemed to skip a beat.

It was a perfect night: the snow fell gently as everyone got ready, skis crunched on snow, and laughter rang out. Gail had never felt as thrilled and happy and tender as when she and Chris led the parade down the mountain. Hand in hand, holding their torches high, they skied almost as one, the wind in their faces, the snow falling, soft pink light all around them.

Chris took her in his arms when they reached the bottom and tossed their torches, which landed in the snow with a hiss just as he kissed her. Arm in arm they went back to the lodge, planning a toddy by the fire, a candlelight supper and then . . .

They were told that Chris's office in Tampa had called. Another emergency had arisen, and Chris was needed immediately at home.

LATE THAT SAME NIGHT, the caller finally got through to Wade Sutton.

"I've been trying to reach you all day," he complained. "I've got news."

"Van Der Kellen isn't my only project," Sutton growled. "I've got other things to do. What news?"

The caller took a deep breath. "He's definitely decided to buy the Kalliste chain."

"So?"

"I thought you'd like to know that he's going to expand it immediately."

Sutton's tone sharpened. "Oh? What location?"

"Somewhere in Hawaii."

"*Where* in Hawaii?"

"I don't know yet. I'm working on it."

"You called to tell me nothing?"

The caller winced at the sarcasm. "It's not *nothing* when you find out that wherever he's going to build, he's put a nonrefundable deposit on the land."

Sutton was silent. "That puts things in a different light. How much of a deposit?"

The caller told him. Sutton was silent again. "I see," he said finally. "Then obviously our work is cut out for us. I want that land."

"Yes."

"And in the meantime—what news about Volker Steel? Has Horst done what I asked?"

"Chris is on his way back to Florida right now."

"Well done."

Surprised at the rare compliment, the caller preened. "I told you you'd get your money's worth."

The moment had passed. "I'll be the judge of that," Sutton grunted, and hung up the phone.

CHAPTER THIRTEEN

THE TRIP BACK TO FLORIDA seemed endless. Gail didn't know what the new emergency was at VDK because Chris didn't tell her, but one look at his tense face, with most of the color leached away because of some sustained, inner anger, and she thought it wise not to ask.

Besides, she had her own problems as a result of this new twist. After eavesdropping on his conference call before they had left Kalliste Caballero, she'd thought her job was over. Chris was going to buy Damion's chain of resorts, expand in the future, and that was that. Now she wasn't certain he'd still do that. If the new crisis was going to affect Chris's plans, she couldn't report back to Damion just yet. She had to know exactly what he was planning to do, and she couldn't just ask. Not now, anyway, when Chris looked so angry and troubled. Even she knew that the last thing on his mind was Kalliste International.

So that meant that she had to go on with him to Florida, and despite herself, her heart leaped at the thought. It meant that she could prolong the inevitable parting a few days, at least, and she was grateful.

What she wasn't so pleased about was the deep-down knowledge that she'd do anything at this point to stay on with Chris, even lie to herself. She didn't know if she was using VDK's new emergency as a reason to delay going home, or if it was a legitimate excuse. She couldn't trust herself anymore, not where Chris was concerned, and that raised another unpalatable question. Was she using this delay as a way of avoiding the truth? She knew she had to tell him who she really was, but every time she thought she'd drummed up the courage to confess, she hadn't been able to make herself do it. She knew how angry he'd be to find out she'd duped him; he'd feel like a fool and not want to see her again. Nothing she could say would change the fact that she'd lied to him, and she felt backed into a corner, with no place to go. She couldn't tell him, and she couldn't not. So what could she do?

Glumly, she stared out the window. They'd left the mountains behind, but she hadn't the foggiest idea where they were. Darby had just come over the intercom to say they'd arrive in Tampa shortly, but the flight seemed to be taking forever—and ending too quickly at the same time—and she stole another glance at Chris. If she wasn't going to come clean and tell him her sad story, she still had a job to do, so instead of feeling sorry for herself, she thought, she should think of some excuse to go to the office with him. Once there, she could somehow find a way to snoop around again, and hopefully learn something that would help.

Help who? she wondered. *Chris or Damion?*

She wasn't sure about that, either. Lord, what a mess. Things had gotten so much more complicated than she'd ever intended, and she knew that if Roger found out about her involvement with Chris, he'd blow a gasket— or at least, order her back to New York so fast her head would spin. She'd be demoted down to...heaven knew what. Probably dusting the office at night—if he allowed her to stay on at all, that was. Either way, her investigative career would be over, and it hadn't even really begun.

Gloomily, she looked out at the clouds scudding by down below. Then she sat up. Roger didn't have to find out about this, did he? There was a way to turn things around; there had to be. If she managed to find out what was really going on here, she could do her job, help Chris, save face and solve the case—all in one fell swoop! All she had to do was figure out how to go with Chris to the office. Once she was there, she'd handle things somehow.

"Gail?"

Startled, she looked up. She'd been so deep in thought that she hadn't realized Chris had left his seat and had come to sit beside her on the couch.

"I'm sorry I've been so rude," he said, taking her hand. "I know I've got a lot on my mind, but that's no excuse to leave you sitting here by yourself. Forgive me?"

Why was it that even the sound of his voice made her feel tender and protective? "You don't have to apologize," she said. "I understand."

Looking relieved, he said, "Thanks. It seems that it's been one thing after another these past few months."

Trying to remember why she was here instead of how tired he looked, how tense and drawn, she said, "Sometimes business is like that."

"If it were only normal business crises . . . But it's—"

When he stopped suddenly, she knew she couldn't just let it go. She was still on the job, and a lot was at stake—for both of them. Cautiously, she said, "This is different?"

"Yes," he said, glancing away, out the window. He suddenly looked remote. "This is different."

When he didn't explain, she knew she couldn't prod further—not without raising his suspicion. But as she looked at him, she wanted just to forget all this pretense and *tell* him. It was so awful not being honest, not confiding in him; it was even worse to know that the fault lay with her. Given their new relationship, Chris might have asked her advice, or even her opinion—if he hadn't believed she had her own ax to grind. He still thought she was Damion's representative, here to see through a big business acquisition. He could hardly admit to someone in her supposed position that his own company was vulnerable.

If only she could tell him! she thought sadly. But she had her own responsibilities, and as much as she longed to just blurt it all out, she knew that doing so would only complicate an already difficult situation.

"If you're wondering whether this is going to affect my decision about whether or not to buy Kalliste International," Chris said, interrupting her thoughts again as he turned back to her, "please don't. One has nothing to do with the other."

"Oh, Chris," she said. "I wasn't thinking of that."

"Nonsense," he said, smiling slightly. "Of course you were. I would have been, in your place. I'm just sorry all this is happening now. Believe me, I usually run VDK's ship a lot tighter than this."

"I believe that," she said, and made herself try again. "But everyone has crises to deal with in business. Sometimes it seems as though the bad times come all at once."

"That's for sure," he said, and gave her hand a squeeze. "I'm sorry this business took us away so quickly from Kalliste Snowball," he said softly. "I never got a chance to tell you how much I enjoyed that twilight ski run."

Remembering, she smiled in return. "I did, too. It was one of those..." She hesitated, searching for words that wouldn't sound too fatuous and foolish. Then, when he said them, they didn't sound that way at all.

"One of those perfect moments?"

"You felt it, too?"

He held her eyes. "I've been feeling a lot of things since we met."

Her throat suddenly felt tight. She wanted to say something, but she couldn't seem to make her voice work. Then she didn't know what she'd say even if she could. How could she tell him what she felt? If she confessed that, she'd have to reveal all the rest, and she'd already decided that now just wasn't the time.

What a coward you are! a voice whispered at the back of her mind. And where Chris was concerned, she knew it was true.

He hadn't said anything, and he looked at her curiously. "You haven't felt it, too?"

"Of course I have. It's just—" She stopped, knowing she couldn't say more without revealing her true colors. Wondering if every conversation was going to lead to a verbal trap, she swallowed and tried again. "It's just that things seem so complicated now," she finished weakly.

"I know. But—" he reached for her other hand, holding both tightly as he went on "—Gail, I won't lie to you. There have been problems at VDK, as I know you're aware. But I promise you, it's nothing I can't straighten out, nothing I'm not working on right now, in fact. And when it's all over, I ... I'd like us to take some time together. No, don't say anything yet," he said, when she tried to protest. "But something is happening between us, something that doesn't have anything to do with you representing Kalliste International, or with me wanting to buy Damion's resorts. I'm aware of it, and I know you are, too. So when I get things straightened out, I'd like to just go away, the two of us. Because the truth is, I think I'm falling in—"

Now she did protest. Not wanting him to say it because that would require a commitment from her, too, she put her fingers over his mouth. "Please, Chris. You don't know—"

He put his hand over hers, turning it up so that he could press his lips against her palm. A thrill went all the way through her, right down to her toes. His eyes held hers. "I want to know," he said. "I want to know everything there is to know about you."

She shook her head wildly. "No, you don't, Chris. You don't understand...."

Slowly, he released her hand. "I think I do," he said.

"What...what do you mean?" she stammered, alarmed. Was this all a ploy? Had he found out about her? But how? When?

He shrugged, as though it was obvious. "Well, for one thing, we're both right in the middle of a possible business transaction. You're Damion's representative. I understand that you don't want to let personal considerations interfere with your job." He smiled, bleakly. "I admire that."

"You...do?" She felt almost faint with relief. The denouement was postponed. She didn't have to face his contempt—or his wrath—just yet.

He looked rueful. "Sure I do. Not that I *like* it, you realize. But I understand, and admire your stand."

"Oh. Well, I'm...glad," she said weakly, and thought, *This is awful. He's being so generous, and I'm betraying him with every word.*

He leaned forward abruptly, taking her chin in his hand so that she had to look at him. "But that doesn't mean," he said, staring into her eyes, "that as soon as I get this problem at VDK straightened out, I'm going to let you off as easy as that. If I have to, I'll storm Harlan Damion's corporate offices in New York and carry you off myself!"

"Oh, you don't have to go that far!" she exclaimed, trying not to show how horrified she was at the thought. She could just imagine what would happen if he actually did go to the Damion building to look for her and she wasn't there. Hastily, she added, "I'll be happy to meet you somewhere!"

To her relief, he laughed. After a moment, when she had regained her composure, she laughed with him. Then Darby's voice came over the intercom to announce that they were on final approach, and soon after that, they were on the ground again.

Feeling as though she'd been careering from one crisis to the next, Gail tried to marshal her whirling thoughts. She had yet to come up with some reasonable excuse to accompany Chris to his office, and despite her precarious emotional state, she still had a job to do.

But then Chris gave her the opening she was looking for. "I'm sorry, Gail," he said, turning to her as they taxied to one of the private hangars. "I guess I'm not thinking too clearly yet. I suppose I just assumed you'd want to come back to Tampa with me, but I should have asked what your plans were. Do you—do you have to go back to New York right away, or could you stay another day or so?"

The last thing she wanted to do was head back to New York. The thought of leaving Chris like this, without anything resolved between them, was too depressing. She knew that if their involvement became any more intense, she would have to confess everything, but that was—mercifully—at some future date. She couldn't worry about that now; she had a job to do. If she was going to find out anything that would help, she had to make use of this chance.

"Well, I suppose I could stay on," she said slowly, as though just pondering the idea. "But I'll have to talk to my office first. How about if I come to VDK with you? I could make arrangements from there."

The look on his face was nearly her undoing. He looked so pleased and happy when he took her arm that she nearly blurted out the horrible truth right there. "Wonderful," he said. "Now you'll be here for our festival!"

"What festival?" she asked. She didn't believe she'd heard about that.

"Oh, it's a celebration we have every year at Kellen Key," Chris said. "Sort of a traditional holiday that was started by my grandfather. Everybody on the island comes, and people from neighboring keys. It's quite a thing. You'll enjoy it."

"But what's it for?" she asked, confused.

"You'll see," he said with a wink, and then they were both distracted with saying hello to Max, who had brought the car around.

She didn't get a chance to find out any more about the island festival, for both Patrick Delaney and Daniel Harris were waiting anxiously when they arrived at the VDK office. Max took the car off somewhere after depositing them outside, and Chris didn't waste words as they headed into the building.

"Where's Nick?" he asked his hovering executives.

"He's here, don't worry," Daniel Harris said nervously. "He had a call to make, but he'll be right along."

"Chris—" Patrick began.

Chris interrupted him curtly, gesturing to a secretary who came quickly from her desk at his signal. "Charlene, please show Ms Sullivan to an empty office," he said, and then turned to Gail. "I'm sorry. Will you be all right?"

"I'll be fine," she said, feeling as though she were lying through her teeth. Now that she was here, she felt even more like a traitor, and she had to make an effort to give him a reassuring smile. "You go ahead. Don't worry about me."

"I'll always worry about you," Chris murmured. Then he turned to his two executives. "Get Nick. Meet me in the conference room in five minutes. I want a little time in my office before we get going."

With another quick smile at Gail, Chris started off. Watching his abrupt departure, the long strides, the broad, tense set to his shoulders as he headed down the hall, Gail felt her heart constrict. How was she ever going to explain to him her part in this? Watching him turn just now from a loving companion to a ruthless-looking industrialist was a little chilling. She'd seen that hard look come into his eyes before he turned away; how would she feel if—when—he looked at her like that?

"If you'll follow me, please, Ms Sullivan?"

She'd forgotten the secretary was still there, waiting to show her to an office. Forcing a smile, she indicated she was ready, and, distracted, she followed the woman down another hall. She'd never been to VDK's corporate headquarters, but like everything else Chris seemed to touch, this building emanated quiet luxury. The hall carpet was a pale ivory, and the walls were painted a deep forest green. Modern original paintings here and there provided great slashes of color, and all around were vast panoramas of tinted windows, letting in light without glare. She noticed an absence of background music, but she was sure she felt a distinctive throb of power, and as she walked along, she thought how perfectly the surroundings suited Chris. She was so bemused that she nearly bumped into the secretary when she stopped by an open door and gestured.

"Will you be needing anything, Ms Sullivan?" she asked.

"No, I'll be fine," Gail said, feeling a distinct sense of déjà vu. Hadn't she been through this routine before? "I'll be making a few calls, so I'd prefer not to be disturbed."

She nodded. "As you wish. The phone lines here are on a separate trunk from those on the other side of the building where Mr. Van Der Kellen and the others will be, so there will be no conflict. In fact, these offices are all empty at the moment, so no one will intrude."

"Fine," Gail said, and waited until she was sure the young woman had gone before she went to the desk. She'd already planned how she would handle the situation: she was going to take the receiver off the phone so that the call button for that line would light and it would look as though she were making a call. Then she could slip out and prowl around, hoping to find something that would make all this cloak-and-dagger business worthwhile. She was just reaching for the phone when she realized that one of the lines was already lit.

What was this? She frowned. Charlene had just told her that the offices on this side of the building were empty, and that the phone lines were separate, but someone was obviously here, making a call. Biting her lip, she stared at the phone. Should she?

It's your job, she told herself, and before she could think about it, she reached out, punched the lighted button and, ever so gently, inched the receiver out of the cradle and put it to her ear.

"... yeah, just got in," she heard a voice say. "I tried to hide it as long as possible, but one of the others caught it and sent for him. What do you want me to do?"

"Nothing," a second voice, one she couldn't identify, rasped. "He can't do anything about it now. It's more important to find out about the Hawaii business. Has he said anything about the location yet?"

"No, but I'll find out at the meeting right now—somehow," the first man said. "I'll get back to you."

"See that you do—pronto. I've almost got him where I want him. On top of these latest two, losing the Hawaii deal would be the coup de grace. I want it to happen."

The first voice laughed. "Don't worry, Wade," he said. "It'll happen. I promised that, didn't I? And I've kept up my end of the bargain."

"Not yet," the second man grunted. "And it's *Mr. Sutton* to you. Don't forget who's paying who."

"Yeah, right," the first man said angrily. "Well, I got a conference to attend. I'll get back to you."

"Make it fast and there's an extra fifty grand in it for you."

There was a barely muffled gasp. "In that case, I'll talk to you tonight."

There was a click, and before she knew it, Gail was listening to dead air. Quickly, she replaced her own receiver so the light would go out, then, her heart pounding, she sank down in the chair behind the desk.

There was no doubt that the conversation she'd over-heard just now was real, she thought shakily. Those men couldn't have known anyone was listening, and it hadn't been a joke. Remembering that raspy voice, she shivered. No, *he* hadn't been joking. Nor had...the other man. *Oh, Chris!* she thought, thinking of that other voice, the one she had recognized from the first word. *Oh, Chris!*

It was clear now that there was a conspiracy to bring down VDK and Chris with it; she knew beyond a doubt because of what she had heard. The question was why. And, she thought, did Chris know? Thinking back to the times when he'd looked so troubled, so preoccupied and sad, Gail was sure he did—or suspected, anyway. But why hadn't he done anything about it?

Because he hadn't been able to identify the traitor, that was why, she thought, and straightened, thinking, *But I can.*

Then she slumped again. She didn't have any proof of what she'd heard; she couldn't go to Chris with nothing. She looked at the phone again. She'd call Roger and ask him to find out everything he could about this Wade Sutton. And while he was at it, he could get additional information about the other man. Oh, why hadn't she put it together before now? Remembering the travel mix-up, and those odd expressions on his face at different times... No, there was no doubt about it. Once she had what she needed from Roger, she'd go to Chris and...

And what? Tell him that she'd called her boss at Brenner and Company and put her fellow investigators on the case? She couldn't do that. By admitting her connection with Roger in New York, she'd expose herself, and then what would happen? Would Chris be so grateful to her that he'd conveniently overlook her own little deception? Wincing, she shook her head. Knowing Chris, it didn't seem likely.

Well, then, maybe she should just go to him and tell him, she thought hopefully. She could say she'd over-heard this strange conversation and let him take it from there. VDK was his company, his responsibility. If she handled it that way, she could stay out of it, keep her cover intact, and everything would be just fine.

But if she did that, what about her own responsibili-ties? Personal considerations aside, she had still taken on an assignment, and now she had an obligation to her client, who had hired Brenner and Company to obtain information that might affect his own business dealings with Chris and VDK. How could she ignore that?

"Oh, damn!" she muttered, putting her head in her hands. She was so confused, and she didn't know what to do. She'd never expected things to get so complicated; this assignment was supposed to have been so easy!

But then, she'd never expected to get involved with her subject. So it was no one's fault but her own that she was in such a mess. She couldn't ignore her obligations; peo-ple were depending on her. She had to act like a profes-sional and put her own feelings aside.

Sighing heavily, she lifted her head and reached for the phone. There was no use postponing the call to Roger in New York. When he answered, she said, "I think I'm on to something, Roger. Can you do something for me?"

He didn't hesitate; it was obvious he felt she'd uncov-ered a break in the case at last. "Sure," he said immedi-ately. "What do you need?"

She told him, adding, "And I need it yesterday, Roger. I've got a feeling that things are going to be happening very soon."

"I'll get on it right away," he promised. "Where can I reach you?"

She hesitated. But she was already in so deep that it couldn't possibly matter. "I'll be at Kellen Key," she said. "But I'll call you. I think it will be safer that way."

She was just hanging up when someone knocked on the door. Thinking it was Charlene, Gail said, "Yes?"

To her surprise, Chris opened the door and poked his head in. "Sorry to bother you—"

She felt so guilty that she sprang up. Had he heard anything? Willing herself not to flush, she said, "No bother. I was just finishing up. What can I do for you?"

He gave her a strange look. "Are you all right?"

"Of course," she said nervously. "Why?"

"Because you seem... Is everything all right? Are there problems at your office?"

She seized on the excuse as though it were a lifeline. "Oh, you know. There are always problems. One of the secretaries... well, it doesn't matter. It's nothing I couldn't handle from here. How about you?"

Frowning, he came into the room. "My problem's not so easily solved, I'm afraid. It looks like I'm going to be tied up here for a couple more hours at least. I'd like to have Max take you home—back to Kellen Key, if that's all right. I can't imagine you want to sit around here, if you've finished with your office."

She was caught in her own trap. After admitting that she'd taken care of things back home, she didn't have an excuse to stay and snoop around. But maybe it didn't matter now, anyway. She couldn't do much more until Roger collected that information she'd asked for, so she said, "Well, all right. If you think that's best."

He smiled tiredly. "I wish I could go with you. I'd much rather be relaxing on the beach with you than trying to deal with things here."

She had to ask. "Is there anything I can do?"

He shook his head. "No, I'm afraid I'm going to have to handle it."

He looked so drawn and unhappy that she knew she couldn't just walk out without telling him *something*. "Chris—" she said, and stopped, biting her lip.

"What?"

She couldn't tell him, not until she knew for sure. Reluctantly, she shook her head. "Never mind. It's just that I wish I could help somehow."

Reaching for her hands, he drew her gently toward him. "You are helping," he said softly. "Just by being here."

That made her feel even worse. Trying to find a way around her dilemma, she looked at him anxiously. "Maybe it would help for you to talk about it."

When he hesitated, her heart gave a little leap. Maybe he'd give her the opening she was looking for, she thought, and then had to hide her disappointment when he shook his head. "Maybe I will, when I get things straightened out. Right now, I don't want to burden you with my problems—especially when they don't have anything to do with you and Kalliste International."

"I wasn't thinking about the resort sale!" she protested. It was true. The damned hotel chain had been the last thing on her mind.

He laughed, pulling her even closer. "You know," he said, "you're a very special lady. And a good sport. I want you to know I appreciate it."

As always when she was near to him, she seemed to be having trouble focusing. More than anything, she wanted to fling herself into his arms and ask him to take her away—far, far away, where there were no problems and they could spend all day, every day, making love. But even as she looked up into his shadowed eyes, she knew that was impossible; they both had too many responsibilities, too many secrets between them, too many obstacles to overcome. And nobody ever outran problems, no matter how many speedboats or fancy private jets they owned. What was the saying? *No matter where you go, there you are.* She'd never felt that so keenly as she did now, this very moment, when she longed to tell him everything and couldn't.

"Oh, Chris," she said helplessly.

He held her tightly to him for a moment, then he gently pushed her away. "Don't tempt me," he said hoarsely. "Or I'll never be able to get back to my meeting."

She didn't want to let him go, but she couldn't keep him here—not under false pretenses. If she wasn't going to tell him what she had learned, she had no right to keep him at all. Reluctantly, she stepped back, if only to put some physical distance between them. "You're right," she said, and tried to smile. "Don't worry about me. I'll go back to the island with Max."

He smiled tiredly in return. "And if I don't get home until tomorrow, have Max take you to the costume shop in the morning."

She was sure she'd misunderstood. "The costume shop?"

For the first time since entering the room, he looked amused. "I told you about the celebration."

"Yes, but—" She looked at him suspiciously. "Maybe you'd better tell me a little more about it."

"Well, surely you know about the pirate Respina?"

She didn't trust that sudden wicked glint in his eye. She'd seen it right before he suggested they go parasailing, and horseback riding and—

"The pirate Respina?" she repeated. "Are you making this up?"

He held up a hand. "I swear. You're always telling me stories. Now I've got one for you."

Leaning back against the desk, she crossed her arms. "I'm listening."

"Well, he's really a takeoff on José Gasparilla," Chris said, and saw her expression. "Oh, you've never heard of José Gasparilla, either? How come you know all those obscure tales about Great Spirits and vengeful Indian goddesses, and you've never heard of the pirate who once captured Tampa? There's a big festival in February every year, with the pirate himself sailing into the bay in a full-rigged ship, his crew brandishing cutlasses and kegs of ale."

"And capturing fair damsels, to boot, I'm sure," she contributed, not believing him for an instant.

"That, too," he agreed.

She looked at him suspiciously again. "You said this guy's name is Gasparilla. What does that have to do with Respingo?"

"Respina," he corrected. "Gasparilla arrives in Tampa in February, but our pirate comes to Kellen Key in October. We avoid a conflict of interest that way, you see."

This was too much. Sure he was making up all this, she said, "And this pirate of yours arrives at Kellen Key tomorrow night, is that right? How does he arrive, by sailing his own galleon into the bay?"

She'd been kidding, but he seemed to take her seriously. "No, a galleon is too cumbersome for our Respina. He captains a much faster, two-masted schooner—downsized, of course." He grinned. "There aren't as many pirates these days as there were of old. Crews are harder to come by."

"I see," she said, and then decided to play the game, too. Innocently, she asked, "And do any female pirates ever join in the celebration?"

He seemed to consider the question. "Aside from Anne Bonny and Mary Read, I don't believe I know about any genuine female pirates."

Now she gave him an incredulous look. "You've never heard of the piratess Henriette?"

"The piratess Henriette," he said, trying not to smile. "Why, I don't think so. Who's she?"

"Maybe she'll come to your celebration tomorrow night and you'll see."

He bowed. "I'm sure Respina will be pleased to make her acquaintance."

"Who is this Respina?" she asked.

He winked before he went out again. "Come to the party tomorrow night and you'll see."

Intrigued, not knowing whether to believe Chris's story or not, she asked Max when he came to take her back to the key.

"Oh, yes, it's a big festival," Max said. "The whole island celebrates. People even come from neighboring keys."

"And everybody comes in costume?" she asked, still not sure whether he was in on the joke or not.

"No admission without it."

"And who plays Respina?"

Max turned in the front seat of the car and grinned. "Can't you guess?"

She could, indeed. So it wasn't a joke, after all, she thought, and smiled to herself as she made a decision. She couldn't do anything about her situation until Roger had time to collect her information, so she might as well join in the fun.

"In that case," she said to Max with a grin, "let's stop by the costume place and see if they've got something for a piratess."

"A lady pirate?" Max asked.

"Yes," she said, enjoying herself thoroughly. "I think it's time your Respina met his match."

CHAPTER FOURTEEN

CHRIS WAS TIRED when he headed home the next night. The current crisis had taken much longer to resolve than he had anticipated, and after calling Gail to apologize, he'd slept on the couch in the office and started early again in the morning. The last thing he wanted to do was don a pirate's costume and launch Kellen Key's annual festival by playing Respina, but the people on the island who depended upon the Van Der Kellens for their livelihood looked forward to this gala every year, and he couldn't disappoint them—or those who always came from the neighboring keys to help celebrate. A Van Der Kellen male had sailed into Kellen Bay as the pirate every year for the past fifty years. He couldn't ignore tradition just because he was dead on his feet.

"You want to drive, boss?"

Chris had laid his head back against the car seat while Max had driven from the office to the dock. Surprised, he looked up and saw where they were. The *Kellen Two* bobbed gently in the water, and for a moment he was tempted. Piloting the boat always relaxed him; sometimes he took over the helm even when Max was there.

But not tonight. The way he felt, he'd probably fall asleep halfway there and ram the boat into one of the buoys that marked the entrance to the bay.

"No, you take it, Max," he said. "I'm beat."

"Long day, huh," his driver said sympathetically once they were ready to cast off. "Too bad you've got Respina's Return tonight. There is one thing, though...."

"What's that?"

"You got one mighty-fine-looking lady pirate waiting for you when you get there," Max said, and switched on the ignition.

Chris didn't reply; the roar of the boat's engine would have drowned out his voice, anyway, so he grinned and braced himself as they headed sedately out. But once on the open water, Max gave the *Kellen Two* her head, and as the boat's nose lifted, Chris could feel his own spirits rising. He always felt good out here; something about the wind and the sky and the sea—not to mention the powerful throb of those engines behind him—made him feel calm again. Out here, he could think, breathe. Things didn't seem so bleak as they had back at the office.

And things were bleak, he thought with a frown. Damn Volker anyway! Whoever betrayed him had done a hellishly good job. If he hadn't had Allied as an alternate, he really would have been in a bind. As it was, it had taken all his powers of persuasion—and the mention of a big bonus—to talk Allied into coming through in time to save his neck. If he hadn't been able to rely on them, he thought, taking off his coat, he didn't know what he could have done.

Well, it was taken care of now, he told himself, pulling at his tie and stuffing it into his pocket. And now his other plan was in motion. He'd called his old friend in Hawaii as soon as he reached Tampa, and Matsu, bless his heart, had already set things up.

"I've got phony real estate companies all over the place," Matsu had told him, chuckling. "The lure is out.

Now all we have to do is wait for the fish to come along and take the bait.''

"I just hope it's soon," Chris said. "VDK isn't going to be able to take much more."

"Your company is strong," Matsu said. "Like its president."

Hoping that was true, he'd thanked his old friend, and then made arrangements. When his three suspects arrived at Kellen Key for the celebration tonight, he intended to tell them he wanted the Hawaii deal to go through. Since all three would be there the entire weekend, the traitor would have to contact his partner from somewhere on the estate, and when he did . . .

Reminded of something, Chris went forward. He'd asked Max to help out, and he tapped his friend on the shoulder, shouting over the roar of the engines, "Did you set up that recording equipment like we discussed?"

"Yeah, I did it this morning," Max shouted back.

"Any problems?"

"Are you kidding?" Max said indignantly. "It was a piece of cake. Now any calls made from anywhere on the estate—even the guest houses—will be on tape. I put the recorder in that corner cupboard in the study, so you'll be able to play it back whenever you want."

Chris clapped him on the shoulder. "Thanks, Max. I don't know what I'd do without you."

"Fortunately for you, you don't have to worry. You think I'd ever give up a cushy job like this?" Max said, grinning. Then he frowned. "Besides, I want to catch the bastard just as much as you do. I only hope you give me five minutes with him after we find out who it is."

"Sorry, as tempting as the offer is, I think we'd better pass."

"Aw. Just let me at 'em. I'll teach 'em conspiracy!"

Chris laughed and clapped him on the back again. By this time they were approaching the entrance to Kellen Bay, and as always when he saw his home after even a short absence, he felt a thrill of pride. He never tired of gazing at the long, low lines of the house—or seeing the sun glinting off the prowlike windows in front. It looked so peaceful, so serene. The only thing missing was someone standing on the dock, waiting for his return. Celeste had never come out to welcome him home, but he'd always secretly wished she had, and—

With a start, he realized that someone *was* waiting for him. Even at this distance, he knew it was Gail, and as he stared at her, he felt his heart constrict. She looked so perfect standing there, her skin bronzed by the setting sun, her long skirt blowing about her ankles as she shaded her eyes with one hand, that he drew in a breath. She was so much like the vision he'd imagined all these times that he felt choked with emotion. Wouldn't it be wonderful....

Max had seen her, too. Looking a little misty-eyed himself, he glanced toward Chris. "I told you, you had one hell of a woman waitin' for you tonight, didn't I, boss?"

Chris put a hand on that beefy shoulder, but he couldn't take his eyes off Gail, who had seen the boat, and started to wave. Lifting his own hand in response, he said, "You did, indeed, Max. And what a sight."

"Somethin' to come home to, all right, that's for sure," Max said approvingly, and accelerated so that they practically flew over the water the last few hundred yards home.

GAIL HADN'T INTENDED to go out to the dock to wait for Chris, but for some reason, the instant she'd heard those mighty engines, she had dropped what she was doing and practically flown out to the pier. By shading her eyes, she could see them coming, and when they got closer, she waved before she realized what she was doing. She had no right to feel such a thrill now that Chris was home, and hesitantly she dropped her hand.

She'd had a lot of time to herself to think about the situation with Chris, but it seemed that no matter how she tried to approach the problem, she reached an impasse. She wanted to tell him everything—the whole story, from the time she'd met Harlan Damion in the New York office, to overhearing that conversation at Chris's office yesterday afternoon. But it wasn't that simple. She had responsibilities, duties—to everyone but herself.

"Ahoy, there! Can you catch this line?"

Relieved to be doing something other than just standing there, she caught the rope Chris tossed to her, and made it fast to the pier. He swung up beside her, smiling.

"Nice welcome home," he said.

She felt suddenly shy. "Oh, I . . . heard the boat and came out," she said, avoiding his eyes.

"I'm glad you did," he said. "It's been a long time since anyone waited for me to come home."

Wondering how Celeste could have stayed away, she forced herself to speak lightly, to defuse her growing emotion. She knew he wanted to kiss her; she wanted to kiss him, too. But they were both very aware of Max, shuffling around the boat, pretending to examine the life jackets, trying his best to make himself invisible. So she said, "Then I guess it's time someone did."

He looked down into her eyes. "I'm glad that someone was you."

She didn't know what to say; she was suddenly thinking how wonderful it would be to greet Chris like this every night for the next hundred years or so. But she knew that if she kept thinking along those lines, it was going to be impossible to leave him at all, so she turned to Max as he came up beside them.

"Max, I made some appetizers and canapés this afternoon to help Hana. Would you like to be my official tester?"

The sturdy driver looked wistful for a moment, then reluctantly shook his head. "No, I'd better not, Ms Sullivan. With the party and all tonight, I've got a lot to do to make sure everything's ready."

"But Raphael and Hana have had everyone in sight bustling around like bees all day," she said, laughing. "Including me."

Chris frowned slightly. "You didn't have to help."

"Oh, but I wanted to," she said as Max hurried off. Smiling, she linked her arm with his. "Besides, I couldn't see lounging around on the beach all day when everyone else was so busy."

"That may be so, but I usually don't allow my guests to be pressed into service."

"It's okay, really, "she said, teasing him. "Stop being so stuffy." She gave him a sly glance. "That's no way for the pirate Respina to act."

"Oh, so my secret is out, is it?" he said with a rumbling laugh. With Gail by his side, it was especially wonderful to be home.

"I'm afraid so," she said, and then glanced around, as though preparing to share a secret. Lowering her voice to a whisper, she said, "I've heard that the piratess Henriette is in the area."

"Oh, really?" Chris said, trying not to smile—trying not to swing her up into his arms and head for the trees to make mad, passionate love right on the ground. "Do you think she'll come to the party tonight?"

"We'll just have to wait and see," she said, and left him with a laugh just as he started to reach for her, so she could go and get dressed.

But she wasn't smiling when she finished with her makeup at dusk. It was time to call Roger, but as she reached for the phone, her hands were clammy and she realized she was nervous. And she knew why. She'd have to tell Chris what Roger had found out for her, and she knew that no matter how she tried to present the information, it wasn't going to be pleasant. *It never is, when a trusted friend is discovered to be a traitor,* she thought grimly, and gave herself a last check in the mirror while she waited for the call to go through.

For the party tonight, she was wearing what she was sure was the perfect lady pirate outfit. The big round earrings she'd gotten yesterday added the final touch to her outfit, which consisted of a billowing long-sleeved white shirt, a divided leather skirt with a wide leather belt, boots and a scarf tied pirate-fashion around her head. She really looked the part, she mused, or would, she amended with a smile, once she put on the three-cornered hat she'd found in the costume shop. Then she'd be transformed into her lady pirate, all right. She smiled again. The piratess Henriette. How Max had laughed at that.

She tensed as Roger picked up the phone.

"Brenner here."

"Hi, Roger," she said. "This is Gail. Listen, I don't have much time to talk. What did you find out?"

"I'm still working on it, *Agent* Sullivan," Roger said testily. "Remember, around here, the difficult we can do immediately. The impossible takes a little longer."

"I seem to remember quoting that to you on several occasions," she retorted. "So *have* you found out anything?"

"Not much," he said, to her disappointment. "But we're still digging. Additional background checks on Delaney and Harris didn't yield a thing. Both men have been working for VDK for years, in highly trusted positions. There's never been a whisper about either of them."

"And Nicolas Sierra?"

"He's a little more difficult to get a line on. Seems he and Van Der Kellen have been friends for years—since they were kids."

"Yes, Chris mentioned that they grew up together. In fact, most of Nick's relatives live right here on Kellen Key. It seems the two families have been involved for many years—the Van Der Kellens as employers, the Sierras working for the family. That could be the connection."

"What do you mean?"

"Well, think about it," she said, having thought long and hard about it herself. "Two boys, almost the same age, growing up together. One having everything he could ask for, the other tagging along—sort of the poor relation, but not really a relation at all. That could cause a lot of resentment, don't you think?"

"I think you're reaching."

"I don't," she said. "I know what I heard."

"Yes, but why the connection to Wade Sutton?"

"More to the point, what connection does Sutton have—or want to have—with VDK? Or maybe it's Chris this guy Sutton's after. Have you found out anything about that?''

"As a matter of fact, we have unearthed a few interesting details. Once you gave us the connection and where to look, we saw the pattern right away. Sutton Incorporated—or one of its subsidiaries—has picked up the ball on every contract VDK has dropped this year. Conveniently, they just happened to be in place at the right time—with the cash or the goods—and they moved right in to take up the slack. It couldn't have happened without inside information—just as you said.''

"So I was right."

"Yes, you were," Roger agreed. "The only problem now is proving it."

She sat back. "Damn it, I wish I'd recorded that conversation!"

"It would have helped, I agree. But only to put the squeeze on these guys. It wouldn't have held up in court."

"We don't need to go to court. I just need something to give to Chris."

"Chris?" Roger repeated, his tone sharpening. "Aren't you confused? Our client is Harlan Damion, remember?"

She straightened again. "We're not going to let him in on this!"

"We certainly are—once we get proof. He's the one who hired us, or have you forgotten?"

She had forgotten. But she wasn't about to admit that to Roger, so she said curtly, "No, I haven't. But Damion doesn't need such highly sensitive information. It's none of his business!"

"It is if it affects the sale of Kalliste International."

She didn't know what to say to that. Fortunately, she didn't have to think of a reply, for just then she heard distant shouts and cheers and the start of music. The party was beginning; as Hana had told her this morning, the music was the signal for Respina's ship to come sailing into the bay.

"Roger, I've got to go now," she said hurriedly. "Keep digging, will you? I'll call you." She didn't know when she'd get another chance to call, so she added vaguely, "Later." She hung up before he could remind her again—as she was sure he intended to—just who they were working for.

The music and the sounds of revelry were getting louder, and she snatched the tricorn off the bed and jammed it on her head. As she did, she caught another glimpse of herself in the mirror. Her talk with Roger had heightened her coloring, and she really did look a little wild-eyed, just like a piratess. Hoping Chris would think it was excitement instead of nerves, she grabbed a shawl and raced out just as the lighted schooner sailed into the bay.

A crowd had gathered on the edge of the sand, and she started to join them as a cheer went up. A man dressed in tight breeches and a billowing white shirt had leaped onto the deck and up into the rigging of the approaching ship. Looking very piratical indeed, he was brandishing a cutlass and holding a long, wickedly-curved knife between white teeth.

"Behold!" he bellowed, his voice amplified by speakers obviously hidden somewhere on the ship, "the pirate Respina!"

As renewed cheers went up, another man who was obviously Max, dressed as the first mate in breeches and a striped shirt, dropped a small rowboat into the water to bring the pirate captain to shore. Watching, Gail stopped where she was. She couldn't take her eyes off Chris, who had swung out over the water by rope, dropping gracefully into the waiting boat below. He had never looked so handsome, she thought with a thrill of pride, and without realizing it, she clapped her hands and laughed in sheer delight. She didn't care how many people were here, or how many saw them, or what they might think. As soon as he came ashore, she'd run right down there and throw herself into his arms.

"Er...Gail?"

As excited as she was, as loud as the cheering and shouting were around her, as entranced as she was by the sight of Chris standing in the bow of that boat, one booted foot resting on the rim, a fist on one hip as Max rowed them to shore, she was still able to recognize that voice....

"Gail, that is you, isn't it?"

She couldn't believe it. Whirling around, she looked straight into his eyes. "Stanley!" she groaned. "Oh, no! Not again!"

He seemed oblivious to her dismay. "Oh, I'm so glad I found you!" he said. "I thought that was you, but I couldn't be sure. You look so...different, Gail. I don't think I've ever seen you like this."

She didn't want reasons, or explanations, or answers as to why he was here again, not with Chris moving ever closer to shore in that boat. But as she looked at him, she couldn't help but see that he had at least dressed for the occasion. To her amazement, he even had a gold earring dangling from one ear.

She was still staring at him, openmouthed, when she realized she was wasting time. Grabbing his arm, she dragged him out of sight. "Stanley, you have to go—right now," she said, one eye on him, the other on that boat. If Chris saw him here, what would he think?

"Go?" Stanley said, bewildered. "But I just got here!" He looked at her earnestly. "And it wasn't easy, either, let me tell you. I had to go through—"

"Stanley, I don't *care*!" she said desperately. "I know you went to a lot of trouble, but you're just going to have to leave. Right now. Right *now*!"

To her horror, he grabbed her by the arms. "I can't leave!" he announced dramatically. "Not until I say what I've come to say!"

She wanted to tear at her hair. "Stanley, we've already been through this!" she cried. "I'm not going to marry you! I don't love you! It just isn't going to work, no matter how hard—"

"That's not what I came to say," Stanley said, looking hurt.

She was too distraught to pay attention. "I've told you and told you!" she went on. "Oh, why can't you under—" She stopped, realizing suddenly what he'd said. "What?"

He was looking at her earnestly again. "If you'll just calm down a minute, I'll try and explain."

Renewed cheering went up again down by the beach, and when Gail glanced that way, she was galvanized to see that Chris was almost ashore. Oh, she didn't have *time* for this! she thought in a frenzy. Whirling around to Stanley again, she said, "All right, I'm listening! What *is* it?"

"Well, Darla and I agreed that—"

Despite her distraction, she caught that. "Darla?"

Stanley's face cleared. "Oh, she's the most wonderful girl I met, Gail," he enthused. "I want you to meet her, really I do. And she's anxious to meet you. In fact, she wanted to come with—"

She was sorry she'd asked. "Go on, go on," she interrupted hurriedly, aware of Chris's impending approach.

Obediently, he began again. "Well, as I said, Darla is this wonderful girl I met." He beamed. "She's working at Brenner and Company, in fact," he said. "Temporarily, of course. But—"

The light dawned. "Darla!" she exclaimed. "Is that the girl who's been telling you where to reach me? The one who sent you down with that courier package the first time?"

"Yes, that's the one," he said, obviously proud and pleased at how clever he and his new girlfriend had been. "How do you think I found you those times? Didn't you ever wonder?"

Obviously Stanley didn't remember his slip. She *had* tried to remember to ask Roger about the secretary who had been substituting for Jean. But there had always seemed to be something else, something more urgent to discuss when she had talked to Roger. Finally, the matter of Jean's substitute had completely slipped her mind. Wondering what else this Darla had blabbed—and to whom—she was just about to insist he tell her every detail, when she heard another cheer from the beach. Oh, Lord! she thought, looking that way. The pirate Respina had landed. She had run out of time.

"Stanley, you've got to get out of here!" she said urgently, turning to him again.

"But don't you want to know why I've come?"

She closed her eyes, seeking strength. But she knew he wouldn't leave until he told her, so she decided she'd better ask. It seemed simpler this way. Maybe, if Chris found them, she could say Stanley was a demented relative who had just happened by.

"Why, Stanley?" she said.

"Because I wanted to give it one last shot, Gail," he said sincerely. "Darla made me promise to do everything I could to make sure it was over between you and me before she agreed to go steady with me." He beamed again. "Isn't she wonderful?"

Now she could bundle him off. "Yes, Stanley," she said hurriedly, grabbing his arm and turning him toward the—how *had* he gotten here, anyway? Deciding she didn't have time to worry about it—if he had gotten onto the island, he could get himself off again—she said, "Just wonderful. I hope you two will be very happy. Now, if you don't mind—"

"But don't you want me to tell that man what a great job you're doing?"

She looked at him, wide-eyed. "What man?" she said. And then her voice rising. "You mean, *Chris*?"

"Well, yes," he said, faltering. "I thought that since I was here, I could...I could..." He saw her appalled expression and shook his head. "I guess not."

"Good*bye*, Stanley," she said. Chris was coming up the beach; in seconds, he'd be on them. She had to get rid of Stanley right *now*.

"Goodbye, Gail," Stanley said, rising on his tiptoes to give her a peck on the cheek. "I just wanted to say, it's been swell. And when you get back to New York, maybe we can get together for lunch or something. I really would like you to—"

"I'll call you, all right?" she said, pushing him to make him go away. She didn't know how she'd explain him to Chris, and it would be just like Stanley to say something...unfortunate. She didn't want that to happen, not now, not tonight.

"That would be—" Stanley started to say, and then his eyes widened as he looked over her shoulder. Fearing the worst, Gail whirled around and nearly fainted right there. Looking every inch the fierce pirate in his costume, Chris was striding purposefully toward them. Stanley's eyes widened even more when he saw the cutlass Chris was casually swinging; even to Gail it looked dreadfully real, and they realized at the same time that it was indeed, when the blade caught the light from the torches placed all around.

"Uh, Gail, I think I'll leave now," Stanley said, and disappeared practically at a dead run into the trees just as Chris came up.

"I've been looking all over for you, Gail," Chris said, looking beyond her in the direction Stanley had gone. "Who was that?"

She tried to shrug casually. "I'm not sure," she said. "Someone from…around, I guess. He didn't tell me his name."

Chris still looked puzzled, and after a hasty glance over her shoulder to make sure Stanley had truly disappeared, she took Chris's arm and practically hauled him after her down toward the beach. She wanted to get as far away from Stanley as possible, and she had to resist another quick look around as she said, "You looked wonderful piloting that ship into the bay. For a minute, I really did think you were the pirate Respina."

Mercifully, he appeared to forget all about the strange visitor. His approving glance swept over her. "For me, on the other hand," he said, "there's no doubt in my mind that I have the honor of meeting the piratess Respinette."

Forgetting Stanley for the moment herself, she smiled up at him. "Henriette," she corrected him. "And don't you forget it."

"Oh, I don't know," he said, putting an arm around her waist as they started to join the other revelers down by the picnic tables that had been set up on the beach. "Respina... Respinette. It has a certain ring to it, don't you think?"

She didn't know what to think. With his arm around her like that, and his voice so appealingly husky, she was having a hard time remembering her own name. Her voice trembling slightly as she looked up at him, she managed to say, "It does, at that."

He stopped, holding her with him. For a moment, he didn't say anything, but gazed down into her face. "You look beautiful tonight," he said finally. "But then, you always do...."

She couldn't look away from that dark gaze. Her heart was starting to pound again, for he was so handsome in that flowing white silk shirt, unbuttoned to the waist and tucked into tight breeches; he truly looked like a swash-buckler. Never mind the truth about pirates, she thought dazedly, caught up in his glance; no matter what anyone said, they had been a romantic breed—although she was sure none had been as romantic as Chris seemed right now, with the torchlight bronzing his lean face, and that look in his eyes that told her he wanted her as much as she did him. There'd been so little time... so little time.

"Chris, I—" Just then the band started up, interrupting her with a blare of happy music. His expression wry, Chris looked down at her as people started shouting for the master of Kellen Key to open the buffet.

"Duty calls—again," he said, and put his fingers briefly under her chin. "But not for long, I promise."

She didn't know what to reply to that; she was feeling so confused right now that she was almost glad of the interruption. *Tell him now,* she told herself, but knew she couldn't do it. Not yet.

As though he sensed her turmoil, Chris hesitated. "Gail, are you all right? You seem so... nervous tonight."

"Nervous?" she repeated, wondering if she sounded as shrill as she felt. She couldn't rid herself of the feeling that Stanley hadn't really gone, but had changed his mind and decided to come back after all and tell Chris what a wonderful job she was doing here.

"No, I'm fine," she said, and knew right then that whether he had intended to or not, Stanley had ruined her night. His appearance had underscored how guilty she felt at continuing her deception, and she wasn't in a party mood anymore.

"I'm sorry, Chris," she said unhappily. "But I guess I've got too much on my mind to enjoy myself. Would you mind if I left the party and went back to the guest house?"

He was instantly concerned. "What is it? Don't you feel well? I'll call a doctor...."

She knew no doctor would be able to cure what ailed her, and she shook her head quickly. "Oh, no, it's nothing like that, really. Maybe I'm just tired. I'm sorry—I was looking forward to the party. You stay and enjoy yourself."

"No, I'll come with you."

She didn't want that at all. In her fragile emotional state, who knew what she would say or do? She might blurt out the whole awful truth, and then what would happen? She'd be in the first boat back to the mainland, that was what. Quickly, she shook her head. "No, I wouldn't think of it. You can't leave your guests."

"Don't be silly," he said. "I'm the pirate Respina. I can do what I like. Besides, I've fulfilled my obligations. No one will notice if I'm gone."

"Oh, that's not true!" she protested, and then saw him looking in the direction of the crowd surrounding the buffet tables. Following his glance, she saw Patrick Delaney, dressed as a preacher of all things, and Daniel Harris beside him, looking like Ichabod Crane in breeches and high stockings and a frock coat. She wondered suddenly where Nick was. Now that she thought about it, she hadn't seen him all night. But then, she decided, she'd been too busy with other things to notice.

"Chris, really," she said again. "Your guests—"

He shook his head. "No, I've done my part. No one will miss me. And I . . . I don't feel like partying tonight myself."

She hadn't dared ask until now. "Then things aren't going well at the office?"

He looked even more grim. "I've been wanting to talk to you about that, Gail. Maybe now is the time. I know with all the problems VDK has been having, especially lately, you're wondering where I stand about Kalliste International—"

"Chris, about that—"

"Let's not talk about it here," he said. "I'd rather say what I have to say in private, up at the house."

She didn't care at the moment if he went forward with the purchase of the Kalliste resorts or not; she was much too concerned with where their own relationship was going. She'd never felt like this about a man before, and she knew he felt something for her, too. But they'd never been able to take the time to discuss any kind of future; there had been too many other things in the way, too many problems, too many situations to deal with. Her own assignment was one, she thought, and realized she'd finally come to the end of her rope where that was concerned. She was so tired of lying to him, of keeping up pretenses; she wanted to tell him the whole story and just let the chips fall where they might. If that meant she'd never see him again, well, somehow she'd have to accept that. If it meant losing her job, well, she'd have to deal with that, too. But she couldn't go on lying to him—she couldn't!

At the house, Chris led her to what was obviously his study—a room she had missed the morning she'd searched the place. Even then she'd been an inept spy, she thought. She should have taken that as a sign that she might not be cut out for undercover work. A quick glance around revealed leather-bound books and various knickknacks; a globe under the window, a model of Chris's schooner on a shelf, a case full of sailing trophies. Then she saw a painting of a beautiful woman over the fireplace mantel, and without realizing it, she gasped.

Chris followed her glance. "My mother, Evangeline," he said.

"She was lovely," she murmured, awestruck. Now she knew where Chris had inherited his dark coloring. He might look like his father, but the black hair, the fierce dark eyes and proud lift of the head had come from his mother.

"I haven't been completely honest with you, Gail," Chris said just then. Startled, she looked away from the painting, at him. Wasn't that her line?

"What . . . what do you mean?" she asked cautiously.

He hesitated, as though making up his mind that he really wanted to tell her. Finally he sighed. "I know it's no secret that VDK has been having...problems this past year," he said. "But what no one knows—or what I hope they don't know—is that the company's problems have been engineered from the inside.''

She wasn't sure what to say to that. Should she admit that she already knew, that she had found out herself just the other day? It seemed wiser to say nothing at this point, so she just said, "I see."

"You don't seem surprised," he said.

She made herself shrug. "It was obvious that something was wrong, Chris. But why are you telling me?"

Abruptly, he left the position he'd assumed in front of the desk and made her sit beside him on the couch. Taking her hand, he looked into her eyes. "Because something's happened here, Gail," he said, "something that means more to me than even the future of my company. I knew from the moment I saw you that you were special, that you'd be special to me. I just didn't realize how much. I don't want any secrets between us, Gail, even if it means that you'll have to tell Damion that VDK isn't such a good risk right now. I'll understand. But I can't go on deceiving you like this. It just isn't fair."

She felt as though a knife had been plunged into her heart. *He* was talking about deceiving her, when she'd been dishonest with him from the beginning? Ashamed and guilty, she couldn't look him in the eye.

He mistook her reaction. "I'm sorry, Gail," he said. "I didn't mean—"

"I'm the one who's sorry," she said thickly, and made herself look at him. She had to say it now, or she'd lose courage. "Because I haven't been completely honest with you."

He was taken aback. "You haven't?"

Briefly, she shut her eyes. *I'm sorry, Roger,* she thought, and then looked at Chris again. How to say it? she wondered, and decided just to plunge right ahead.

"No, I haven't," she said. "We knew you were having internal problems—"

"We?" he said. "Oh, you mean, Harlan."

This was more difficult than she had ever imagined. Her heart was pounding so hard from nervous anxiety that she felt it might jump out of her chest. Would he understand? Briefly, she shut her eyes again. *Oh, please let him understand!* she thought, and said, "Yes... Harlan, and... others."

"What others?" he asked, and then shook his head. "No, never mind. I know how the business community works. If rumors are so rampant that they've reached my ears, everybody in the country must know."

"That's not—"

He didn't hear her faint protest. Continuing, he said, "But what they don't know is that I've spent the past few months trying to identify the traitor, and now I've narrowed it down to three men."

It was now or never. "I know. Patrick Delaney, Daniel Harris and... Nick Sierra."

He looked startled. "Yes. But how did you know?"

She was beginning to wish desperately that she'd waited until Roger had gotten her the information she needed before she'd started this. Hoping Chris already had proof of his own so she'd be let off the hook, she said, "Trade secret. Anyway, it's not important. Go on."

He looked at her strangely, but to her relief, he was too intent on getting his own story out to question her. "I should have done something about the situation when I first realized what might be happening," he said. "But I couldn't believe it at first. Then, when I narrowed it down to those three, I was sure it had to be some kind of mistake. I've trusted those men, as my father before me did. But when I started looking at ruin, I knew I had to do something—fast. That's when I set a trap."

Hope rose in her. "A trap?"

Briefly, he told her about the Hawaiian deal, the one he'd set up with the help of someone named Matsu Yokomoto. "And tonight," he finished, "when Pat and Dan and Nick all got here for the party, I told each one privately that I was going ahead with the Kalliste deal, including the expansion I'd already told them about."

She tried to hide her disappointment. "Oh, I see. That's why you're telling me. You didn't want me to think that the resort sale was set, in case anyone mentioned it to me."

"No, no, it was more than that," he said. "I told you, I don't want any secrets between us. I do intend to go ahead with the Kalliste deal—but after I smoke out the traitor. You see, each of the three believes that the land is located on a different island, and that there's a deadline. Whoever it is is going to have to move before the weekend, contact his partner from here. And when he does, I'll know which one it is."

"How?"

"Because I'm recording all calls made into or out of Kellen Key."

"What!" Remembering the call she'd made earlier to Roger, she nearly shot to her feet.

Again, he mistook her reaction. "I know, I know, it's an underhanded trick." His expression became grim. "But what they're doing is underhanded, too. Look, I'll show you how it works."

Before she could stop him, he got up and went to a cabinet she hadn't noticed behind the desk. She knew she had to tell him about her own part in this before he listened to a recording of her call with Roger, but she couldn't get out the words. Her throat seemed to seize up on her, and she could only watch helplessly as he reached down and opened the doors of the cabinet. From her position on the couch, she could see the recording equipment, the big reel of tape, the glowing dials.

Chris turned to look at her, but she had to swallow twice over the lump in her throat before she could speak. Hoping against hope she'd been spared, she asked, "Chris, which lines are taped? Only those in the main house—or all the phones on the estate?"

"All of them, of course. Why?"

She couldn't answer, she could only shake her head and watch helplessly as he looked back at the machine that was going to play out her doom. "Well, well," he said, spying the used tape. "It looks like someone has already made a call."

"Chris—"

"Let's hear it, shall we?"

"Chris, listen—"

But he had already reached down to rewind the tape. When he punched the play button, she knew it was too late. Much too late. Dully, she listened as her voice and Roger's filled the room.

Recognizing her voice, Chris looked over his shoulder. "Oh, sorry. I'm sure this is a personal—" he began. Then he realized what she and Roger were saying. Slowly, he straightened, his face turning red, then white with anger as the conversation Gail had had earlier with Roger seemed to go inexorably on...and on...each word more incriminating than the last.

"I'm still working on it, Agent Sullivan.... Once you gave us the connection and where to look, we saw the pattern.... It couldn't have happened without inside information—just as you said.... Aren't you confused?

Our client is Harlan Damion, remember... He's the one who hired us, or have you forgotten?"

Even Gail's protest sounded feeble. *No, I haven't. But Damion doesn't need such highly sensitive information. It's none of his business!*

And Roger's final statement, one she hadn't countered: *It is if it affects the sale of Kalliste International.*

His expression stony, Chris reached down and switched off the machine. Instantly, Gail sprang to her feet. "I can explain, Chris—"

He was so angry his voice actually shook. "I don't think any explanation is necessary, *Agent* Sullivan," he said. "Unless it's to tell me just who you work for. It certainly isn't Harlan Damion, not as his executive vice president, anyway. Is it?"

Oh, why hadn't she spoken up before now? "No, it isn't, Chris," she said, and was so anxious to make him understand that she finally just blurted it out. At that moment, she didn't care about Roger or corporate secrecy or intelligence or obligations or even her job; she had to make Chris understand!

"I work for Brenner and Company, an intelligence-gathering firm in New York—" she started to say, and then almost quailed at the look on his face. His eyes were nearly black with rage.

"As one of their operatives, right?"

"Yes," she said, trying not to cringe at that terrible tone. Because she was so frightened and nervous, she started to babble. "But Damion really did hire us, Chris. With all the rumors about VDK, he wanted to make sure the sale would go through. And when we took on the assignment... I mean, when I said I would..."

A muscle leaped into a knot on Chris's jaw. "And so you came down to spy on me, to find out whether I was serious or not!"

"Yes, but—"

His eyes might have been black, but his face was white with fury. "And was sleeping with me part of the assignment, *Agent* Sullivan?"

She shrank at such contempt. It was far worse than shouting, cursing and damning her to hell for deceiving him would have been. Blanching, she forced herself to lift her head. "No, that had nothing to do with it, I swear to you," she said. And then, despite herself, her voice broke. She couldn't bear the look on his face. "Chris, please listen to me," she begged. "I didn't intend for this to happen—"

"No, I'm sure you didn't," he interrupted harshly. "No good *agent* likes to get caught."

"No, I didn't mean it like that." To her horror, she was nearly in tears. But she had to convince him; she had to *try*. "I didn't intend for us to get involved—"

He made a gesture that silenced her. Looking as though he hated her, he said, "Then you have nothing to worry about, do you? As far as I'm concerned, nothing happened between us."

She looked at him in disbelief. "But—"

"God!" he shouted suddenly. "What a fool I was! When I think how I sat here just now and told you that I didn't want any secrets between us—" Choking, he banged his fist against the desk, scattering some papers. "You must have laughed at that, right? Knowing what a scam you were working on me!"

She was almost afraid to go to him, but she did. Reaching for his arm, she tried to make him look at her.

"Chris, please, it wasn't like that," she said. "I did intend to tell you. Please believe me!"

He jerked his arm away. "Believe you!" he said incredulously. "How can I believe anything you say? You've lied to me from the beginning. I'm not even sure Gail Sullivan is your real name!"

"Chris, please—"

Abruptly he reached for the phone. In a voice that chilled her to the bone, he said, "I think you'd better get your things together and leave, Ms Sullivan—or whatever your name is."

She was desperate enough to try again. "Chris, please, can't we talk about this?"

"I think we've said all there is to say," he said coldly. "I'll have Max take you to the mainland. But you'll forgive me if I leave you to make your own arrangements about getting back to New York. At present, I'm a little busy trying to salvage my company."

Right now, she didn't care if she had to walk back home. Reaching for his arm again, she said, "Chris, if you'll just listen—"

His eyes were like hard chips of ebony. "I think we've concluded our business. Except for one thing."

She looked at him, hope springing up. "What's that?"

"Tell your boss—whoever that is—that I won't be buying Kalliste International after all. Not because I can't afford it, even now. But because I don't deal with dishonest men who send women to do their dirty work."

That did it. She'd tried to explain and been rebuffed; she'd begged him to understand and been rejected. But his final remark was the last straw. It was a little late, but she'd finally found her misplaced pride. She'd beg no more; anger was uppermost now.

"In that case," she said, her voice starting to shake, "you can take the listening devices off your phones so your guests won't be subjected further to *your* deceit."

His lip curled. "Well, that's just about what I'd expect from someone like you!"

"Someone like me?" she said. Her eyes blazed. "You mentioned a while ago that you didn't want any secrets between us. Well, I think that's just fine. So, just to set the record straight—in case you haven't already got it on tape, that is—you might like to know that your traitor's partner is a man named Wade Sutton."

Despite himself, Chris drew in a sharp breath. "Wade!"

"Ah, I see you're familiar with the name. Well, that doesn't surprise me. From your actions just now, it's obvious that you're two of a kind." She went to the door, where she turned to deliver a parting shot. "Oh, and your traitor? In case you want to know that secret, too, *his* name is Nick."

She had the satisfaction of seeing him blanch, but it was small gain. Wanting to hurt him now as much as he'd hurt her, she went on cruelly, "Goodbye, Mr. Van Der Kellen. It's been...an experience I don't care to repeat."

And with that, she walked out, not slamming the door but closing it quietly, with finality, on that part of her life.

CHAPTER FIFTEEN

GAIL MADE IT ALL THE WAY to the Tampa airport ladies' room before she burst into tears. The trip back to the mainland had been a nightmare. She hadn't expected sympathy from the loyal Max, but she hadn't expected such granite-like disdain. He'd ignored her all the way, depositing her at the pier, where by some previous arrangement a taxi was waiting. Before she could thank him, he'd roared off in the boat again. The taxi driver took one look at her set face before silently loading her luggage in the trunk, and as she climbed in the cab, Gail thought bitterly that as angry as Chris had been, he hadn't forgotten the proprieties.

Well, bully for him, she thought, and felt the quick sting of tears behind her eyes. She wouldn't cry, she told herself, not now. She ordered the driver to take her to the airport as fast as possible. She couldn't wait to leave Florida behind; she didn't care if she had to take a cargo plane out.

Sensing her mood, the driver said nothing, but stepped on the gas. As they sped along, Gail looked out the window and thought fiercely how glad she was she'd left all those clothes behind. In her frenzy of packing after the terrible argument, she'd been careful not to take anything she hadn't brought to the island herself. If Chris wanted to burn everything, she didn't give a damn. Oh, she *hated* that man.

A sob escaped her, and as she searched vainly in her purse for a handkerchief, she knew it wasn't true that she hated Chris. It was just the opposite, in fact. She loved him. Her situation was all her fault, and that made it even worse. She should have told him who she was much earlier, but she hadn't had the courage. She had known that once he found out the truth, she wouldn't have any reason to stay, so she just hadn't said goodbye. She'd never known a man like Chris, who could thrill and excite her with just a look, and it wasn't his money or his power or his position that attracted her. She would have felt the same way if he'd been as poor as the proverbial church mouse. Material things didn't matter to her, only Chris.

Miserably, she endured the rest of the cab ride, but rushed to the ladies' room as soon as she entered the airport. Burying her nose in a tissue she grabbed from the box on the counter, she leaned against the sink and thought miserably what a mess she'd made of things. Not only had she acted in the most unprofessional way possible by getting involved with her subject; she hadn't even asked to be removed from the case when she had. She knew she should have told Roger she couldn't handle the assignment; the first time she felt that powerful attraction to Chris, she should have asked Roger to send someone else in. But she'd been so sure she could manage . . . somehow. . . .

Oh, what a fool she'd been! Stupid pride and ambition had made her stay, and now look what had happened. She'd never felt so miserable in her life. Alone in the rest room, she looked at herself in those awful fluorescent lights over the sinks, thought how horrible she looked and burst into tears.

She was still sobbing when her flight was called, and only the thought that this was the last plane out tonight enabled her to walk on board with her face blotchy and her eyes practically swollen shut. The flight attendants, tactful as always, waited until the twinkling lights of Tampa were being left behind before one of them diffidently approached and asked her if she'd like a drink.

It was tempting, but she shook her head. "No, tea will be fine," she said, and thought, *Gallons of it*. It was going to be a long flight home.

Seemingly an endless time later, she finally arrived at her own apartment. She was so exhausted by then that she didn't even notice the musty, unaired smell, but just dropped everything in the entryway, took a shower and went to bed. Two hours later, she was up again, sipping some hot chocolate she'd made, sitting by the darkened living room window, staring out unseeingly at streetlights haloed by her tears.

She didn't sleep that night at all, but sat by the window until dawn, mourning the end of a beautiful, doomed love affair. At first light, she finally dozed off right there in the chair.

Roger called at eight in the morning, jerking her out of an exhausted sleep. Only half-awake, she flung herself out of the chair and across the back of the couch to get to the phone. "Hello?" she said hoarsely, after picking it up on the fourth ring.

She so wanted it to be Chris that at first she didn't recognize Roger's voice.

"Gail?"

"Yes?" she said, trying to clear her head. Then she realized who it was and she winced. It was Roger, and he was mad.

"Where in the hell have you been?" he shouted, as soon as he knew for sure he was talking to her. "Do you realize I've been trying to locate you since last ni

What happened? Why did you come back to New York without telling me?''

Wishing she'd never picked up the phone, because now she'd have to think of some explanation, she grabbed the quilt from the back of the couch and wrapped it around herself. Now that she was awake, she realized how cold it was in the apartment. Along with everything else, she'd forgotten to turn on the heat.

"Calm down, Roger," she said wearily.

"Calm *down*? Do you realize what a scare you gave me?"

That touched her; he'd been worried was all. "I'm sorry," she said contritely, and didn't add that phoning him had been the last thing on her mind when she came in. "But I had to leave the island in a . . . in a hurry. . . .'' Was it only last night? Already it felt like a century. . . "I . . . I didn't get a chance to call."

"Well, thanks a lot," he said, still annoyed. "I wish I'd known before *I* called and got an earful!"

She sat up a little straighter at that, pushing a strand of hair out of her eyes. "What do you mean?"

"What do you think I mean? How was I to know you'd blown your cover and had to get out of there? When I called with the information you wanted, Van Der Kellen himself answered. To say he was upset is the least of it."

Oh, this was too much. On top of everything else that had happened, she couldn't take the blame for being discovered. "In the first place," she said hotly, "I didn't exactly blow my cover. It seems we're not the only ones who know how to tap into phone lines. Chris decided to catch his traitor himself and had all the estate phones bugged. He recorded our little conversation last night."

There was a silence. "Oh," Roger finally said. "Well, in that case, I'm sorry. And I didn't mean to yell at you. I guess I was just worried."

His apology took the wind out of her sails. "Well, thanks," she said grudgingly. Then she added, "I would have called you last night, but I didn't get in until late, and I..." There was no use going into all that, she thought, and took another tack. "I planned to come in this morning to write up my report," she said instead. "We might as well call Damion and tell him that Chris has decided not to buy Kalliste International, after all."

"Yes, he told me."

Wincing, she thought she might as well learn the rest of it. "What else did he tell you?"

"In between all the shouting, you mean?"

She grimaced. "Maybe I don't want to know."

"Oh, come on," he said, deciding to be expansive, as only Roger could be. "It wasn't your fault. And you did a good job."

"You don't have to say that to spare my feelings, Roger. I know I made a mess of things."

"Not really. You got the information Damion wanted. And exposed a traitor in Van Der Kellen's company to boot. He should be grateful to you."

"Well, somehow I get the feeling he's not."

"Can you blame him? It's not the most pleasant prospect in the world—having someone close to you betray you like that."

"That's true," she said with a sigh. "Why do you suppose he did it?"

"I don't know. Money would be a good guess. Another would be that resentment you told me about."

"And Sutton?"

"Same thing. All that digging you asked us to do turned up some interesting facts about old Wade. It seems he and Van Der Kellen, Sr. used to go to the mat quite a bit in the old days. Kerstan won a lot of contracts Sutton had bid on, and at one point, Wade had to declare bankruptcy because he couldn't come up with the cash at the last minute and VDK could."

"But why did he wait so long to get his revenge?"

"Because Chris is a hell of a businessman. My guess is that Sutton didn't have a chance until he turned someone at VDK. The only way he could beat Chris Van Der Kellen was to have inside information about which direction the company was going to take—and when."

Gail shivered. "When I think what might have happened if I hadn't overheard that conversation—"

"Maybe, maybe not," Roger said philosophically. "Chris was obviously on to the scheme before that. Remember, he did bug the estate phones."

"I'm not likely to forget that," she said. "If I had known, I would have just kept my mouth shut."

"You mean and not called me last night?"

She felt near tears again at the irony. If only she'd waited! she thought. "I mean and not have told him that his traitor was Nick—and that his trusted assistant was dealing with Wade Sutton. With the phones bugged, he would have found out soon enough for himself."

"So, you told him a little ahead of time. It didn't change anything—he was still being betrayed. As I said, he should be grateful you were so sharp."

"Yeah, right," she said dully. She knew the last thing Chris felt right now was gratitude. "Well, I'll be in this morning to type up my report—"

"No, you don't sound so good. I want you to take some time off."

"Oh, but—"

"Hey, let the boss shower a little largess, will you? You did a good job. I want to reward you with a vacation. Take a couple of weeks. You haven't had any time off, and you deserve it."

"But—"

He wouldn't listen. "I'll see you then. Until that time, I don't want to see your face around this office, got it?"

How could she refuse a gracious offer like that? Thanking him, she wondered all the same what she was going to do with herself for the next few weeks. She'd counted on being occupied with work so she wouldn't have time to mope—or think about what a mess she'd made of things with Chris.

"So have a good time," Roger said. "Don't worry about anything here. We'll still be chugging along when you return."

She was just about to hang up when she remembered something else. "Roger, did Jean ever get back?"

"Yes, thank the Lord," he said. "God, I missed my own secretary! That Darla was about to drive me nuts! Questions, questions, all the time! You'd think she wanted to be an operative herself—she, who doesn't have the brains of a gnat!"

She had brains enough to find out where I was, so Stanley could decide between us on his own, Gail thought. "Well," she said, "I hope everything worked out for Jean. Did you send Darla back to the secretarial pool?"

"What? No, she quit. Can you believe that? She called in this morning to say she wouldn't be coming in anymore. Says she's going to get married. What do you think of that?"

All Gail could think was that she wished Stanley well. She got a chance to tell him so later that day when he called and told her his wonderful news.

"And it's all due to you, Gail!" he said enthusiastically. "If you hadn't insisted on taking that stupid job, I never would have met the girl of my dreams! Boy, you were right. You and I *never* would have made it. Darla is just perfect for me."

"I'm glad, Stanley," she said sincerely, and felt like crying again when she hung up the phone. Things had worked out for Stanley, and she was glad. But why couldn't they have worked out for her?

Not even Suzanne could cheer her up. They went out one night to a new restaurant and the next to a movie, and although her friend succeeded in worming part of the story out of her, Gail couldn't tell her the whole truth. Her reticence didn't have anything to do with client privilege, not now. She just couldn't talk about Chris without feeling a lump in her throat that made conversation impossible.

"You're really in love with this guy, aren't you?" Suzanne asked sympathetically one night.

"I *was*," Gail muttered, telling herself she would *not* cry. She'd wept too much as it was these past few days. "I *was* in love with him."

"Oh, yes, I can see that," Suzanne said, tactfully handing her a tissue and pretending not to see when Gail furtively dabbed at her eyes. She waited a moment, then said, "I think you need to get away. All this moping around your apartment isn't good for you."

"I haven't been moping," Gail denied. "And besides, I've just *been* away. That's why I'm in such a mess!"

"Yes, that's true," Suzanne said briskly. "But you don't need a vacation right now, you need a . . . a haven.

Why don't you drive up and see your parents? Your mom and dad are so understanding. You could brood around there all day, and all your dad would do is pat you on the shoulder, and your mother would bring you another cup of tea. You need a little pampering. I'd love to do it, but things at the shop are chaos. One of the girls quit, and I've had to work extra time, and oh, it's just too much. Promise me you'll go, Gail. It'll do you good."

So the next morning Gail found herself in the car on the way to Albany.

Her mother had sounded pleased when Gail first called, but as always was so sensitive to her daughter's voice that she soon asked what was wrong.

"Nothing's wrong," Gail had lied. "I just had some time off and realized it's been a long time since I visited with you and Dad. Can't I just come up for a visit?"

"You know you're welcome any time, dear," her mother said. "Is . . . Stanley coming with you?"

She closed her eyes. She'd forgotten to tell her parents about Stanley. "No, I'm afraid not. Stanley and I aren't seeing each other anymore."

There was a silence. "Oh, I see. Well, I can't help but think it's for the best, darling. I didn't say anything before, but I never did think you and that boy were suited."

Gail had to smile. Her mother was rarely so outspoken. "Does Dad feel the same way about 'that boy'?"

"You know your father, dear," her mother said comfortably. "He's certainly old enough to speak for himself."

Gail laughed. Suzanne was right; going to visit her parents was just the tonic she needed. "I'll ask him when I get there, then," she said.

"Drive safely, darling. We've been here twenty-five years. We'll still be here the next few days or so."

"I'm on my way," Gail said, and went to pack.

It was snowing when she arrived in Albany, huge flakes that covered everything with a beautiful blanket of white. Reminded poignantly of the first snowfall in Colorado when she and Chris had led the twilight parade of skiers down the mountain, Gail got quickly out of the car. She didn't want to start crying again, not when she'd just arrived.

Her parents' old collie, Lad, stood up on the porch as she took her suitcases from the car. At fifteen years of age, he was now a dignified old man who could no longer come bounding down the steps, so she went to greet him. Dropping to one knee as he came stiffly up to her, she scooped him into her arms and buried her face in the thick ruff of fur at his neck.

"Oh, Lad," she murmured when he nuzzled her with his cold nose and then licked her cheek in welcome. She laughed shakily. It was good to be home.

FAR AWAY IN KELLEN KEY, where it never snowed, and tropical breezes blew through the open windows, Chris Van Der Kellen stopped pacing long enough to look across the desk. Nick was sitting in the chair opposite him, and the reel of tape on which was a recording of another conversation lay on the desk between them.

"Why, Nick?" Chris asked. "Just tell me why?"

His dark face suffused with anger and insolence, Nick stood, too. His hand were clenched. "Because I wanted to, that's why," he said. "Because all my life, I've *wanted* to."

Chris felt as though he'd just been punched. "I don't understand. We've always been friends. You've always had everything I've ever had."

Nick looked disdainful. "Everything you've ever had?" he repeated. "Think again, old buddy. *You* were the one with the Van Der Kellen name. I was just one of the stupid peons who worked for you."

Chris paled. "What are you talking about? That's not true. I never felt that way. Neither did my father!"

His lips drawn back from his teeth, Nick leaned over the desk. "Well, *my* father didn't either! But I did! You think it was my decision to stay home while you went off to college? No! I wanted to go, but my family couldn't afford it!"

As shocked as he was, Chris wouldn't accept that. "That's ridiculous!" he said sharply. "Aside from the fact that it's not true, all your father had to was ask for a loan. My father would have given it eagerly. Hell, he'd probably have made it a gift. I don't—"

Nick looked at him with loathing and hatred. "And that's just the problem, don't you see? You had it all. You had so much you wouldn't even have missed that kind of money. Well, somewhere along the line, I got tired of it, tired of hearing how great the Van Der Kellens were, tired of hearing my parents say, 'Don't offend the *padróne* Nikko,' don't say anything, don't *do* anything, don't *breathe* the wrong way to make the white father angry! God!" he cried suddenly, "how you make me sick!"

Chris was stunned. For a moment he didn't know what to say. Then he said, "I'm sorry you feel that way, Nick."

Nick had gone to the big windows in the study. The wind was calm today; the waves barely made it to the shore before kicking over and dissipating into nothingness. "Sorry," he spit contemptuously without turning around. "Sorry! That's all you can say?"

Chris took a deep breath. "I'm not going to apologize for what I am, Nick," he said. He waited a beat. "I'm sorry you feel you have to."

Nick whirled around, his face twisted. "Oh, I might have expected you to say that, you condescending son of a bitch! God, you're just like the old man, aren't you? Just like him!"

Chris's jaw tightened. Nick knew how he hated to be compared to his father; to him, it was the ultimate insult. His dark eyes darkened even more, but he held on to his temper. "And I'm sorry to say you are *not* like your father. Esteban was a fine man. He would not have been proud of you this day."

Nick made another crude sound. "My father was proud of only one thing—his servitude to your family. I only wish I had managed to bring down this cursed company before you found me out. But it's just like everything else, isn't it, Chris? You always were a clever, ruthless bastard, just like your old man."

Chris didn't trust himself to say much more. His jaw stiff with anger, he said, "Get out, Nick. I never want to see you on Kellen Key or at VDK again. Don't even bother to clean out your things. I'll have then sent to you—care of Wade Sutton."

Nick glared at him balefully. "Don't bother," he grated. "There's nothing here worth taking. Burn it all— or give it to charity. You Van Der Kellens are good at charity. You've kept everyone here in your debt for years."

"But not you."

"No, not me," Nick said, going to the door. He turned back. "And believe me, if I get another chance, I'll bring you down, Chris. I swear on my father's grave."

Chris just looked at him. Softly, he said, "Your father deserves better than that. Beware of oaths you haven't the balls to keep."

They looked at each other for a long moment, two men who, Chris realized suddenly with a sharp pain, had never been friends despite what he had thought.

"You bastard," Nick said, and walked out.

As soon as he was gone, Chris looked down at the incriminating reel of tape on his desk. Then, with a sudden, violent curse, he swept the thing into the wastebasket before throwing himself into the chair, his head in his hands.

He sat like that for a long, long time, unmoving, pictures of himself and his boyhood friend, Nick, flashing through his mind. He saw them playing in the surf at Kellen Key, or skipping stones across the water, trying to best each other; he saw them fishing from the boat, and carousing around Miami in his convertible, calling out in youthful exuberance to all the good-looking girls. He'd wanted Nick to go to college with him; he'd begged him to go. But Nick had stayed home, and Chris remembered all those eagerly awaited school vacations, when he'd rush home so they could be together. He'd never had a friend like Nick Sierra, and now . . . now it seemed that he'd never had Nick as a friend at all. He still couldn't understand why his boyhood chum had turned against him; he thought that he probably never would.

Finally, Chris raised his head. That was another situation he couldn't avoid any longer; he'd spent nearly a week trying not to think about it, but he couldn't pretend anymore. He'd taken care of Nick; now he had to face someone else.

It was snowing in New York when he arrived, but Chris hardly noticed. Terrified that he might be too late after all, he hadn't even taken time to throw some things into a duffel. Shrugging into the light jacket he'd grabbed when leaving Kellen Key, he turned up the collar and started toward Gail's apartment. On the way he practiced what he'd say, but when he finally knocked on her door, she didn't answer. With a sinking heart, he knew he'd waited too long after all. Gail wasn't here, and he didn't know where to find her.

He was just trying to think what the hell he was going to do when someone came up behind him.

"Hi," Suzanne said. "Can I help you?"

HER HEAD DOWN, wearing one of her father's parkas with a scarf her mother had knitted around her neck, Gail was taking the dog for a walk. She'd been in Albany two days, and already she felt better—almost ready to go back to New York and take up her life again.

But not yet. She hadn't told her parents much about Chris, only that she'd met someone and it hadn't worked out. But they were both too perceptive to believe that was all there was to it; they knew her too well not to recognize the facade she was trying to keep up, even though they pretended along with her that she was just here for a visit.

Every morning, she told herself that it was going to be all right, but deep inside she doubted that things would ever be right again. How was it possible, she wondered bleakly, to love a man so much after knowing him such a short time? There were moments, like right now, with her boots crunching in the snow, when she felt his absence almost as a physical pain, an ache she knew would never go away. She felt so empty, as though nothing would ever matter much again; as ridiculous as part of

her knew it to be, she was sure she'd never love anyone
the way she loved Chris.

But he's gone, she told herself fiercely, and tried to
smile as the old collie, who had gone foraging ahead,
came tottering back to make sure she was all right. Why
weren't men as faithful and uncomplicated as dogs? she
wondered, patting the panting collie on the head. Lad
would never judge her as Chris had; he would continue
loving her no matter what she did.

But not Chris. He hadn't even given her a chance to
explain, to justify, to apologize, to beg his forgiveness.
He hadn't given her a chance to do anything but lose her
temper. Even now she cringed when she thought of that
clever parting remark about Nick. She couldn't have
chosen a better way to hurt him than to fling the knowledge in his face that the man who was betraying him was
his best friend.

Oh, what did it matter anyway? she asked herself dismally as Lad gave her hand a last push with his nose and
turned to go on ahead again. The relationship was obviously not meant to be. She and Chris moved in different circles, they came from different backgrounds; they
had different goals, different friends, different everything.

But it didn't matter for those few glorious days, did it?
she mused, and felt like crying again. She hated to cry,
she thought, brushing away tears, but lately it seemed
that was all she'd been able to do. She missed him so
much. If only she could get another chance, she could—

She shook her head. She couldn't blame Chris for
being so angry with her. She couldn't blame him for not
listening to her explanations. What explanation could
there be for lying to him, deceiving him and pretending
to be someone she was not? There was no denying that

she'd gone to spy on him. What explanation could there be for that?

But even that might have been forgiven if she'd only confessed herself as a fraud once they started getting involved. That had been her big mistake; she never should have convinced herself that *somehow* things would work out. She had wanted it both ways, so she had only herself to blame for her predicament.

Feeling overwhelmed by that empty sense of loss again, she decided to cut the walk short. It was getting cold, and she was worried about Lad being out too long. Wiping away the last of her tears, she looked around for the dog and finally saw him some distance up the path. She was about to call him back when she realized he had assumed a guarded stance. What was it? Had he spotted a raccoon? Praying that he wouldn't try to chase it and break one of his feeble old bones, she hurried toward him.

"Lad, what is it?" she called. "Lad!"

He didn't even look around, and she felt another stab of alarm. *Oh, Lord,* she thought, *maybe it's a bobcat.* She hadn't seen any around, but you never knew.

"Lad!" she said, more sharply, and then saw what was claiming his attention. She skidded to a stop on the snowy ground, sure she was seeing things. "Chris?" she said disbelievingly.

She still thought she was dreaming even when he straightened from his leaning pose against a snow-covered tree. Like her, he was dressed in jeans and boots, and his parka was an indigo color that made his eyes seem even darker. He wasn't wearing a hat, and his black hair was dusted with a scattering of the snow that had started to fall again. Hands in his pockets, he began walking toward her.

Standing guard on the path between them, Lad whined uncertainly, looking from Chris back to Gail for a sign to tell him what he should do. At the moment, Gail didn't have a clue. She just stood there, her mouth open. Was this happening? Was he really here? Was it true?

Chris stopped about halfway to her, asking with amusement, since it was obvious Lad was very old, "Can I come closer, or will your dog attack me?"

Gail didn't know what to say. She'd been thinking of nothing but Chris and what she *would* say if she ever saw him again, and now he was right here in front of her, and her mind was a wasteland. Blankly, she looked down at the dog, who wagged his tail doubtfully.

"Lad won't hurt you," she said stupidly. "He's fifteen years old."

"Old enough to recognize a fool when he sees one, then," Chris said.

She just looked at him. "What...what do you mean?"

His hands still in his pockets, he didn't move. He looked so handsome standing there, those long, strong legs of his encased in tight jeans, his jacket broadening his shoulders and setting off his eyes and hair, that she felt her heart lurch. What was he doing here?

"Just that," Chris said. Taking his hands out of his pockets, he took another step closer. Lad backed up a step toward Gail, and whined again. She glanced down at him. "Lad," she said. "Heel."

Seeming relieved that a decision had been made, the dog came eagerly, circling around as he'd been taught and sitting straight, his nose exactly by her knees. She put her hand on the old collie's head, as though that would give her strength, and looked at Chris again, trying to steel her treacherous heart. She still didn't know why he had come, and because she wasn't sure she wanted to know, she said, "How did you find me?"

He smiled, a smile that made her breath catch. "Trade secrets," he said. "You have yours. I have mine."

"Yes, and yours was Suzanne, right?"

"How did you know?"

"How did you get her to tell you? My whereabouts were supposed to be a—"

"Secret?" He smiled that smile again. "I persuaded her by saying I'd camp on her doorstep until she told me where you were."

She wanted to laugh, and couldn't because of the lump in her throat. Why was he really here? Unfinished business? Remembering that last awful quarrel, she said, "Why did you come, Chris? I really don't want to talk about...about that night we heard the tape."

He sobered instantly. "I don't either. But I think we have to, don't you?"

"No," she said. "We agreed I was wrong to deceive you like I did, wrong to lie to you like that. I can't blame you for the things you said. I would have been furious in your place, too. There really isn't any excuse."

"I should have listened."

She shook her head. "To what? I had no explanation for the things I did. I...I broke all the rules getting involved with you. I knew it was wrong, that I couldn't be involved with you and do my job at the same time, but I—" the words were out before she could stop them "—I couldn't help myself."

Something leaped in his eyes. "Nor could I," he said, never taking his glance from her face. "And I still can't.... Gail, can you forgive me?"

She looked up disbelievingly. He wanted her forgiveness? But she was the one who had deceived him!

"You want..." She couldn't say the words. Was this really happening? She didn't know whether to believe it or not. She couldn't bear to be separated from him again. If she had misinterpreted...

He saw the look on her face, the terrible longing she could no longer hide. With two strides he covered the distance between them, and neither of them heard Lad's tentative bark when Chris gathered Gail up into his arms.

"Oh, God, I thought I'd lost you forever!" he cried, burying his face in her hair. He was trembling, but not from cold—from the yearning she felt so deeply herself. "I was such a fool, Gail. I...I don't know what got into me. Even before Max took you off the island, I knew I'd made a terrible mistake, but I was too proud to admit it. I'm sorry, I'm so sorry."

He was holding her so tightly that she couldn't see his eyes. She had to see his eyes. Pushing herself slightly away, she looked up into his face. What she saw there made hope fly.

"I'm the one who's sorry, Chris," she said shakily. "I hated deceiving you. I hated pretending to be someone I was not. I thought—somehow—I could make it work, but I knew I couldn't. Still, I had to try. I had my job, responsibilities...and you."

"And I made it worse," he said.

She shook her head. "No, you had your own problems to deal with," she said, and remembered again that last awful scene. Lowering her eyes in shame, she said, "I'm the one who made it worse. I never should have told you about Nick like that. But I—I wanted to hurt you the way you'd hurt me."

Grief flashed through his eyes, and was gone. "But you were right," he said. "Nick was the one. I...I listened to the rest of the tape later. There was a conversation on it between him and Wade Sutton. There was no doubt."

She looked up at him. "I'm sorry."

"So am I," he said regretfully, and then shrugged. "But it's done. That's when I realized how good you were at your job." He smiled slightly. "In fact, that's why I came."

"You came about my job?"

"No, I came to offer you one."

She blinked. He'd come all this way for that? "What?"

He looked wry. "Well, it's obvious that my internal security is a disgrace—you proved that."

"But—" She felt near tears again. He'd come all this way because of some stupid job offer? This wasn't what she'd thought, hoped, dreamed—at all!

Seeing her dismayed expression, he held on to her more tightly, as though afraid she might break away. His eyes starting to dance, he said, "It's a good deal, Gail. Head of security at VDK—or Kellen Key...or both. Your choice. Please, darling, what do you say?"

Darling. He'd never called her that, but she didn't know whether to trust her heart or not. Was he really saying what she thought he was? She knew him well enough to read between the lines, but still, she had to be sure. Very sure. She couldn't survive another parting like the one they'd had; if they got together again, it had to be...forever.

"Oh, Chris, I don't know," she said, pretending to think. "I'm not sure you need a head of security. After all, you found out where I was. If you could do that, why do you need me?"

This time there was no laughter in his eyes. "Because I need someone to watch over me, Gail," he said. "Because I need someone to be there, waiting for me on the dock at Kellen Key when I come home—like you did for me that day. Because...because I so desperately need you.''

Emotion was threatening to overwhelm her. She couldn't joke with him any longer; she was too relieved that things had worked out at last, too overcome with love for him to play games. Against all odds, he had come back to her, and now they'd have no more secrets. But still...

"If I agree," she asked shakily, "will you do one thing for me?"

Those dark, dark eyes held hers. "Anything," he said fervently. "Just name it."

She smiled. "Will you let me drive the *Kellen One* sometime?"

He looked at her blankly for a moment, without saying anything at first. The *Kellen One* was his premier racing boat. Then, as comprehension dawned, he gave a great whoop of delight, grabbing her up so exuberantly that her feet left the ground. With Lad barking excitedly around them, sure something wonderful was happening but not sure what it was, Chris swung her in a circle.

"You *are* a lady pirate!" he said with glee. "But yes, you can drive the *Kellen One*! You can have it, for all I care, just as long as you marry me!"

Only then did she dare believe it. Oh, she had wanted excitement and thrills and adventure, she thought—and she had found all three. Wanting to laugh and cry at the same time, she hugged him back.

"In that case, my love," she said, "No matter where I am, I'll always be there for you...."

Harlequin Superromance

COMING NEXT MONTH

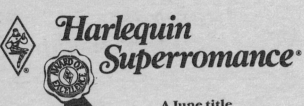

Harlequin Superromance®

A June title
not to be missed....

Superromance author Judith Duncan has created her
most powerfully emotional novel yet, a book about
love too strong to forget and hate too painful to
remember....

Risen from the ashes of her past like a phoenix,
Sydney Foster knew too well the price of wisdom,
especially that gained in the underbelly of the city.
She'd sworn she'd never go back, but in order to
embrace a future with the man she loved, she had to
return to the streets...and settle an old score.

Once in a long while, you read a book that affects you
so strongly, you're never the same again. Harlequin is
proud to present such a book, STREETS OF FIRE by
Judith Duncan (Superromance #407). Her book merits
Harlequin's AWARD OF EXCELLENCE for June 1990,
conferred each month to one specially selected title.

S407-1

You'll flip . . . your pages won't!
Read paperbacks *hands-free* with

Book Mate • I

The perfect "mate" for all your romance paperbacks

**Traveling • Vacationing • At Work • In Bed • Studying
• Cooking • Eating**

Perfect size for all standard paperbacks, this wonderful invention makes reading a pure pleasure! Ingenious design holds paperback books OPEN and FLAT so even wind can't ruffle pages— leaves your hands free to do other things. Reinforced, wipe-clean vinyl-covered holder flexes to let you turn pages without undoing the strap . . . supports paperbacks so well, they have the strength of hardcovers!

Pages turn WITHOUT opening the strap

SEE-THROUGH STRAP

Reinforced back stays flat

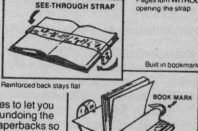

Built in bookmark

BOOK MARK

BACK COVER HOLDING STRIP

10 x 7¼ opened
Snaps closed for easy carrying, too

Available now. Send your name, address, and zip code, along with a check or money order for just $5.95 + .75¢ for postage & handling (for a total of $6.70) payable to Reader Service to:

Reader Service
Bookmate Offer
901 Fuhrmann Blvd.
P.O. Box 1396
Buffalo, N.Y. 14269-1396

Offer not available in Canada
*New York and Iowa residents add appropriate sales tax.

BM-G